THE NEXT FITHIAN

AN ORDINARY TEEN ON A STRANGE, NEW WORLD

RICK BARRY

FITHIAN
Publications

The Next Fithian: An Ordinary Teen on a Strange, New World

Copyright © 2021 by Rick Barry, www.rickcbarry.com

Published by Fithian Publications

ISBN 978-1-7355886-3-6 (paperback)

ISBN 978-1-7355886-2-9 (ebook)

Cover art copyright © 2008 Focus on the Family; cover design by Sarah Slattery.

Dedicated to you readers who hold
more God-given potential than you realize

ACKNOWLEDGMENTS

I didn't create *The Next Fithian* alone. Years ago, then-editor of Focus on the Family's *Breakaway* magazine, Michael Ross, telephoned. Michael asked me to brainstorm a big, bold, new adventure for teens: "Maybe fantasy. Maybe science fiction. I don't know—maybe both mixed together. Just make it big!" It was a tall order, but I accepted the assignment and created a three-part sci-fi story titled *The Next Fithian*. Those three installments reaped fun feedback from readers. However, after I submitted Part Three, that assignment was done. I moved on.

As time passed, my *Fithian* characters refused to let me forget them. They kept coming to mind, urging me to create a novel-length adventure for them. At first I refused. My novels about World War II airmen received priority. At last, though, I yielded and allowed my imagination to travel back to the planet Zemna. The book you're holding is the result.

Special recognition goes to fellow author Sharon Hinck for doing the line edit and substantive edit. Although Sharon spotted errors and contributed ideas for strengthening the manuscript, she greatly encouraged me by declaring the story a pleasure to work on.

Emily Krajci performed the final proofreading. Volunteer

readers who offered objective feedback on early drafts are the following, in alphabetical order: Dan Anderson, Leslie Black, Stephanie Clapp, Lauren Ruark, Travis Crawford, Kaden Evers, Jay Faubion, Linda Glaz, Lois Hudson, Darren Kehrer, Lara Luke, Pam Luttenberger, Shae Mallory, Ethan Nottingham, Serena Nottingham, Erin Prater, Colleen Shine, Jane Simerman, Victoria Shanks, Rachel Slutz, Marali Sargent-Smith, Marc Stansberry, Jude Urbanski, and Rachael Wolfenden.

I express special appreciation to Focus on the Family for granting permission to reuse two images from the original short stories for the cover and promotional purposes. Graphic designer Sarah Slattery accepted those images and created the book's cover.

In addition, Thomas Umstattd, Jr.—"the Vulcan of Book Marketing"—provided indirect inspiration via his Novel Marketing and Christian Publishing Show podcasts. Thomas commands a wealth of publishing and marketing knowledge. I highly recommend his podcasts for fellow authors.

Of course, you readers inspire me to keep writing. Your enthusiastic emails, online reviews, and the way you recommend my books to friends and family are invaluable. Bless you!

To God be the glory!

1

BOOM!

Boarding pass in hand, I quicken my pace through the airport. After months of waiting, it's hard to believe I'm finally heading to an archeological dig in Israel—and I'm going solo! Excitement building with every step, it's all I can do not to run.

However, beside me, Grandma Johnson shuffles to a stop. With a teary sniff, she points at the security sign:

Indianapolis International Airport.
Ticketed passengers only beyond this point.

"Oh. Yeah." It's the moment I've been dreading.

Grandma wipes her eyes with a pink hanky. "Well, Rankin, I guess this is where we say goodbye."

So awkward. Ignoring that fearful little tremor in her voice is impossible. "Don't worry. Remember, it's only six weeks. Then I'll be back."

"I'm sorry. It's just that Israel is so far. You're the only one I have left. I've worried about you for all of your seventeen years.

I don't know what I'd do if anything happened to you." Her lower lip begins to quiver, making me feel slightly guilty.

I set down my backpack and pull Grandma into a tight hug—partly to comfort her, but also to avoid seeing that quivering lip. During the hug, I notice how the grandmother who once seemed so big and strong now feels so petite, so frail.

Beyond the security sign, passengers are pulling off shoes and stepping into metal detectors. My sense of adventure urges me forward, but I force myself to clamp it down. No way I'm going to stomp the heart of my last living relative in my rush to leave.

"Don't worry. I'll be back in time for cross country practice. After all, it'll be my senior year—last time to be captain of the team."

Of course, it's not my flying to Israel that really bothers her. Grandma was the one who drove Mom and Dad to the airport that last time. Simply standing here must dredge up the heartbreak of everything that happened next. If only she wouldn't dwell on it every day, keeping the sting of their deaths alive. Me—my game plan is just the opposite, staying sane by trying not to think about them. Even though I never really succeed.

I take a deep breath to fight the tears trying to well in my own eyes. "Besides, you're set up with Facebook now. You can check my status every day. If I dig up anything cool, you'll be first to see the photos. Who knows, maybe my team will discover something really mysterious."

A dozen chattering travelers flow around us. Most of them grip passports and tow carryon bags behind them. Their excitement is infectious. But Grandma is delicate. She deserves extra kindness, even if it's killing me to stand here talking.

She tucks the handkerchief into her purse and stands a little straighter. "Time for you to go. But Rankin, whatever it is your heart is looking for, I hope you find it. And I'm not talking about broken pottery at some archeological site."

I stiffen. Grandma doesn't usually mention "the topic." I don't either. But now she's done it. Well, almost.

I pick up the backpack and heave it over one shoulder. "I can't have what I want, Grandma. It doesn't exist. At least, not on this side of Heaven. But you pray for me, and I'll pray for you. Deal?" I back away.

"Rankin …"

"Look for my emails!"

I force a wide grin and give her a final wave goodbye. With that, we part. Me, to join a team of volunteers sifting through ancient dirt in Tel Jezreel, and Grandma to her Garden Club and Ladies Bible studies.

As I approach the first TSA guard, my stride is quick and bouncy. At last, my overseas getaway is beginning. Yet, as I pull the passport from my back pocket, my fingers are trembling. I still picture Grandma's quivering lip. Maybe there's just no way to bury your feelings entirely.

* * *

After one layover at John F. Kennedy Airport and endless hours over the ocean, the Fasten Seatbelts light dings on. "Ladies and gentlemen, we're beginning our descent to Ben Gurion Airport in Tel Aviv …"

Finally. The ache in my back is more than ready to escape the cramped seat. Economy class, they call it. More like cattle class. Worse, the industrial-strength perfume of the elderly woman beside me has numbed my nostrils.

Then—a scream rips through the passenger compartment. In the next instant, a muffled explosion erupts outside the airplane.

"They're shooting!" someone shouts.

Instantly, the passenger cabin transforms into an uproar of shrieking voices.

"Look!"

"What's happening?"

"Who's shooting?"

I twist and turn in my seat, trying to see out the little windows on either side. From where I sit in the middle section, I can't see whatever has terrified everyone. Is it a fighter jet? Maybe Stinger missiles shooting up from the ground?

An explosion rocks the Boeing 777. We plunge into a gut-wrenching dive as freezing wind whips through the compartment.

My elderly neighbor grips my arm and digs in with claw-like fingernails. With panicky, panting breaths, she declares, "We're going to crash. I just know it."

Only seventeen—and I'm about to die?

Yellow oxygen masks drop from overhead. As I fumble for mine, a second explosion blasts open the airplane. Just that quick, the airliner is gone! I glimpse alternating blue sky, brown earth, and billions of bits of tumbling wreckage as my body—still buckled to the seat—cartwheels through icy air. My lungs gasp for breath.

Terrified, I blurt the one thought that springs to mind. "God, I'm yours!"

Next—nothing.

I open my eyes. Silence. No wind. No noise. My heart pounds like crazy, but I'm no longer falling. Instead of plunging to the ground, I find myself surrounded by—what?

The airplane seat has vanished. Neither standing nor sitting, I'm floating upright in white mist. Absolute peace has replaced the chaos.

"I'm dead."

"To the contrary, Rankin. You have never been more alive."

Through the haze a blond man comes straight toward me. Or is it a man? His sky-blue sport jacket fades into nothingness below the waist. Could he be a—?

"That's correct, Rankin. I'm an angel. My name is Jaylel. You may call me Jay, if you prefer."

He offers his right hand, and I take it. Despite its warmth, goose bumps prickle my skin.

"But angels live in Heaven, right? If I'm not dead, where am I?"

Jaylel smiles. "That's difficult to explain to someone with your limited experience. Geographically speaking, you are nowhere. Chronologically speaking, you are in every time, but no time."

"Huh?"

His smile widens. "Perhaps it will help to think of yourself as inside a bubble. The physical universe did not come into existence by itself. All the particles that make up physical matter were created—"

"Yeah, I know. By God."

"Precisely. Your knowledge of God and your faith in Him are partly why you have been chosen. But have you ever considered that time itself is not a normal condition? Our Lord created time for the convenience of His creation. Here, you and I occupy an exception—a bubble, if you will—in the fabric of the universe."

My panic drops, but only half a notch. "Why all the mumbo jumbo? Does everybody who dies pass through one of these bubbles?"

"No. And I repeat—you are not dead. I created this artificial environment to protect your fragile body. Now, it preserves you in the transition from your previous world into another. Rankin Johnson, you are a chosen vessel. The next Fithian. You will bear witness for God in another galaxy. Or, more precisely, in another dimension."

My stomach performs a sick flipflop. This has got to be a nightmare. That's it—I must've fallen asleep on the plane. None of this is really happening. Moving my right hand to my left, I pinch the skin on the back of my hand—*hard*. But I don't wake up. It's no dream.

Unblinking, Jaylel stares at me. "May I continue?"

In other situations, I might crack a joke. But this is no time for joking. "Yeah. Go ahead. You said I was the next Fido or something."

The angel suppresses a grin. "Not Fido. You are the next Fithian."

"What's a Fithian?"

"*Fithian* is both a name and a title, somewhat like the word *Caesar*. It signifies a chosen messenger of the Light. Not simply an evangelist from one city to another, but a messenger from one dimension to the other. From this point onward, you are no longer Rankin Johnson. You will be called Rankin Fithian."

"Another dimension?" I hate asking questions. I don't even ask for directions. Maybe it's a pride thing. But here—wherever this bubble is—I have no choice but to ask or stay ignorant.

"Your understanding of the physical universe, from the farthest star in one direction to the farthest star in the opposite direction, comprises only one facet of God's creation. However, there is a parallel dimension, like two sides of the same coin, only separated by a buffer zone. That alternate dimension is where I'm taking you right now."

"Why me?"

"Why you? For starters, you have a sense of adventure."

"Wait a minute. I'm not all that adventurous. I just like to look cool."

"You also have personal faith in the Son of God. Plus, you possess an inner fortitude even you do not recognize."

"What's that mean?"

Jaylel ignores my question. "In addition, because your parents are already in eternity, you have fewer ties to Earth than most others. The death of your parents has also matured certain aspects of your personality."

I stiffen and clench my jaw. Not even Grandma gets permission to touch my wound about Mom and Dad. But since Jaylel is an angel, I bite my tongue. This time.

"Let's change the subject. What happened to the airplane?"

"The typical story. Human nature erupting in violence.

Except for you, no one survived. But you, Rankin, surrendered yourself to the Lord's will. You shouted, "God, I'm yours." He is pleased to accept your living sacrifice and to set you on this fresh mission."

"Surely some other guy could do your mission better than me?"

"There was one more factor in your favor. Difficult puzzles intrigue you. That quality will be helpful."

"Puzzles? What do puzzles have to do with anything?"

In reply, he simply grins and winks. This Jaylel sure knows how to push my buttons.

"Okay, at least tell me something about this place where you're taking me."

"Excellent request. In your dimension, sin entered soon after Creation. Satan tempted, and the first man and woman fell into sin, affecting every descendant on Earth. In the alternate dimension, it was not so. There, on the planet Zemna, humankind and created creatures lived in joyful innocence and harmony with the Creator until about ten of your earth years ago. That is when the enemy discovered the other dimension. At their tempting, many Zemnans turned away from blissful innocence to their own pride, rebellion, and misery. Spiritual death resulted."

My heartbeat and breathing finally slow down. But the sick feeling in my gut grows worse. What happens if I vomit in this bubble thing?

"Rankin, the people of Zemna need your knowledge of the Savior. The Son of God was crucified once—but only once—to save the souls of all humans who trust in Him."

"Sure, but that was on Earth. What's that got to do with a totally different planet?"

"Faith is not limited by distance. Your home in Indiana is far from Israel, where the Son of God was crucified and rose again. Yet you believe, and that is enough. Zemna is much farther, but the same principle applies. Zemna simply needs a Fithian—a messenger who can explain the Way that God provided."

In the next moment, the soles of my Nikes touch down on something. Like a soap bubble popping, the protective thing around me vanishes. Suddenly I'm standing in a grassy, bowl-shaped depression in the ground. Overhead stretches a pale-purple sky. The scattered clouds look light and feathery, as if an artist airbrushed them.

"Welcome, Rankin. You've arrived on Zemna."

I turn and find Jaylel standing beside me, this time in a completely visible body, sport jacket, pants, and shoes. Like me, he must not care for neckties.

He points up the grassy slope. "Walk that way. You will discover some who need to learn of the Savior."

"Aren't you going with me?"

"This is your assignment, not mine." He steps backward.

"Just a minute. I still haven't agreed to this job. I mean, yeah, I love God and everything, but don't tell me I have to spend the rest of my life here?"

"Do you make a request?"

My mind races. "Even missionaries get to go home. You know, furlough. If I do this—if I travel around and explain the Gospel to aliens—can I go back to Earth some day?"

Jaylel crosses his arms. "Your aircraft was destroyed. How could you reappear alive and well at some point in the future?"

"Look, God can do anything, right? He can send me back to Earth and make it so I never got on that airplane. Maybe Grandma can get a flat tire on the way to the airport."

Jaylel's eyes flit upward, as if he's listening to something I can't hear. "You surrendered your life to God. Humans don't cut deals with the Almighty. However, I'm instructed to say we can proceed with the following understanding. If you perform the work of a Fithian and win at least seven thousand Zemnans to the truth of the Gospel within one year, then you may return to Earth. At that point, you will be replaced with another Fithian. However, be warned—if you ever go back, you will have no memory of your time on Zemna. Not a single souvenir.

No one on Earth would ever know you've been here—including you."

Seven thousand? I swallow.

Once again, he points up the grassy slope. "Let the mission begin. Head that way. Share the Gospel."

"Wait! How will I communicate? Don't tell me aliens on Zemna speak English?"

"No. They speak First Tongue, the original language your own planet once spoke. Here, no Tower of Babel took place to confuse the languages. We are now speaking that language too, although you are unaware of the change in your mental process-es." He takes another step backward.

I pull the New Testament from the pocket of my hoodie and flip it open. "But this is in English. I still understand it."

The hint of a smile reappears on Jaylel's face. "True, your brain can decipher the written Word from English. You need that ability for the mission. Yet, your thought and speech patterns are now in First Tongue. Trust me."

"There must be some mistake. I'm no preacher. I've never even been to Bible college."

"That doesn't matter."

"I only became a Christian a few years ago. There's a lot I still don't know."

"True, but that doesn't matter either."

"My Grandma Johnson—she'll be heartbroken when she thinks I'm dead."

"The Lord is not without compassion. Make no mistake, He will comfort in ways you don't imagine. Besides, most of Olivia Johnson's earthly days are complete. Tell you what—if she departs for Heaven, I will personally tell her where you are and give her your love."

I'm running out of excuses. "Look, I'm not good at talking in front of people."

"Neither was another fellow I recall. His name was Moses. It worked out."

Jaylel's body rises into the air. He points a final time. "That way, Rankin. People need to hear what you know."

"But I still don't totally get it. What should I do?"

"The same as on Earth. Live for God. Stay pure. Share the Good News of the Savior's life, death, and resurrection with anyone willing to listen. Lead them to faith in Him."

A final question springs to mind. "Hey, you called me 'the next Fithian.' What happened to the Fithian guy before me?"

Jaylel's body becomes transparent as he ascends. However, his reply rings out clearly. "He was killed."

"Huh? Stop! What do you mean, killed?"

The lavender sky is empty. He's gone.

So, I'm alone on an alien world—and somebody here might want me dead? My dry mouth barely manages enough saliva to swallow. With my stomach nauseous, I'm not in the mood for adventure.

For a long while I stand rooted to the spot. This whole scenario is way beyond weird. Worse, a fuzzy feeling in my brain keeps me from thinking clearly. I read about jet lag in the airline magazine. Could that explain the sensation of cotton stuffed into my brain? Space-bubble lag? I pat my pockets for my iPod. Gone. My wallet and passport are missing, too. Probably flung into the sky when I was cartwheeling. Other than my clothing, the New Testament is my only possession.

Finally, as if waking from a dream, I suck in a breath and hike up the slope. The blades of grass are an inch wide, knee-deep, and incredibly thick. Pushing through the stuff takes an effort.

"I've got a bad feeling about this."

At the rim of the depression, I gasp. In the distance lie the blackened remains of a town. Here and there, wisps of smoke curl upward. Am I in a war zone? The thought of people wounded and bleeding brings back memories of the First Aid course in summer camp. I quicken my pace.

"This is worse than a bad feeling."

When I enter the smoking outskirts, I find no dead bodies as I expected. The style of architecture is bizarre, unlike anything I've ever seen on Earth. Every charred building is—or was—circular. Round towers, round buildings. There's not a square corner in sight. Between scorch marks, the original green and orange wall colors still show. No streets are in sight. Just narrow, brown footpaths that look like they were poured into place and left to harden.

No cars? No trucks? How do these aliens get around?

High-pitched whining breaks out overhead, growing louder by the second. I look up but see nothing.

Jaylel's voice blurts inside my skull. *Run!*

No sooner do I dash across the street than a series of explosions shatter the stillness behind me. Adrenaline kicks in. I bolt over a scorched plaza and race down a walkway, hurdling broken chunks of debris as I go. Trembling and gasping for air, I duck into the protection of a building. When I halt, my breath comes in fast gasps. My ears are alert for danger. So glad I'm a runner. But what I wouldn't give to be back on Earth.

Outside, steady droning rules the air, as if an enormous dragonfly hovers out there, searching. Not wanting whatever it is to find me, I press deeper into the building's dim interior.

So freaky. Like being swallowed alive by a sci-fi flick.

"Stop right there, or I'll vaporize you."

My heart lurches. I freeze as commanded. When only silence follows, I dare to peek. Behind some sort of console crouches a man, grimacing in pain. His hand clutches a gadget the size of a TV remote.

The guy's skin is darker than mine. His eyes seem slightly Asian. But he's human. As if too exhausted to hold it anymore, he lowers the gizmo. "I thought you were one of them. But they don't wear garments like those."

I glance from my blue jeans, hoodie, and tee shirt to the man's clothing, which slightly resembles a tan karate outfit. I've never thought of blue jeans looking strange, but here I am, a visitor from another planet dressed in Levi's.

"You thought I'm one of who?" I listen to my own voice. To me, it sure sounds like I'm speaking English.

"One of them." When the man slumps, I notice a woman on the floor behind him. She's gorgeous, but her eyes are shut.

"Is she ...?"

"Not yet. We're both dying, though. The sickness is upon us. Flee. Save yourself."

The word *save* sparks a connection in my brain. The mission. Even though I don't understand a fraction of this alien situation, my mind carries information a dying person needs. "Listen, I've come here to tell you a story. It's important. This is about God."

"A story? Are you insane? We're dying, and you stand there blabbering about the Creator? He doesn't care about us anymore."

"No. There's a Way. Listen to me."

Even as I say these words, I reach toward the man for emphasis. The guy's eyes latch onto my left hand and grow wide. "The Intersection of All Things. You're a Fithian?"

Confused, I twist my hand to see my own palm. Something new is there—not a scar, not a tattoo, but a symbol covers my entire palm. Its main tint is burgundy, yet it shimmers with iridescent flecks of sapphire, ruby, and gold that change as I twist my hand. Space hieroglyphics? Since I can't even feel it, I'm not sure whether the symbol exists under my skin, on top of it, or whether it has replaced my natural skin. And what did he mean, "the Intersection of All Things"?

The woman's eyes flutter open. She, too, stares as if I've turned green.

"Yes, I'm a Fithian. I've come a long way to tell you something important. Now listen."

Step by step, I explain how God—the Creator—sent His Son to open a way for people to join His family. About how people rejected and crucified that Son of God. As I talk, I don't go into detail about Romans or Jews or even where all of these events happened. Keeping the whole story as generic as possible, I simply emphasize it did happen.

Despite obvious pain, the man and woman hang on every syllable. I've never seen anyone so eager to hear anything I have to say. But, by the time I get to Jesus' burial in a little cave, the man collapses. "I'm finished. Save yourself, Fithian."

The exertion of speaking proves too much. He sprawls beside the woman. Eyes closed, she wraps her fingers in his. "We die together."

"Hold on! You need to hear the rest of the story. The Creator wants you to live with Him—"

With a final effort, the couple embraces. Their breathing stops. Limp hands flop to the floor.

Creeped out, I back away from the corpses. It's the first time I've seen anyone die. And if those two carry a disease, I sure don't want the germs.

Just that fast, I want to kick myself. Two people died in front of me, and all I can think about is my own health?

"What a failure. I blew my very first assignment." Lifting my eyes to the ceiling, I shake my head. "God, what am I even doing here? I'm no preacher. I can't be the right guy for this Fithian job."

But God doesn't reply. Neither does Jaylel.

I lower my eyes just as a yellowish glow envelopes both dead bodies. A second later, with the slightest puffing sound, they wink out of existence.

Whoa. I've sure got a lot to learn. Starting with, what does a Fithian do now?

2

TERRA INCOGNITA

As I stand there, some fragment of my brain clings to the hope I'll wake up and find myself back in my airplane seat after a nap. But no dream ever felt so real. The solid floor, the holes blasted in the walls, and the charred odor in the air convince me this place is real. I'm literally exploring a strange new world called Zemna.

I venture around the console to where the couple collapsed. It strikes me as some sort of entertainment center—comfortable chairs behind an array of electronic equipment. Panels, buttons, but no TV or monitor.

Scrounging through shelves behind the console turns up only cases of black, shiny octagonal disks. They aren't plastic, like CDs. They feel heavier, denser, but they're not metal, either.

It's like something Luke Skywalker might buy for his living room. Not knowing what the various buttons and panels operate, I decide not to mess with it. Somebody powerful destroyed this town. I don't want to advertise my presence by blaring space music or flicking on strobe lights. Yeah, I might be a Fithian, but that doesn't make me bulletproof. Or laser proof. Whatever.

The man mentioned "the sickness" before they died and vanished. Is a deadly virus floating in this air? I back away.

My question dangles, still unanswered: what on Earth do I do next? Well, no, not on Earth, but what on Zemna should I do?

Jaylel made it sound easy. Live for God. Talk to people. Lead seven thousand people to Jesus in one year, and I can go home. Is that even realistic?

In the back of my mind, guilt tugs. Yeah, I told this couple about Jesus. Maybe just in time, who knows? But for the first time, the main reason I had talked about God was to earn something for myself—a return ticket to Earth.

Dad never did that. The shining example of a self-sacrificing missionary, Dad told Africans about God for their own sakes, not to get something. But if talking to people is the only way to go home, what choice do I have?

My growling stomach breaks the silence. I've been so distracted that the hunger pains startle me. Fithian or not, I need food. Plus, my mouth is dry as sandpaper. My last snack was a packet of roasted peanuts and a plastic cup of Coke. That was about thirty minutes before the plane exploded. But I ate that stuff clear across the galaxy. I mean, in the other dimension. So how long has it been in Earth time?

I don't have a clue. All I know is that I want to pour something cold and wet down my throat and fill my stomach with anything that will keep it from growling. So, what do people on Zemna eat? They're still human. At least, they looked human. They must keep food someplace.

Tiptoeing through interconnecting chambers, I can tell I'm in a dwelling place, similar to an apartment. A smoky odor lingers. One room suggests a kitchen, with a table and molded chairs of unknown material in the middle. My eyes land on a panel recessed in the wall. Beside it are two buttons.

Doesn't look too dangerous.

I press the top button with my thumb, and the panel hisses sideways into the wall.

Jackpot. A fridge!

One after another, I pull out the contents and set them on the table. A glassy vase with a removable top contains aqua-blue liquid.

Please don't be water from a fishbowl or cleaning supplies. I dip in a finger do a test lick.

Fruit juice. I can't name the flavor, but it's sweet and super tangy.

Finding a stack of cups, I fill one with juice and drink it, slowly at first, but with growing confidence as the sweet flavor flows over my tongue. Definitely fruit juice. Next, I study the other items. Not a speck of meat, so no roast beef sandwich today.

What I find is a block of stuff that smells a little like cheese, plus a loaf of something that must be bread, even if the aroma reminds me of new leather. I try a bite. Not bad. It's tastier than some of the dishes I've tried overseas. At least I won't starve.

I wolf down the whole loaf with more sips of juice.

My stomach satisfied, I explore the remains of the building. No paintings or artwork decorates the walls. Instead, various colors merge and separate as they ooze from wall to wall, room to room, in ultra-slow motion. Only around the jagged holes blasted in the exterior walls do the colors fade into dead gray.

I brush my fingertips against one wall. It isn't paint or wallpaper. The moving hues seem embedded in the surface. So, are the walls themselves living artwork? Do they function off a power source, or are the colors somehow alive?

I search for more people but find only empty chambers, and I can't imagine what some of these rooms were for. What did that guy say when he ordered me to halt? He thought I might be "one of them." Obviously, dangerous beings lurk nearby—close enough that he expected me to be one.

If only I had a light saber or something.

That notion sparks another idea. The dying guy pointed a

gadget at me, threatening to "vaporize" me. Retracing my route, I search the floor for the weapon, but don't find it.

Either it vanished along with him, or somebody else picked it up while I was exploring the building. That possibility sends a shiver down my spine. Time to get out of here.

Maybe I can sneak around Zemna for a while. Lie low and scope out the place? I need to get my bearings in order to figure out my next move. What's the army expression back home, when soldiers creep around observing the lay of the land? Mentally I can picture camouflaged men doing it, but for some reason I can't think of a word to describe it. Maybe my thought patterns really have changed to fit this new planet, except no such word exists here?

Or maybe I'm just freaking out a little.

Stealthy as a ninja—and much more nervous than one—I pad to a rear exit and study the terrain outside. Uppermost in my mind is Jaylel's tip that somebody killed the previous Fithian. I don't want to suffer the same fate—especially not during my first hour on Zemna.

Outside, a faint breeze nudges clouds through the pastel purple sky. Nothing else stirs. Also, the droning sound has disappeared. Only the charred and broken remains of a once-magnificent town meet my eyes. Now it lays silent, eerie, as if waiting.

"No guts, no glory." I step outside.

Our youth leader back in Indiana once told me, "Rankin, you're a great guy. But you try to accomplish things on your own strength. Remember to go to God first. He never intended prayer as a last resort."

Even now, Pastor Eric's advice stings my conscience. Yeah, I do that. How did anyone in Heaven ever decide I'm worthy enough to get promoted to Fithian? I look upward.

"God, I have no idea what I'm doing. Please don't let me do anything stupid."

Senses on red alert, I hike over crunching rubble as I pick my way out of town. That's when another feature of this place strikes me. Nowhere do I see the least sign of personal security. No fences. No barred windows. No locks or keyholes on the doors.

It's as if citizens of Zemna never heard of burglars and murderers.

Jaylel said sin didn't enter Zemna as early as it did on Earth. Here, the inhabitants had lived in peace with God and each other for generations. So, did God conceal this dimension of creation from Satan and demons all these years?

Still scanning left and right, I exhale a frustrated breath. "What I need is a guidebook. Like, *The Complete Idiot's Guide to Planet Zemna*. Or *How to Be a Fithian for Dummies*."

On the outskirts of town, the buildings end. A reddish-brown walkway that feels like hardened rubber runs around it like a border. Standing on the walkway, I pause and look back. Like the architecture of the individual buildings, the whole town seems constructed in a circular shape. From overhead, this curving pathway must form a perfect ring.

Again, I study the new emblem on my left palm. A cross embedded in interlocking circles. Licking my opposite thumb and rubbing the emblem accomplishes nothing. Not even a smudge. The thing is there to stay. What did that guy call it? "The Intersection of All Things"?

Feeling as though I'm being watched, I follow an extension of the walkway that veers away from the settlement. It cuts through a grassy meadow and plunges into a forest. Not a yellow-brick road, but the walkway must go somewhere. I follow it. The trees will provide a welcome shield from hostile eyes, if anyone is paying attention.

When I step into the woods, the beauty of the forest slows my feet to a complete stop.

The overall impression is that each tree trunk, each branch— literally every twig—grows in a predetermined place and way for ultimate beauty. Quite a few trees have leaves with silver edges, and that lends the whole scene a shimmery effect as they reflect twinkles of sunlight.

Here and there, stream-like patches of colorful flowers crisscross one another like threads of a living tapestry.

Overhead, birds of every imaginable hue flit from branch to branch. They trill back and forth with notes that seem to pass right through me.

"Absolutely, totally, one hundred percent awesome!"

Sure, I loved nature back home. On Earth I'd enjoyed every chance to camp or hike or go fishing. In the Sangre de Cristo Mountains of Colorado, I even climbed Crestone Peak and went rappelling with the church youth group.

But this place ...

Never before had I gazed on an entire forest that looks as if an artistic genius designed it. The whole experience is calming, almost hypnotic. I could stand and stare forever.

In various places, I notice weeds and briers fighting for territory. My impression is these are latecomers, not part of nature's original blueprint.

I shake my head in fascination. Did the forest just grow this way? Or did Zemnans spend their lifetime cultivating it? Even the Garden of Eden couldn't have looked more amazing.

Maybe this place resembles Eden the way it looked when God first created it? Not until Adam ate the forbidden fruit did God curse the ground and make it sprout thorns and thistles.

My hand touches the New Testament in my hoodie pocket. Too bad I didn't bring a whole Bible. Wouldn't it be cool to reread Genesis 1, to compare its words with the beauty of these woods?

Keep walking, an inner voice insists. I obey.

Despite the danger, I laugh when the lines of a poem pop into my mind. It's Bilbo Baggins's rhyme about the road going ever on.

"Yeah, it does. But at least Bilbo knew his destination. Plus, he had a bunch of Dwarves for guides."

Despite my doubts, something about this fantasy landscape energizes me. I'm taking longer strides, marching into the future. Sure, I'll need to stay alert until I figure out this world. But God is on my side, right? For now, I'll play the role of a soldier scouting the terrain, get to know the lay of the land.

I can do this. At least, if nobody "vaporizes" me.

In time, the forest yields to fields teeming with vegetation similar to wheat, beans, and other crops that are different, yet reminiscent of plants back home. Rows of ornate trees add a decorative flourish to the borders of each field. And these trees don't merely stand in rows. Their branches have been grafted together to form living barriers, almost as if they're all holding multiple hands. Unlike the trees in the forest, these bear fruit. The round pods resemble turquoise apples. Others resemble coppery bananas or flat, plate-shaped things that appear in more colors than a bag of M&M's.

Are they edible, or poison? Resisting the temptation to take a bite, I keep walking.

Occasionally I spot animals, too. Despite their white fur, smaller ones remind me of squirrels as they frolic around, playing tag. Larger creatures resemble distant cousins of deer or ostriches. These graze in scattered clusters.

Here and there, other walkways bisect my road. From a hilltop I spot another town off to the left. It, too, has suffered some destructive attack. But what kind of artillery aims so accurately that it hits only buildings and never disturbs surrounding trees and fields?

Should I head over there?

No audible answer comes, but my heart feels no particular reason to go there. Months earlier, I had memorized Proverbs 3:5-6, but now the words crystallize as never before: "Trust in the Lord with all your heart and lean not on your own understanding; in all your ways acknowledge him, and he will make your paths straight."

Straight, huh? Okay. I'll keep walking straight. However, the sun dips toward the horizon. Will I find a shelter before night?

Senses alert for danger, I'm tramping along when a sparkle in the sky catches my eye. Like an aircraft without wings, a silvery needle soars high overhead.

Danger?

I leap from the walkway and dash through a patch of black-petaled flowers to the shadow of a tree. Whatever that thing is, it isn't natural. Somebody or something is piloting it.

The object glides along, curving this way and that, as if searching.

"I don't think we're in Kansas anymore, Toto." Joking with myself doesn't lessen the tension. Instead, my stomach knots and my skin breaks into a cold sweat. So much for boldly marching into the future.

Plip. Pip.

I've been so busy studying the flying object that I nearly miss the delicate sounds. When I turn, I'm startled to see a trail of black-tinted bubbles the size of marbles hovering above the flowers I ran through. They trace my exact path from the causeway to my hiding place under this tree.

Pip. Plip. Now the flowers around my Nikes are releasing bubbles too. With one finger, I poke a flower. A dark-tinted bubble wells up from its center. *Plip.* The bubble lifts off.

I glance up again, to where the needle in the sky performs a gentle turn. Nah, these bubbles can't give me away. They're too dinky. Still, I wish a breeze would blow them away.

For fun, I spear a bubble with my finger. When it pops, my nostrils detect a fragrance sweeter than a fresh-peeled orange. Such a refreshing scent. I pop another. Then another, enjoying the smell of each one.

Before I realize what's happening, my legs collapse. The next instant I'm on my knees. I want to stand, but murky fog invades my brain. So groggy. Summoning all my will power, I force my legs and crawl toward the roadway.

Next my elbows thud into the grass, bringing my face into full contact with black blossoms. Bubbles burst into my eyes and nostrils, making them sting. I inhale the sickly-sweet scent.

"They're ... poisoning ... me."

I struggle to rise. My efforts prove worthless. Instead, my head sinks, crushing more petals.

Plip.

3

THEENA

When consciousness creeps back, my sense of hearing returns before my paralyzed muscles respond. I'm numb and sightless. Metallic clanging. Garbled shouts. A cry of pain. Weeping, echoing as if from a distance.

With all my might, I will my eyes to open. They won't budge. I'm drugged. But I sense that I'm moving. Two people are carrying me.

"Throw him in."

My body goes airborne. Just as quickly, I thud onto a solid floor. The impact—and the pain it causes—jar some of the grogginess from my brain. At last, I can crack my eyelids.

Metal bars?

Guttural laughter. "Aha. The new one has finished napping." A pause. "Look at me, you maggot."

Lightning streaks up my leg. My eyes shoot wide, and I finally locate the source of the voice. On the other side of vertical bars stands a huge, broad-shouldered man gripping a metal baton. He glares at me through eyes the color of steel.

"Welcome to your new home, fool. This is where you will live and work for the rest of your life—which won't be long if you don't obey. From now on, Lotan is the name of your god. You live to worship and serve me."

Howls of laughter erupt from unseen mouths.

One lone thought comes to mind: *Lord, help me.*

Lotan shoves the metal rod between the bars a second time. A bolt of pain shoots into my shoulder.

"Argh!"

Lotan's laughter sounds as if it resonates through iron vocal cords. He tosses something that bounces off my head. "Eat. I prefer my slargs alive. Dead prisoners do nothing but leak and stink."

After he stalks away, I dare to glance around. I'm alone in a metal cage consisting of a metal deck plate, vertical metal bars, and a metal ceiling to match the floor. The sides look roughly five feet high by five feet wide. Outside my cage are rows of identical cages. They're empty, but the floors of many bear stains that might be dried blood along with other body fluids. That would explain the reek in the air.

Stand up and stretch? Not yet. My leg muscles feel like Play-Doh. Let them recover while I eat.

With difficulty, I reach for the loaf and nibble as best my semi-numb mouth and throat muscles permit. Swallowing proves difficult. Bits of grass poking from the sour-smelling bread make it even less appetizing. I barely finish when a new figure clumps up to the cell door. Dressed in black and gray, the newcomer sports a mane of inky black hair and a square chin.

"Back away."

I obey.

The man removes a glittering disc from an armband around his bicep and traces a circle in the air. The door springs open.

"Out. I am Karnag, your section commander. I will assign you to your labor."

"My name is Rankin."

Anger kindles in Karnag's eyes. He raises a shorter version of the metal baton Lotan zapped me with. "Silence! You no longer possess a name. You are Lotan's property, a slarg. You will serve him in silence—or die."

I step from the cage but say nothing.

Play along. Act submissive. If they relax their guard, maybe I can find a way to escape. I hang my head.

"Better. If you learn all your lessons that quickly, you might live. Follow me."

Two beefy guards flank me as Karnag leads the way. Other prisoner-filled cages line both sides of the corridor. Quite a few captives are unconscious. All of them bear bruises, scorch marks, or blackened eyes. Are they slaves, or prisoners of war?

The four of us exit the building to an interior courtyard. I gaze upward. The surrounding walls with their circular windows stretch above me, at least fifteen stories high. Only directly overhead is there a patch of lavender sky. Full sunshine. I must've been unconscious all night.

Karnag and his two guards lead me to the middle of the courtyard. Parked on the ground are four gleaming objects. The largest one resembles a silvery airplane, but it has no wings or tail. Clearly though, it's a vehicle. It has a large windshield up front. The flying thing I spotted before passing out.

However, the big, silvery tube is not Karnag's destination. Instead, he strides to a smaller contraption the size of a school-yard merry-go-ground, only it features waist-high metal sides and a circular seat that runs most of the way around the interior. The upper half is open to the sky. Three bruised-up prisoners and a hulking guard already sit aboard, waiting for us.

I hesitate in the doorway. What is this thing? Obi-Wan's convertible?

"Into the samka!"

A foot kicks me from behind. Iron-strong hands pluck me from the floor and crush me onto the seat.

An automatic harness snaps over my body from behind and holds me tight. Similar harnesses lower over the guards when they sit.

Karnag takes the single seat facing what must be the "front" of the round samka. Once again, he withdraws the glittery disc from his armband. The moment Karnag presses the disc onto the control panel, the samka pulsates.

I watch, fascinated. Where's the steering wheel?

Onto his head Karnag lowers a transparent helmet that reminds me of Plexiglas. When he spreads his palms on the control panel, the vehicle shoots straight upward, leaving my stomach somewhere below. About a thousand feet up, we stop rising and begin cruising forward. The impression is that all Karnag needs to do is turn his head, and we move in that direction.

Don't tell me he's guiding this flying thing with his thoughts?

The next sight makes me catch my breath. Outside the citadel we've just exited stands an enormous construction project. Atop a base shaped like a pyramid rises a forbidding monolith of black stone. The structure is tall—an alien skyscraper. Even though it's constructed of massive stone blocks, a pattern of intertwining ribbons and rings runs up and down the exterior. Even uncompleted, the tower impresses with its size and complexity.

I nearly blurt, "What's that?" but bite my tongue. Who knows? These clowns might toss me overboard for speaking without permission. Lotan must be planning a loftier residence from which to rule his empire. Aren't all dictators full of themselves?

Taking advantage of our altitude, I study the countryside spreading beneath us to the horizon. Scattered here and there in the distance are circular areas that I recognize as towns like the one I visited. Patches of woods and fields occupy the spaces between these towns. Stretching between each settlement are long, dark lines that must be more walkways.

What's the deal with all the circles? The towns are round. That disk key that Karnag carries is round. The windows in

Lotan's citadel are round. This flying "samka" thing is also round.

I open my left hand enough to glimpse the new symbol embedded there. Even the mark of a Fithian consists of intersecting circles.

Again, I wish Jaylel had given me more information about Zemna. Should I flash my palm to my captors? Would they respect me, offer better treatment? Deep inside, something says that would be incredibly stupid. It's a long fall to the ground if these guys hate Fithians.

God, I have no clue what's going on. Please help me.

When Karnag guides the samka to a landing, we descend into a rock quarry. Thousands of men and women in tattered garments chip away at massive stone blocks as black as obsidian.

Karnag raises his hand in greeting to a burly man who is likewise garbed in black and gray. "I bring fresh muscles for the labor. Count these slargs as part of my entity."

"We'll put them to work."

Without even entering the samka, the muscular man releases my harness and hauls me out of the vehicle. When my eyes meet his, a massive fist slams down on my head. My knees buckle, and I crumple into dust and stone chips.

"Slargs don't look overseers in the eye. Whoever you were in your old life is over. You worship Lotan, but you answer to Karnag. Serve him, and you will eat. Slack off, and your bloody corpse will be strung up as an example. Understand?"

With a million questions whirling through my mind, no, I don't understand. But I don't want another whack either. I just nod.

"Finally. A slarg with a brain." The overseer shoves a hammer and chisel into my hands. "Work with those slargs on top of that block." He points. "Imitate what they do. The block must be smooth before transport."

I nod and mount the ladder. I don't know which is shakier, the flimsy ladder or my jittery nerves.

For hours, I breathe dust while chipping massive stone blocks. My fingers ache from gripping the tools. Stinging sweat from my brow drips into my eyes. The urge to pause and strip off my hoodie is powerful. However, the sight of overseers kicking, punching, or zapping slow workers—slargs—with their batons keeps my hammer tapping at the chisel. Maybe I can pull off the hoodie during a break time.

Back in Indiana, I never realized how trouble-free life with Grandma Johnson had been. If I could go back right now, no way I would ever gripe about mowing the lawn or taking out the trash.

What a mixed-up planet. These people can pilot flying-saucer convertibles with their brains, but they force their slaves to fashion stone blocks in the most primitive way possible. Why don't they give us some kind of laser tools for this work?

In the next second, I realize what a dumb question that was. If these oppressed workers ever got ahold of lasers—if such things exist here—the overseers would be smoldering mincemeat. Yeah, as a Christian I'm supposed to love my enemies, but if I had a light saber, Boss man wouldn't conk me on the head anymore.

God, did I take a wrong turn? Surely, busting rocks isn't the reason I'm on this planet. Did I goof up?

As if in reply, my mind gravitates to characters in the Bible who loved God, but who still ended up in stinking circumstances. People like Joseph, Daniel, Jeremiah, and the apostle Paul. For that matter, even Jesus got whipped and spat on and nailed to a wooden cross. Each of them stayed faithful, even though some didn't understand what was going on. Okay, if those Bible-time guys endured prison for God without whining, I can, too.

After a while, a female slarg works her way toward me. Dark hair hangs halfway down her back in a ponytail. Grit clings to her face, hands, and tunic, but not enough to hide her high cheekbones and dimples. I try to focus on the rough crag I've been smoothing. Letting myself get distracted by a cute face could earn more zaps from King Kong's magic rod.

Under her breath, the girl whispers while chipping. "Your clothes. Your complexion. You're not from this ward, are you?"

Ward? What's a ward? I glance left and right. No overseer watches, but I keep chiseling. "No. I'm from far away."

"From Taralah?"

I risk a glance into her face. Yes, she's pretty despite the coat of dust and rings under her eyes. Her dark bangs are trimmed straight across, just above the eyebrows. I'd like to see her in clean clothes—maybe a dress—after a shower and full night's rest. Then—incredible—her eyes have purple irises. It's as if someone squeezed some of the alien sky into concentrated liquid and applied a dropper to each eye. I blink. A guy could get lost in those beautiful eyes. Forcing my gaze back to my chisel requires all the self-discipline I can muster.

"From much farther," I say, still chipping. Of course, I have no inkling where Taralah might be. But if it exists on the planet Zemna, I'm definitely from farther away.

When I glance back, she studies me with awe. "They call me Theena."

"Rankin."

"Before lights out, some of us gather inside the mine." Her eyes flick toward a hole cut in the face of the cliff. "It's a safe time to talk. No overseers enter so late. Please come. Others are curious about you."

"Why do you gather?"

A sigh. "To worship in vain. Even though we're no longer one with the Creator, some of us remember Him. We gather to mourn the light we have lost, and to cling to faded memories of how the world used to be. Will you come?"

My heart leaps. Is this group the reason I'm here? Some kind of underground church? "I'll come," I whisper between taps on the chisel.

Just before Theena edges away, I take a gamble. "Wait. Do

you recognize this mark?" I set aside my chisel long enough to wipe my left hand on my jeans and reveal the symbol emblazoned in my palm.

Astonishment springs into her wide eyes. She brushes her fingertips across my palm. "The Intersection of All Things! A Fithian—*here?*"

"Yes, here. I have much to tell your friends."

"Praise the Creator for not abandoning us! We will listen."

4

INTO THE MINE

Late that evening, after a supper of watery gruel and sour bread, the guards permit the slargs some free time while most of them tramp away for their own meal. Despite sore muscles, I meander in the direction of the mine entrance. Both male and female slargs have been glancing around before slipping inside. I do the same.

Cool darkness engulfs me. It's a refreshing change after the heat of the day.

Someone takes my elbow. "This way," says a male voice. "The overseers cut the lights when the workday is over."

My escort, whoever he is, leads me over an uneven stone floor through inky blackness. Either this guy has built-in radar, or he has plenty of experience in the mine.

Eventually we round a corner into a tunnel where a dim light becomes visible. In an alcove, a couple dozen slargs huddle around a small panel that pushes back the darkness with a pale-green gleam.

Theena steps forward to meet me. "Everyone, I present Rankin, the Fithian. Come, Rankin. Stand in the center, where all may see you. Tell us what you have to say."

I step to the middle of the group and try to swallow. I clear my throat. This is so not me. Doesn't God realize how much I can't stand being the center of attention?

"Just a moment. My name is Prahv," says the man who had guided me by the elbow. "First, show us the sign."

Someone in the rear says, "He's right. Display the Intersection before you speak."

I raise my palm and move it in a slow arc so everybody can see its faint sparkle in the dim light. Many squint and lean closer.

Beside me, Prahv examines it. He twists his head back and forth, then mashes his full palm into the Intersection, twisting his hand back and forth. "It's true."

"A genuine Fithian?"

"We have little time," Theena says. "The guards will soon summon us for evening count. What is the message from the Creator?"

As I did the previous day, I retell the old story of another place, where people had rebelled and lost fellowship with their Maker. By ignoring myself and my loathing of public speaking, I simply concentrate on sharing the message of the One that God sent to bear the penalty for people's sin and to restore fellowship with Him.

Just like yesterday, my ragged audience listens with rapt attention.

"So, it was the same in the other place," someone murmurs. "People took their eyes off the Creator and elevated themselves to become their own gods."

I nod. "Sad, but true."

Another voice from the dark, outer ring says, "But how does the Creator's incarnation as Jesus on your world help us? We are not from your world."

"What a great question. And God has a great answer. You see, this is the Creator's message for all people, no matter where they live. The key is faith in the Lord Jesus Christ and the way of salvation He has provided. If you believe, you can receive forgiveness for your sin and renew fellowship with God. Does anyone want to pray and do that?"

Eight listeners in the chamber drop to their knees and lift their faces toward the rocky ceiling. One after another, they pray, asking their Creator's forgiveness and professing their faith in Christ, "whom Your Fithian has proclaimed."

Your Fithian? I swallow. This whole scenario feels way too heavy duty for a guy from Indiana. It's like getting called "his royal majesty Rankin" or something. Part of my brain tallies these eight decisions to my credit for eventually going back to Earth. But another part of me absorbs the incredible sight of these people sincerely calling on God. And I was part of that. Goose bumps rise on my arms.

Other slargs hang back in the shadows. When the final prayer ends, a figure in the rear grumbles. "It seems easy. Too easy."

"I'm not so sure either," says a dark silhouctte. "If you represent the Creator, why are you here, toiling as a slarg? Why aren't you free? Is the Creator so frail that He cannot protect you?"

His questions dredge up a memory, the explanation of a gray-haired evangelist who had once been imprisoned in Soviet Russia. On the spot, I adapt his illustration. "If a person walked up to Lotan and requested permission to deliver a message from the Creator to you, would Lotan agree? No. In God's mercy, He has allowed me—a messenger of His light—to become one of you to deliver His Good News. I can't force you to accept God's love and mercy. All I can do is deliver the message. The choice is yours."

Many shake their heads and mutter. Even some who don't scoff aloud study me with doubtful eyes. Darkness has dragged them into slavery. God offers spiritual freedom, new life in Him, but still they resist—just as I used to do. I end our meeting with a prayer for them and for all the other slargs in the quarry.

* * *

After that first meeting, every evening I sneak back to the mine, where I repeat the story to desperate listeners. Each time, a few accept the message and pray. Others reject it and trudge away.

"He's a deceiver," a woman objects. "There's no life on other planets."

Another man says, "Perhaps he's raising an army to rebel against Lotan. If so, that's the path to an early grave."

At first, the number of those who reject the message discourages me. Am I messing up? After all, I'm no theologian. All I can do is share what I know, even though I have Bible questions of my own. On the other hand, I notice that some who hesitate to accept Christ return on following evenings to listen again and ask me questions. Their curiosity encourages me.

Would Mom and Dad be proud of me for talking about God? As missionaries, they had always been eager to "make a difference for the Kingdom." The ache in my heart returns as I picture them in the photo in Grandma's living room. If only I had talked with them one last time. I didn't though, and I lost my chance. Now that decision haunts me, even on a different world.

* * *

Lotan never sets foot in the quarry. At least, not so far as I see. Occasionally, his scarlet-colored samka cruises above the worksite as he monitors our progress. When it does, slargs quicken their pace, whether they're chipping or hauling away buckets of debris. One morning, I learn why.

Lotan's samka appears and traces a slow circle over the quarry. Then—*whoosh*—it swoops down and hovers over a frail slarg who had stumbled and spilled his bucket of stone chips on the path. Every eyeball in the quarry watches. I continue chipping, but realize I'm holding my breath, waiting for whatever is about to happen.

With an almost majestic flourish, Lotan stands in the samka

and points his metal baton at the struggling slarg. In response, a dozen overseers converge on the man and surround him.

I can't pull my eyes from the drama unfolding a hundred feet away. Lotan holds his baton straight out from his shoulder. It remains motionless for a long, drawn-out moment. Next instant, he lowers it.

As one, all the overseers ram their batons at the fallen body.

Hideous screams fill my ears and start my own hands shaking. I can't imagine such pain. Rather than a quick zap like I've received, the overseers maintain the torture until the victim falls silent, and still they hold position. When at last they trudge away, I don't see the slarg anymore. Just blackened residue on the ground. An odor like charred meat pollutes the air.

When the scarlet samka resumes moving, I pick up the pace.

Before long, a round shadow glides between the sun and me.

Don't look up. Just use the hammer and chisel. Work fast!

Is Lotan eyeballing me in particular? Slargs wear a wide assortment of ragged clothing, but surely I stand out with my tee shirt, blue Levi's, Nike running shoes, and the hoodie tied around my waist to keep anyone from stealing it. Not risking an upward glance, I feverishly chisel and blow away dust until the shadow slides away.

You shouldn't fear any human, I tell myself.

But I do. Before week's end, I've already seen two slarg cadavers hanging upside down and dripping blood from the "Lesson Wire" strung between two posts. I'm not sure who they were or what their offense was. Sure, knowing the Gospel means my soul is ready for Heaven, but I'm not crazy about excruciating pain. So, like a wolf circling just outside the range of a campfire, fear keeps crawling into my heart no matter how often I try to chase it away. I repeat Bible verses. But fear continues to stalk me.

God sent an angel who saved me when the airplane blew up. Couldn't He get me out of here? Yet, He doesn't. Am I going through some kind of test?

A while later, the massive overseer called Gorlic approaches. As always, his head swivels left and right as he clumps along, looking for someone to kick or punch or zap. I can't figure out the ranking system, but he's some kind of special overseer. He doesn't command his own entity of slargs. Instead, he patrols the quarry doing whatever he pleases. Even Karnag bows a little when Gorlic struts past him.

A mountain of muscle with hardly any neck, Gorlic must be the strongest man I've ever seen. But Prahv says he can't utter a word. Totally mute. As far as I can tell, he communicates with grunts, growls, and hand motions.

Gorlic stops on the edge of my peripheral vision. His toes point in my direction. Knowing he's watching makes my skin crawl, even though I don't dare look up. After what seems an eternity, from the corner of my eye I see him lumber away.

Within seconds a human yelp rings out, and I can't help but glance up. Gorlic clutches two slargs by their necks and bashes their heads together. Not even breaking a sweat, he heaves their bodies to the ground. Gurgling laughter boils from his throat.

God, please get me out of here.

* * *

The next evening, no sooner do I approach the feeble light and our group of worshipers when a woman says, "Please, Rankin Fithian, instead of repeating the story of how the Son of God came, lived, and died, may we hear about His first followers? What happened after He rose from the dead?"

"Of course, if that's what you all want to hear."

General murmurs of assent echo in the chamber.

Theena touches my forearm. "Tell us, Rankin. We want to know all we can."

My eyes strain to make out the letters in my little New Testament. I've already shared Acts chapter 1, about how Jesus rose into the heavens while His disciples watched. So, I begin at chapter 2 and start reading, pausing to explain things as I go. Picturing events in ancient Jerusalem is hard enough for me. It must be mind-boggling to Zemnans.

When I conclude with a word of prayer, the slargs hustle toward the exit. They know what happens if anyone is late for the march back to the barracks. Within moments, only Prahv and Theena remain with me. Prahv turns off the light panel. Feeling in the darkness, I help him to hide it beneath rubble until next time.

That done, in the inky blackness, Theena slips her hand into mine. "Come, Rankin. Let me be your guide tonight."

Her move surprises me, since Prahv has always been the one to lead me through the underground maze. But I'm fine with it. What guy wouldn't enjoy holding hands with a beauty like Theena?

As our trio works our way to the exit, I break the silence. "Tell me more about Zemna. I need to understand your world better."

On earlier evenings, Theena and Prahv—her older brother, it turns out—had already clued me in that Lotan isn't the only self-proclaimed deity on this planet. Scores of tyrants all over Zemna have exercised enough power, or charm, or cunning words to recruit followers. They magnify themselves and solidify their power through force.

Prahv clears his throat of mine dust. "What can we say? Zemna was once a unified, harmonious world without rulers or borders. It has disintegrated into petty wards, each with its own sovereign. Few people travel outside their own ward anymore. If the rumors are true, most rulers forbid it. Even if they didn't, fear of the unknown discourages people from traveling. Many of us prefer familiar misery here to the possible worse misery of the unknown."

Prahv's words give me much to ponder as I lay that night on

the canvas-covered board that masquerades as a mattress. Yes, life in this "Ward of Hezkiel" stinks. But slargs cower in the face of rumors that life elsewhere reeks even worse. That whole attitude grates against my patriotic American upbringing. Where's their craving for liberty?

Three nights later, I've shared the Gospel with another cluster of slargs. As usual, Prahv and Theena and I are the final three out of the mine. At that point, Prahv whispers, "You cannot stay here, Rankin Fithian. Uncounted thousands of people in other wards must also hear the Good News you bear. You must go—and soon."

His words catch me by surprise. "What about all the rumors about how life elsewhere is worse? Suddenly you're pushing me into the unknown?"

Theena drops the bomb. "I have heard slargs whispering. They plot to end your life. Whether the rumors are true or not, you must leave, Rankin."

The larger of Zemna's two moons, Feebia, hasn't yet risen, but the little one they call Eenik sheds enough light to show concern on Theena's face.

I tilt my head closer to Prahv to keep other slargs from overhearing. "Why would anybody want to kill me? I haven't hurt anyone."

"It does not matter that you have not wronged them. They are blind, self-centered. Some spout that you are a troublemaker, an ordinary man who has somehow faked the symbol of the Intersection. They fear your presence will ignite the wrath of overseers. Others fantasize about winning special favor by delivering your corpse to Lotan and showing him the symbol. After all, he has declared the Creator his enemy, which means you are the servant of his enemy. Who knows? Lotan truly might reward them for slitting your throat."

I swallow, imagining a sharp blade there as I do. I'll have to stay on full alert.

"We hope you will leave," Prahv says. "Not because we want you gone. We don't. But we care about you, and so many need your message. Will you save yourself?"

By Eenik's meager light, Theena and Prahv wait for my reply. How can I run off and leave them to waste away in the quarry? They've become my best friends on this odd planet. Besides, the very notion of escaping alone into the mysterious unknown knots my stomach. Will I always be a fugitive? Will I constantly share my New Testament, make a few friends, and then desert them as I wander to other "wards"? Also, in the back of my mind nags the biggest question of all—will I manage to convince seven thousand Zemnans of the Gospel and return to Earth within the year?

I clear my throat. "Sounds like leaving is the smart thing to do. Except, I'm not sure how to do it. The perimeter fence looks wicked. Besides, they guard it day and night."

As we follow the path around a huge mound of debris, we cease talking. Often Gorlic sits here on his haunches, waiting to jump on any slarg for the least infraction. On this evening he isn't here.

Prahv lowers his voice to a breath. "I have a plan."

"What kind of plan?"

"I think we can get you away from the quarry under cover of darkness. Sneaking past the guards will be the tricky part. Once away from the barracks, we can guide you to the samkas. By air, you could escape the quarry. In fact, you could leave Hezkiel Ward altogether. With no footprints to follow, no one could even guess which direction you have flown."

"Can we get one of those glittery disks that power the samkas?"

For the second time, my words leave confusion on Theena's face. "Why do you need one? Aren't you a Fithian?" She reaches for my left hand and turns it palm upward. "If the stories are true, this is your gift from the infinite Creator. The Intersection of power is your gateway to all things on Zemna. With this, they say, a Fithian can travel anywhere, power almost any device. You are not only the source for understanding the Creator's grace, Rankin Fithian. You are a living key to this entire planet."

In my brain, a light bulb clicks on. The Intersection of All Things—at last the phrase makes sense. So, I've become a walking, talking access code—like a universal login?

"On Zemna, does anyone besides a Fithian possess such a symbol?"

"Of course not," Prahv replies. "The sign of a Fithian is unique. You understand so many hidden truths, Rankin. How could you not know this?"

I sigh. "Look, even though I'm a Fithian, that doesn't mean I know everything in the universe. I'm new to this role. God is omniscient, but no flesh-and-blood person knows everything. All humans have limitations, even messengers of the Light."

Theena nods. "Yes, this must be true, even for Fithians."

"Right. So, there's plenty about Zemna I don't know. I knew nothing of your world until recently. I'm not even positive which plants are edible and which ones are poisonous. If I leave the quarry, I could use a guide. Or two."

Prahv glances to Theena then back to me. "Are you inviting us to accompany you in your quest?"

I can't stop the grin that grows on my face. "I'd like nothing better. But I don't want to force you or put you two in danger."

The column slows as we approach the counting gate leading to the barracks.

"The years of safety have disappeared forever," Theena whispers. "Merely being alive on Zemna puts us in danger. All right, we will come with you, even though we might prove unreliable helpers. Zemna has changed. It's no longer the place we once knew. Too bad we no longer have Unizem. That would simplify your quest."

"Unizem? What's that?"

She raises her hands and traces a circle in the air. "You know

—Unizem. The unifier that once allowed everyone all around the globe to hear the same voice or same song all in the same instant. Does not your planet have such an invention? In this way, our entire world often knit their hearts together in praise to the Creator."

My heart lurches. There's a system for making announcements to the whole planet at once? What better way to earn my trip back to Earth in no time?

"Quit dragging your feet," shouts an overseer. "Into formation."

We three run to join the procession of slargs assembling for the march into the barracks compound. Meanwhile, my thoughts race. Unizem. Why didn't Jaylel tip me off? That would be the ideal way to accomplish my mission.

As the mass of bodies lurches forward, I whisper, "How does the Unizem work?"

Prahv and Theena lapse into silence and look at the ground as we pass an overseer with an inflictor rod. I do the same.

When we've plodded a safe distance, Prahv continues with lowered voice. "I can't explain how Unizem worked. There's too much knowledge in the world for any one person, and this wasn't my area of giftedness. Friends created it long ago as a method to harmonize our hearts in praise to God. It became a marvelous tool."

Theena continues with more detail. "In several wards around Zemna, a talented team constructed Unizem portals. When the operators calibrated all the variables, any message spoken inside a portal resonated around the globe and was heard in all places where it detected clusters of human life, with no apparatus on the receiving end. What joy we shared as we paused our activities to sync our hearts in a song or a word of edification."

"The Unizem does not function anymore," Prahv says. "It's another shining memory from bygone days."

That fast, my hope goes up in smoke. The best possible way for talking to the whole planet is busted?

No more time for questions. We've arrived at the barracks. Time to split up.

Prahv presses his upraised right palm to mine. It's not a high five, just the Zemnan way of saying goodbye or sealing an agreement. "It will be a privilege to travel with you. We leave together. Expect me tonight."

5

UNDER COVER OF DARKNESS

Long after lights out, in one of the barracks for male slargs, I lie on my canvas-covered board. Around me, heavy breathing, snoring, and a fetid odor fill the air. Although my muscles ache every time I shift, for once sleep doesn't tempt me the slightest bit. In the darkness, tense and alert, I listen.

Come on, Prahv. What's taking so long?

Barely a second later, fingers grip my shoulder. I stiffen.

A breath in my ear says, "Come."

Prahv sure can sneak around on cat's feet. In darkness, we tiptoe out of the barracks. The silhouette of Theena waits near the corner. I can't make out her features, but I'd recognize her slender figure anywhere. She holds something in each hand. Cups? Jars? I'm curious, but this is no place for conversation.

Together, the three of us slink through deeper shadows near walls and under eaves of neighboring barracks toward the vehicle pen. I've never been outdoors so late.

I lean closer to Prahv and dare a whisper. "How many guards patrol at night?"

He places a hand on my back and tilts his head closer. "We'll soon find out."

Oh, great. A possible flaw in the plan, and I'm just now

finding out? *Lord, help us.* I hope the overseers place all their trust in the perimeter fence and the ring of lights that illuminate it.

I risk another question. "What about the samkas? Anyone guard them?"

"We hope not."

My confidence evaporates. What I've assumed would be a well-laid plan relies on a stack of naïve maybes and hopes? A brick settles in my stomach. Is it too late to scratch this plan and sneak back to the barracks? Prahv leaves the normal pathway and cuts across uneven ground, where enormous mounds of useless stone chips offer some cover.

Despite my hoodie, I shiver—more from fear than from cold. How many things can go wrong? Too many.

Tiptoeing, with gravel crunching underfoot, we approach the roped-off samka corral. Here, light from the distant perimeter fence barely illuminates the regular samkas used for personnel and the larger bolsamkas used for transporting massive stone blocks and other heavy loads.

Prahv leans close and places a hand on my shoulder. "The overseers assume no slarg can power the transports. Without you and the Intersection, we could never get off the ground. Before we leave, we must disable the other transports to keep them from pursuing us."

Into my hands Theena presses a cup, plus an object that feels like a paintbrush.

"You go left. I'll go right," Prahv says. "Smear this onto the round indentation of each control panel. It will destabilize the feralin contacts. No power disk will work unless they replace the contacts."

In the darkness, I sniff the mug. "What is this liquid?"

"Blood. It contains the exact chemical composition we need. This afternoon the overseers killed Hindral for stumbling. They strung his corpse to the Lesson Wire. I collected what blood I could to aid our escape."

I yank the cup away from my nose. "That's disgusting!"

"We agree," Theena whispers. "But in this way, Hindral's death can serve a good cause."

Imitating shadows for silence, Prahv and I flit from vehicle to vehicle. As he instructed, I brush the gross contents of my cup into the "ignition" circle of each flying craft. Fortunately, in the darkness I don't have to see the blood. My stomach is queasy enough from tension. If we get caught now, our blood will get mingled with Hindral's.

I step aboard the final samka on my side of the corral.

A sleepy grunt stiffens the hairs on the back of my neck.

The samka wiggles from some unseen shift of weight. Somebody is here.

From the seat where he's been resting rises a silhouette—a gargantuan silhouette. To my horror, the larger moon, Feebia, escapes the clouds in time to illuminate both me and the colossal man with scarcely any neck.

No way. Gorlic!

6

———

ESCAPE

Enraged gurgling shatters the silence. Gorlic sidesteps, blocking the samka's exit. He might be mute, but nothing is wrong with his eyes. Even by moonlight, he recognizes me. The gleam of murder kindles in those eyes.

I spring to vault over the side of the samka. In midair, vice-like fingers clamp around my arm and hurl me onto the seat of the samka. Even though the seat is padded, the impact knocks the wind from me and jars my bones.

Stunned. Can't think. But if I stay here, Gorlic will rip off my arms and legs. Frantic, I scramble to my feet and nearly clear the side of the vehicle when a savage kick catches me from behind. Instead of performing a quick leap to safety, I cartwheel face first into rough gravel.

Another loud crunch tells me Gorlic, too, has jumped from the samka. Before I can rise, he gurgles in my ear. Massive hands grab me under the arms. He hoists me above his head then hurls me to the ground.

Thudding into crushed gravel knocks the air from my lungs. Pain radiates from my back. I want to jump up, flee, but can't. All I can manage is a hoarse plea to my friends.

"Run. Save yourselves."

In a move I didn't realize he could do, Gorlic places both hands beside his mouth and bellows into the night. At such close range, the heinous roar rattles my eardrums and petrifies my soul. If anyone in the quarry was sleeping, they just woke up.

"Run!" I repeat, hoping my friends have already fled.

Desperate, I roll over and scramble onto all fours to escape. Wrong way—the samka blocks my path.

A massive force crunches onto my back, smashing me into the stony ground. The toe of Gorlic's boot slides under my shoulder and flips me over. Eclipsing Feebia's light, he towers above me. This is it. My final second of life.

In a surreal flash, I picture some newbie Fithian getting dropped off, asking what happened to the previous Earthling. "He was killed."

Gorlic raises his boot to stomp my face.

Anger surges. I've come too far to die so fast. I roll to the right just as Gorlic's foot slams down. I barely dodge left as he drives his foot down a second time.

Just as Gorlic raises his foot a third time, a new shadow flings itself onto him, toppling him off balance. The two crash to the ground.

"Take the samka," blurts Prahv. "Go!"

Theena pulls me up and urges me toward the doorway of the samka. In the distance, an unearthly wail splits the night. An alarm.

"Rankin, hurry!"

But I can't leave Prahv. The maniac just committed suicide to save my skin. I turn and see Gorlic heft the shadow of Prahv over his head and slam him to the ground, just as he'd done to me.

"Rankin, now!"

I can't leave. It isn't bravery. Maybe it's stupidity, or just righteous anger welling inside me. Instead, I run at Gorlic, jump, and ram both heels into his kidney. No sooner do I tumble to the ground, than an oversized hand closes around my throat and lifts me. With his other hand, Gorlic picks up Prahv and grins, his crooked teeth glinting in the moonlight. This really is it—head-bashing time. No escape.

From my squashed throat I hiss the word "No" even as I shove my left hand into Gorlic's ugly face. Maybe I can dig my fingers into his eyes. Then—incredible tingling ripples through my palm. For half an instant, Gorlic's face flashes orange red beneath my touch.

With a sound like the blast of air under high pressure, Gorlic's head snaps backward. It's as if I'd smacked him across the nose with a baseball bat. He goes limp. All three of us crumple to the ground. Only Prahv and I rise. Gorlic lies where he's fallen.

"What did you do to him?" The awe in Theena's voice matches my own surprise.

I look at my palm. The Intersection of All Things still glows dull red, but quickly fades and goes dark. "I'm not sure. That's never happened before."

"Whatever you did, I am thankful," Prahv says. "Quick, into the samka."

In the distance we hear shouts. Lights flash. Overseers are hunting for the cause of the commotion.

Once we're aboard, Theena offers me the glassy pilot helmet.

"No. I'm not experienced. Let Prahv pilot. I'll sit nearby, with the Intersection on the panel."

As soon as our harnesses snap on, Prahv nods to me. "Now."

I place my left palm over the round indentation normally reserved for a key disk. Immediately the samka emits a soft hum. Yellow and green indicator lights spring to life all over the panel. Exhilaration wells in my chest. After years of reading graphic novels, I actually have a superpower of my own.

The samka lifts into the air.

"This is so cool."

Theena strains forward and manages to press a fingertip to

the panel. "No, the temperature feels normal. Perhaps using the Intersection causes a sensation of chilliness?"

I nearly laugh despite the danger. "Cool—it's just an expression. Never mind."

"Gorlic?" shouts Karnag's voice below us. "Are you there? Grunt, or bang on something. Make yourself known."

Obeying Prahv's mental commands, the samka elevates higher into the night. Way too late, the darkness around us erupts with orange streaks flashing up from the ground. The shots go wild, missing by hundreds of yards as we zip forward.

I glance overboard and guess we must be two or three thousand feet up. The unfinished monolith of Lotan's future residence rears itself as a deeper blackness against the night. Here and there, pale lights gleam through windows. The diamond necklace of the perimeter-fence lights slides to our rear as the samka glides away. I thank God for the clouds that swallow Feebia and mask our getaway. Are those clouds a fortunate coincidence, or divine help from above?

Once the glow of the quarry lights has receded far behind us, I breathe easier. "Where are we going?"

"We're not sure," Theena says. "All of Zemna has changed. Prahv and I don't know what's happening in other wards. Does it matter, though? The entire planet needs to hear your message. May the Creator guide us."

"You're right. I guess one direction is as good as another." Under my breath, I add, "Ready or not, Zemna, here comes your next Fithian."

* * *

For a long while, we fly in silence. I think Prahv must feel as wiped out as I am after the tag-team fight with Gorlic. My whole body aches. Even swallowing hurts. The unknown future provides another reason for silence. We're cruising into mystery.

"Samkas were never intended for long-distance flights,"

Prahv says at last. "Still, I think we ought to put plenty of distance between Lotan and ourselves."

"Right. The farther from Lotan, the better. That self-proclaimed god will be livid when he learns that three slargs escaped in one of his own samkas."

In the darkness, the silhouette of Prahv's head nods. "I was hoping for a tail wind to push us. Hopefully to some other ward. But I'll get as far as we can."

On we fly. Below, I often see lights, either singly or in clusters. It would be cool to study the landscape by day—better yet, through a pair of high-powered binoculars. So many questions concerning this planet seem knotted together.

I've always been the guy who hates asking questions. Figuring things out on my own is more satisfying. Did Jaylel believe that's a helpful trait? Or is it a character flaw I need to overcome?

Now that we have leisure time to talk, maybe I can coax information from these two. Not wanting to distract Prahv from piloting, I turn to Theena. "Tell me about your planet's—" I stop. I wanted to say "technology," but no equivalent word comes to mind in First Tongue, the language of Zemna.

"About our planet's what?"

I search for a way to rephrase it. "About the newest and most complicated devices your people have created."

She sits in silence a moment, but I notice a slight cocking of her silhouetted head. "Complicated devices?"

"Sure. For example, this flying vehicle. Or those metal batons Lotan's guards use."

"I'm not sure what you mean. These are merely conduits for harnessing various aspects of the Creator's handiwork. This knowledge isn't new, although in the Before Times nobody used it to create inflictor rods, fyotors, and other instruments for violence. In those days, people applied natural principles to constructive applications."

I approach from a different angle. "All right, let's start with something more basic. For instance, how old are you and Prahv?"

"What do you mean?"

I sigh. Even though I've received the gift of speaking this world's language, and these two are extremely intelligent, people on Zemna think with an alien mentality.

"The planet Zemna travels around your sun, Aena, correct?"

"Of course, it does." A playful tone has crept into her voice.

I hope Theena doesn't think I'm an idiot. Whatever reputation Fithians enjoy here, I'm pretty sure they're not supposed to sound ignorant. "Since the day you were born, how many times has the planet Zemna completed its orbit around Aena?"

This time both Theena and Prahv burst into laughter. We fly through darkness, but in the soft glow of the control panel Prahv glances in my direction. "The Creator knows."

"I've never even thought about it," Theena says, still giggling. "Prahv was born before me, so he's gone around more times than I have. But we don't count such things."

"You don't know how old you are? Don't you care?"

She laughs again. "Rankin, every day your eyes blink, right?"

"Of course."

"How many times did you blink yesterday? And how many times have you blinked in your whole life?"

"Huh? I don't know. I don't keep track."

She mimics my shocked tone. "You don't know? Don't you even care?" She bursts into more giggles.

I adore her laughter, even if it's at my expense.

"I have no idea either," Theena continues. "Here on Zemna, we never give thought to the number of times we've circled Aena. Or the number of times we blink or exhale. What could we accomplish with this information?"

I absorb her statement. Theena isn't simple-minded. Back in the quarry, she proved herself as intelligent as she is courageous and cute. I've simply landed in a world with different values and an alternate way of thinking.

Of course, at the root of my question is my curiosity to know whether Theena is close to my own seventeen years. Except for the purple irises in her eyes, her face looks like a college undergrad's. However, something about her hints at more years. How many more?

To save face a little, I say, "Where I come from, we keep track of our age for lots of reasons. For example, when men and women want to become a couple, you know—to get married—they have to be a certain minimum age."

Prahv and Theena remain silent, trying to process my alien way of thinking.

Suddenly I'm fumbling for words. "Well, it doesn't matter."

Both the larger and smaller of Zemna's moons have now broken free of clouds, and before us a pale radiance grows on the eastern horizon. A good chance to change the subject.

I touch Prahv's elbow. "Morning is coming. How about landing somewhere before daylight? Since none of us knows where we are, it might be better if no one on the ground sees our arrival."

Prahv nods. "You are wise in matters of stealth, Rankin." Without even touching the panel, Prahv wills the samka to slow and descend.

A twinge of jealousy seeps into my thoughts. I would love to take a turn piloting the samka. For now, flying lessons will have to wait. But who knows? I just might learn to fly while on Zemna.

As we lose altitude, I consider Prahv's compliment. He's just praised me for knowing how to be sneaky. For the first time, I realize all my experience on the troubled planet Earth might play to my advantage. Sure, these people are now sinners, and they can be violent, just like people back on Earth. But they don't possess my accumulated knowledge of corruption. They're amateurs when it comes to matters of slyness and deception. Is that good, or bad? Whichever it is, I tuck that scrap of knowledge into my brain for future reference.

Obeying Prahv's mental commands, the samka descends toward a vast area of denser darkness below. No lights at all twinkle there. Good. No prying eyes. Uninhabited forest, maybe? It's far better to get a peek at our surroundings before the surroundings get a peek at us.

As the samka lowers toward a black surface, a sound like cascading water grows louder, drowning out the samka's faint humming.

Not until now do I realize how stiff my left shoulder is from holding my hand over the ignition ring all night. I give it a roll to loosen the rotator cuff muscles. "Sounds like a waterfall."

Prahv throws me a glance. "Yes, now I know where we are. I'll settle us in the water."

Sure enough, a moment later, the samka comes to rest on a watery surface. Like a boat, it rises and falls with the waves beneath the hull.

Prahv pulls off the guidance helmet. "You can remove the Intersection now."

The moment I pull away my hand, the green and yellow panel displays wink off. Amazing. Too bad I don't have a user's manual for this Intersection thing. At last I can massage the stiffness from my whole left arm. That done, I pause to study the Intersection again. How incredible that this emblem on my hand can power a flying machine.

Into my mind returns the picture of the glow under my palm right before it zapped Gorlic's face. His motionless body just sprawled there after I knocked him out. I don't think the creep was dead. I'll have to be extra cautious of my own left hand until I figure out what activates the Intersection. Wouldn't be cool to blow my nose and accidentally explode my brains out the back of my skull. Definitely not the way to impress Zemnan girls.

Following Prahv's and Theena's examples, I release the safety harness. Unlike them, however, I don't stand and stretch. I'm tired. Or maybe *drained* is a better description. Does using the

Intersection draw some of my own body's energy? Not until now do I realize how weak I feel.

I stretch out on the circular seat. "All right with you two if I rest awhile? I'm exhausted. Need to recharge."

"Go ahead, Rankin," Theena says. "We've all been through a lot. You especially."

No words have ever been more welcome. My head hits the seat. For an instant it occurs to me that maybe I should do something more spiritual. Perhaps lead us in a prayer of thanks for deliverance? But this is a case of the spirit being willing when the flesh is weak. I simply think, *Thank You, Lord,* and that's all I muster.

7

FLYING LESSONS

"Prahv, I need to adapt to Zemna. The faster I adjust to life here, the more effective I can be as a Fithian. Can you teach me to fly the samka?"

Bright sunlight now washes over our getaway craft, which gently bobs on what Prahv and Theena tell me is enormous Lake Selador. In the distance, the waterfall continues its roaring, but while dozing, we've drifted far out from shore. Theena stirs at the sound of my voice.

Prahv had already been awake, but now sits up. "Of course. I'm the one who taught Theena to fly. Are you ready right now?"

What a question. Learning to pilot the samka will be the coolest thing ever, but I disguise my eagerness. "I'm ready. At least, if you think it's safe. With the sun shining, maybe there's too much danger of attracting attention?"

He picks up the guidance helmet. "Should be fairly safe. The shore along this side of Selador was left wild and undeveloped."

Prahv fits the helmet onto my head. Although it resembles glass or Plexiglas, it's not as heavy as I expected. Right away, the thing seems to cling to me, almost as if it's a magnet and my skull is made of steel. I give my neck a swift twist back and forth, but the helmet sticks tight. A moment later, I "see" translucent controls, which pop into my eyesight. When I turn my head, the see-through controls turn, too. The helmet seems to project them right onto my eyeballs. Meanwhile, the whole world has taken on a yellowish tint. "Wow."

Prahv chuckles. "Looks like the interface will function with brains from your world, too. Good. That was my main concern. As you can see, the helmet interacts with the pilot's mental processes. It also enhances visual acuity to the point where darkness is irrelevant. Wearing that helmet, you can fly through the murkiest night."

"Night vision," I summarize. "Plus, internal mental controls. Incredible. Luke Skywalker never owned anything like this."

"Luhk Skah-wahker?" Prahv and Theena sound like male and female stereo speakers.

"Forget it. He's just a guy on my planet. Sort of." Trying to explain would be a waste of time. I'm ready to soar. "What's next?"

"Merge your thoughts with the projections from the helmet. You'll begin to feel the soft links better than I can explain it. Don't resist. Let your mind relax."

"While you men have fun, I'm going to wash up." Theena pulls off her boots then dives into Lake Selador, clothes and all. For the moment, though, I'm more absorbed with the new "soft links" taking root in my thoughts.

"That's it, Rankin. Let the connections deepen. Don't fight it. You won't lose control of yourself. Rather, the connections will become new hands and fingers, all subject to your mental commands."

A second later, instinct tells me how to elevate the craft. Without consulting Prahv, I press my left palm to the round depression and command the samka to rise a few feet from the water. It responds.

Prahv laughs and gives my back an approving slap. "Perfect. I've never seen anyone merge that fast."

I bask in his praise as I practice maneuvering the samka.

First, I rotate it three hundred sixty degrees. Next, I take it up to about twenty feet and back down. Last, I guide it in a meandering circle around Theena, who stops rinsing her hair to grin up at me. It's the first time I've seen her face without a speck of quarry grit, and even in the yellow tint caused by the guidance helmet, I can't take my eyes off her beautiful face. Hopefully, my quick talent for flying will score a few points after my ignorance of local culture.

"A little higher," Prahv says.

I mentally command the samka up to fifty feet. That is, I think in feet, even though the samka somehow converts to local measurements. It obeys as quickly and smoothly as if I've commanded my thumb to scratch my chin.

From nowhere, a new realization appears in my brain. "Something tells me the samka is low on energy."

"Correct again. I nearly exhausted the tyagil cells during our long flight. Set it back down. The tyagils will automatically absorb gravitational energy and recharge."

Even as I settle the craft onto Lake Selador, my brain—or the helmet—somehow interprets the foreign concept. "Gravity conversion? You mean this thing soaks up energy from gravity and reverses the polarity for flight?"

"Of course. What other energy source would work?"

Wow. Mind blown. Not until this moment does it occur to me that Zemna contains no underground fossil fuels. Noah's Flood never happened here. All the untold trillions of tons of plant and animal life that got buried beneath Earth's surface by a worldwide catastrophe never occurred. Instead of utilizing fossil fuels, Zemnans had to discover alternate sources of energy.

When I tug the helmet from my head, it comes off easy enough. Instantly, the world bursts into brilliant color. The yellowish tint and translucent controls vanish. Still, the sensation of pulling off a molded magnet lingers. Such a bizarre experience.

"Congratulations, Rankin. That was excellent, especially for the first time. Are you sure you haven't flown before?"

"That was my first—" When I glance to where Theena treads water, my answer catches in my throat. She's patting down her tunic sleeves, washing gray grit from the fabric. Somehow, without the yellowish tint from the piloting helmet, the sparkling clean beauty of Theena's face in full color knocks me for a loop.

With an effort, I force my eyes back to Prahv. "Uh, no. I've been airborne before, but never as the pilot. The vehicles I operated at home travel on two or four wheels, and always across the ground."

Prahv is smiling. I'm not sure whether his good humor stems from my successful flying lesson or from noticing my reaction to his sister. Warmth in my cheeks tells me I'm blushing. I order them to stop, but my face doesn't obey like the samka did.

"Let's wash up." Prahv slips off his boots, removes his tunic, and with his leggings still on dives into the lake. He begins wiping his face and running his fingers through his wet hair.

I'm about to do likewise, when I notice a latch inside the samka. A compartment. My experience of merging with the helmet revealed nothing about this door. I pop it open and extract a futuristic-looking rifle. "Look what we have here."

"Gorlic's fyotor." Theena treads water near the opening of the samka. "He must have hidden it there while on guard duty."

"While snoozing on duty, you mean."

The weapon doesn't have a gun sight, so I point upward and depress the firing mechanism.

With a hissing sound, an orange bolt streaks to the sky.

"It works."

Prahv shakes the excess water from his hair. "So it does. But I recommend not firing again. Even without a settlement nearby, there's always a stray chance someone might notice the flash and investigate."

"Right." I stow the fyotor, pull off my hoodie and tee shirt, and kick loose my Nikes. When I knife into Lake Selador, the liquid is cool and incredibly refreshing. Surfacing, I lick my lips. It's freshwater, with no hint of saltiness. Is it truly more invigorating than regular H_2O on Earth? After untold days of chipping stone blocks for Lotan, the experience revitalizes me better than a day at the beach.

After scrubbing my head and upper body, I simply float on my back with eyes closed and pants pockets pulled out. Let the lake rinse my jeans while I bask in the perfect combination of cool water and warming rays from Aena, the sun. Prahv and Theena tread water and chat about other places where they've swum and friends whose names I've never heard. I tune them out. I can almost imagine myself spending Saturday afternoon at Warren Dunes State Park, my favorite beach on the shore of Lake Michigan.

A serpent-like hiss startles my eyelids open. A cloud of steam billows up from the surface.

"What was that?"

Eyes wide as my own, Prahv and Theena glance wildly about.

Another hiss and burst of steam, but this time my eyes glimpse the flash.

Theena points to the sky. "Attackers!"

Sure enough, about a couple thousand feet up and closing, a samka hovers into view. Even from this distance I recognize a fyotor in the hands of the guy riding shotgun.

"They've found us," Prahv says. "Dive deep. It's our only hope to survive a fyotor blast."

8

DOGFIGHT

My friends dive, leaving me the only target on the surface.

But diving isn't the solution. Without air tanks, we can't stay underwater more than a minute. Those guys will boil us like lobsters if I don't do something—and quick.

A hiss precedes another burst of steam gushing from the surface, so close I'm inhaling blistering vapor through my nostrils. Good thing there's no gun sight on fyotors, or the three of us would be poached. The billowing cloud of whiteness provides a smoke screen. I seize my chance.

Heaving myself aboard the samka, I slap the guidance helmet onto my head. Once again, the world takes on a yellowish tint. The safety harness clamps over me. A second later, the samka and I hurtle into the sky like a runaway fighter jet.

The intruders shout as I rocket past, barely missing them. Then they do as I hoped. They ignore my friends and leap into hot pursuit. But now what?

Clad in soggy jeans, I shiver. The wind chill distracts, but I force myself to concentrate. Instinctively—or rather, by interface with the helmet—I realize this craft wasn't meant for high speed. Still, I'm thankful its designers gave the propulsion unit more oomph than needed for normal flight. I order the samka faster.

Orange lightning stabs past me. Thank goodness, they don't rapid fire. Maybe fyotors can't recharge quickly?

Wait. Fyotors. I have Gorlic's.

With my left palm on the control panel, I can barely reach the compartment latch with my right foot. It pops open. I can see the fyotor but can't stretch my toes far enough to snag it.

I bank the samka to the left, and the weapon tumbles out. "Yes!" Just in time, too, because another streak singes the air I just vacated.

Hefting the weapon with my right hand while flying is clumsy. I balance it on my shoulder pointing backward. I can't aim, but I figure they're directly behind me. I depress the firing button and release a shot of my own. A backward glance shows I've startled the pursuing pilot enough to make him back off, but he sticks to the chase.

I depress the button again. Nothing. So, fyotors really do need time to recharge. Awesome. That buys me a few seconds.

Maybe it's the adrenaline, or maybe it's because this is my second experience with the samka, but this time I'm rapidly becoming more aware of its capabilities—and its limitations. I sense that, theoretically, the craft offers more than straight and level flight. More maneuverability is available somehow, but there's a built-in inhibitor. Oh great, a safety feature. My gaze dances over the translucent schematics that scroll inside my eyes.

There's got to be an override, a way to make this thing really perform. But where?

Another brilliant flash narrowly misses.

I break into a sweat. "God, show me what to do."

Still scanning displays, my inner vision halts at a red pentagon. It's marked *Danger, Supercede* in the odd First Tongue symbols I somehow understand.

Supercede? Is that even a word? Hoping it means "override," I decide to find out.

Relying on the helmet's interface, I command Supersede

mode to activate. Immediately, the samka wobbles and bucks against the rushing air. The safety governors have clicked offline. More than ever before, the samka has melded into an extension of my own being. Since I'm buckled in, I dare to experiment with a high-speed barrel roll—rotating the samka clockwise through full inversion. Upside down, I catch a fleeting glimpse of Prahv and Theena treading water far below. Then the samka pulls out of the roll, on the same course and altitude. This is the closest thing to free flight I can imagine!

From the timing of shots behind me, I know they'll fire again within a couple seconds. "Shoot at innocent swimmers in the water, will you? Go ahead. Make my day."

I flip my weapon, pointing it forward instead of backward. Next, gripping the fyotor in the crook of my right arm, I command the samka to veer straight upwards, then over until I'm upside down, then back down. I've seen vintage warplanes loop the loop at the Mt. Comfort Air Show in Indianapolis, but I never imagined myself pulling such a stunt—until now. It works. I come out of the loop dead center on the enemy samka's tail. I see both occupants, one pilot and one fyotor-wielding gunner, both craning their necks my way.

Fire!

My fyotor spits a deadly streak. I'm ready to shout a whoop of triumph, but victory withers in my throat. A miss. My turn to recharge.

The enemy craft is near enough to see the gunner's jaw hanging open. Hasn't he ever seen what a samka can do when all the stops are pulled? Maybe not. The pilot, though, banks a sharp left, then to the right, trying to shake me, or at least to present a dodging target.

"Nice try, but your safeties are still engaged. You can't lose me that way."

The enemy gunner points his weapon my way. The moment I figure he's ready to press the button, I flip the samka sideways, flying vertically. When the shot zips past, I flip back to horizontal flight. Adrenaline pumping, I'm on the guy's tail and closing the distance.

The gunner's jaw drops. Guess he's astonished at my maneuvers. My opponents have murder in their hearts, but when it comes to warfare, these guys are amateurs. I've seen more war flicks and sci-fi battles than I can count, and that doesn't include time spent playing video games. I never served in the Air Force, but I know tactics these guys have never dreamed of. Imagine that—Rankin Johnson, Top Gun.

The red light glowing on the side of my fyotor changes from red to green. She's ready to fire. Still cradling the thing in my right arm, I try to line up my target, which keeps jinking from left to right then back again.

"Eat this!"

My volley nearly misses but grazes the lower edge of the enemy samka. A thin trail of bluish vapor streams out. Suddenly the air stinks like burning plastic mixed with toxic baby diapers. Yee-uck. But, hey, the bad guys are wobbling. Maybe I fried some of the tritantum inside their stabilizers?

That thought smacks home with astonishing surprise. *Tritantum?* Stabilizers? How do I even know this stuff? Incredibly, the helmet must be supplementing my pitiful knowledge from its own database. It's interfacing as if I were a real Zemnan, whether my brain comprehends the lingo or not.

The gunner ahead glances at his weapon and grins. Recharge must be close to one hundred percent. What can I do?

The image that pops into my brain is so outlandish—so ridiculous and risky—that I instantly love it.

I drop the elevation about twenty feet so that I'm lower than my opponents. *Increase velocity. Faster!*

Beneath my left palm, the samka's panel vibrates faster. Yeah, it's just a machine, but the mental merger gives the impression my ride is as eager as I am to try this experiment. Could the craft be vibrating in response to my own adrenaline?

The burst of speed shoots me forward and, just before

catching up to the lead samka, I give the mental command: *Invert!*

My craft flips upside down just as I slide beneath my quarry.

Maximum repeller force!

If my samka had been resting on the ground, maximum grav-repellers would've rocketed me sky-high. However, inverted beneath the enemy samka with anti-grav of its own, my maneuver has placed our grav-repellers facing away from each other, like two electromagnets pushing each other with equal polarity—until mine emanates an irresistible repeller force ten times stronger than theirs. The effect is instantaneous. The enemy samka goes flipping out of control like a giant coin tossing through the air. Meanwhile, my own thrust shoots me downward, but in a controlled maneuver, since I expect it.

"Yes!"

Into my brain pops an urgent message: *Warning. Tyagil mesophylls near depletion.*

I've been so preoccupied with outflying the bad guys that I've ignored my power cells. Using max repeller force drained them. Only seconds of power left. I can't fall two thousand feet and survive.

My brain spits out quick commands: *Level flight. Cut forward velocity. Repellers, bare minimum.*

The craft obeys. I'm right-side up, but it's impossible to descend safely. Only six or seven seconds of juice left before free fall.

My brain flashes through translucent schematics. No parachute. No spare battery. No emergency backup. The peace-loving designers never pictured a hotshot speed jockey burning through tyagil energy at the rate I just did.

What can I do?

It's counter-intuitive, but there's only one tactic I think of to save energy. I yank my left palm off the ignition ring.

9

JAKOR

All systems aboard the samka blink offline. My craft drops faster than Dumbo with frozen ears. My stomach leaps into my throat.

Recharge!

My brain flashes back to an Earth documentary where a helicopter ran out of fuel in midair. That's my predicament, only I'm exposed to frigid, whipping air as the samka rocks and flutters on its downward plunge. Without power, this thing is no more aerodynamic than a playground merry-go-round. Lake Selador spreads directly below, but from this height, that's no comfort. That water may as well be solid concrete if I slam into it at this speed.

"Jaylel, help!" The angel plucked me out of an exploding airplane. Can't he repeat the bubble trick?

The samka rocks violently as it picks up speed. It flips. The fyotor flies out of my grip. The harness holds me onto the seat, but can it withstand the stress? I grab the control panel, just in case. The samka rights itself. Flips another 180°. Then again. And again. My stomach tries to heave, but there's nothing in it.

Dizzy from flip-flopping, I'm losing all orientation. Glimpses of lake and sky alternate through my vision at a quick pace. In the few seconds before impact, the tyagil pods can't regain more than a spark of juice.

Lake Selador rushes up, horribly fast. If I misjudge, I'm a goner. I wait, wait, wait, trying to catch a sense of how fast the vehicle is flipping. Then, just as the samka begins to flip right side up, I slam my left palm onto the ignition ring. Panel lights blink on.

"Max repellers!"

The harness prevents my head from banging onto the control panel as the "brakes" kick in, but the abrupt action whiplashes my neck. Metal joints shriek as the upward burst of anti-grav collides with the downward velocity of my plunge.

Too much stress. But it works. My stomach-churning plummet is slowing, slowing.

Warning. Tyagil pods exhausted. Auto shutdown.

This time the panel lights flicker out even though my left hand is on the ignition.

Again, my stomach lurches upward. I suck in a lungful of air to scream just as the samka pancakes into the water with bone-rattling force. My jaw slams shut so hard I'm afraid I've broken teeth. A circular geyser erupts around me. When my craft finally stops bobbing up and down, I sit there, drenched and panting. Every muscle in my body trembles, and not only from wind chill.

Incredibly, I'm alive. What about Prahv and Theena? I glance around, but don't see them. Then again, the air battle pulled me far away from my friends. The memory of their effortless swimming assures me they'll be fine until I get back to them.

Except for a few fluffy clouds, the lavender sky remains empty, silent. No sign of any angel showing up late for a rescue. With victory adding cockiness to my voice, I call upward, "Hey, Jaylel. Cancel that last request. I handled the situation without your help."

The heavens offer no reply. However, the thought occurs to me that I should've called out to God for help, not to an angel.

Besides, who am I to take credit for escaping death? The fact that my eyes didn't see angelic protection doesn't mean I didn't get any. If the samka hadn't righted itself that final time, I'd be fish bait.

"Sorry, Lord. Guess I'm still wrestling with the pride thing. No matter how it happened, thanks for keeping me in one piece."

What I sense from the guidance helmet tells me the samka is intact. It floats and enters recharge mode as it absorbs gravitational energy and stores that force in the tyagils. Good. I won't go down with the ship. Drained of energy just like my craft, I tug off the helmet and rejoice to see the world resume its normal tint. I fumble for the harness release and stand up.

Recalling those last harrowing moments, I shake my head. "Memo to self: Under *no* circumstances let your fuel run dry while airborne."

But what else could I have done? Those guys would've boiled all three of us if I hadn't led them on a goose chase.

Once more, my concern returns to Prahv and Theena. I'm disoriented. Which direction would they be from here?

Although I don't spot my friends, the rival samka floats about a thousand yards away, upside down and rising and falling on gentle waves. A figure sprawls atop it, face down. His legs dangle in the water. Is he alive? And where's the other guy? A quick scan of the water shows no swimmer sneaking my way.

The sight of one would-be killer this close reminds me of the fyotor. I glance around the samka. Nope. It's gone.

Another glance across the water. The waterlogged figure hasn't budged. His head faces the opposite way. If he's alive, he's oblivious of me. Still, I'm relieved to see his hands are empty. No fyotor.

I won't be able to get the samka airborne for a while, but I'm not the type to just sit around doing nothing. So, I search my craft. Might there be a pair of binoculars onboard? Maybe something to eat? Beneath the seats there are small storage spaces, but each one turns out to be empty. Still cautious, every few moments I observe my enemy on the other samka. If he raises so much as one pinky, I want to know.

My brief search over, I stretch out and study my situation while Aena's rays caress my skin with blissful warmth. Curious —why didn't we Earth people name our sun like Zemnans did? "Aena" sounds much cooler than "the sun." Come to think of it, "Feebia and "Eenik" sound more exotic than "the moon."

Another squint at my foe across the waves. Not so much as a wiggle. Good.

Lying here, I reflect on a similarity between me and the samka. It rests, absorbing gravitational energy, but me—I've always joked that I'm solar-powered. Stretched out, soaking up sunshine while gentle breezes soothe my sore limbs, I imagine myself re-energizing. When I ran cross country for school, I always preferred running on sunny days to cloudy ones. Maybe being solar-powered isn't such a joke after all.

For the first time I notice that my days of toil in Lotan's quarry have re-sculpted my body. Sure, running always kept my weight down. Now, though, my abs stand out with six-pack defi-nition. My biceps, too, have gained more muscle mass than on Earth. But what good are muscles when Prahv and Theena are out there waiting for me? They've already been treading water quite a while.

At this point I stand on the seat and scan in all directions, including the sky. The good news is that no more hostile samkas are visible. However, my friends aren't either. I'm so far out on Selador that the nearest shore is a barely discernible smudge of green on the horizon.

I step down and kick the pilot's seat. If only tyagil cells had some sort of quick-charge mode.

A vision materializes—Theena's sparkling-clean face smiling at me from the water. Would my new physique impress her? Or maybe she goes for the brainy type? I can't guess, but this is no time to imagine myself on the cover of *Muscle & Fitness*.

I'd pace back and forth if I could, but the samka isn't wide enough. How can I distract myself while the tyagils juice up?

The upside-down enemy craft lures my gaze back to it. The figure dangling in the water hasn't moved one hair so far as I can tell. He might be dead. Should I swim over and scope out the situation? Maybe they packed food?

The empty gnaw in my stomach reminds me I haven't eaten since yesterday's gruel. Swimming to the enemy might be dangerous, but once the idea takes root, I can't pluck it out.

Okay, I'll take a closer look. But quietly. No diving or splashing to advertise I'm coming.

Stealthy as a burglar, I ease over the edge and break into a modified butterfly stroke. I take my time and keep my eyes above water, watching the adversary who tried to crash-and-burn me.

As I approach my foe, I curve in a half circle for a complete view. Acrid odor clings to the air. Once again, the stench conjures images of smoldering dirty diapers mixed with molten plastic. I have no clue about the chemistry inside tyagil mesophyll pods, but the stink doesn't encourage exploration. I hope this reeking stuff isn't toxic.

Still seeing only the one enemy, I swim up to the opposite side and drag myself aboard the upside-down samka. Interesting. The underside is battleship gray, with big bumps that look almost like baseballs that have been cut in half, painted gray, then glued on in circular patterns radiating from the center—the anti-grav emitters. My fyotor blast has seared open the emitters in a line straight across the middle. Brownish foam still oozes from inside—the source of the stench.

Not even a twitch from the guy, but up close I'm sure he's the gunner. There's something unnatural about his right arm. It's cocked halfway between elbow and wrist as if there were another joint. I step closer and see the explanation—a split bone juts from a rip in the guy's sleeve. Despite my effort to be quiet, I gasp and wince. In First Aid class, they showed illustrations of broken bones, but this is the first compound fracture I've seen in real life.

"Zephryk? Is that you?"

He's alive. The guy hasn't lifted his head, but he must have heard my reaction.

"Zephryk, help. My arm is broken. One of my legs too. I can't pull myself up." A pause. "Zephryk, speak up, curse you."

Emboldened—or still impulsive—I stand upright. "Zephryk is gone. I don't think he can answer anymore."

My enemy stiffens. He twists his head until he sees me. "You. Come to gloat, have you? Come to mock me in my misery, as if life isn't miserable enough already?"

"Not at all."

"Then what are you doing here? With your demon flying skills, you could be far away instead of standing here smirking in victory."

Apparently, he didn't see how close I came to being in the same condition he's in.

"It's not like that. I didn't want to hurt anyone. You attacked us first."

"Spare me the speech." He squints. "Show it to me. If I have to die, at least let me see it before I go."

Does he think I stole something?

"Look, I know you're in a lot of pain, but I don't think you're dying. Broken bones can be mended. With time—"

"Stop blabbering idiocy. Lotan gave us a mission. We failed. You won. In Lotan's eyes, failure equals death. Slargs told me you claim to be a Fithian. If you are, show me the Intersection before I perish."

Lotan. So, they really had tracked us all this distance. But how?

I raise my left palm. "Satisfied?"

Rather than pleasing him, the Intersection sparks a snarl. "Deceiver. It's all tricks and lies. There never was any Creator. Nobody can know a myth. That dream is over."

"No Creator? You're wrong. Every molecule and every atom had a time of origin. If there's no Creator, where did they all come from? Matter can't create itself out of nothing."

The disgust in his eyes tells me this guy isn't ready for logic. "He'll find you, scum. No slarg can undermine Lotan's authority and steal his property without punishment. You've earned yourself a bigger enemy than you realize. Lotan will find you."

Despite obvious agony, he cinches himself up on his good elbow and places two fingers on a black ring about his neck. There's a click and a flash.

"This is overseer Jakor. Zephryk is dead. My body is broken. I have failed, but now you possess his likeness and his coordinates. The one called Rankin is cunning. Beware his tricks. Also —I have seen his hand. He bears the sign they described. I now commit the final act."

His words chill my bones. Somehow, the guy just shot off a message—plus a picture of me and my location—to somebody else. Probably Lotan.

As a final effort, he makes a grab for my ankle. Just in time I jerk my foot away.

"Save yourself the pain, Fithian-pretender. Vaporize yourself before Lotan catches you. I promise—if you don't, you'll wish you had."

Before I can respond, a glow emanates from the guy's skin and garments. A moment later, with no more sound than a huff of air, he winks out of existence. For a split instant, his disappearance even leaves twin holes in the water where his legs had dangled. Then water collapses into the holes, and I'm alone on the overturned samka. No trace of him. Only a wet spot proves a person's body had lain there. It's the same puffing out that happened to the dying couple I found that first day on Zemna. Except Jakor's ending is more pitiful.

I scan both lake and skies. Not another sign of life. How did they trail us? Some kind of GPS? I don't understand their science, but even Prahv didn't think they could track us. I shiver.

In light of Jakor's parting words, I'm more than a little creeped out standing here alone.

Time to check for supplies then get out of here.

I dive over the side and stroke to the underside of the demolished craft. Anything that was left on deck is gone, of course, but I'm hoping these men stashed away food for the journey. Maybe even a spare fyotor. Disoriented a moment, I feel my way. Although the day is pure sunshine topside, in the shadow of the overturned samka the water is darker than expected.

My fingers locate a compartment latch. It's jammed, maybe from the brutal impact with the lake. I push and yank with my fingers. Still stuck. If I can't open it soon, I'll have to surface to gulp more air.

I flip backward and kick at the latch with my bare heel. Once. Twice. On the third try it pops open. Before I can check out the contents, I freeze. Cold fingers trace along my bare back. I whirl and come face to face with the corpse of the pilot, floating freely, his shocked eyes large and bulging toward me. His whitish fingers sway in the current, beckoning me closer.

Screaming underwater is nothing like screaming in air, but a garbled shriek rips from my throat in a whirl of air bubbles. The next instant finds me clawing to the surface and onto the bottom of the samka.

My skin shared the same water with that ghoul.

Up here, Aena continues to shine. The breeze ripples the water, same as always. When my pulse and breathing calm down, my thinking clears.

Well, sure, it was a weird surprise. But a corpse can't hurt anybody. He's no zombie. Dead guy or no dead guy, we need food and water.

Revolting though the notion is, I steel my nerves then dive back in. This time I keep an eye on the corpse as I kick my way under the craft. Zephryk's body sways with each movement of the water. But if just one of those spine-chilling fingers makes a move toward me, I'll break an Olympic swimming record back to my own samka.

Sure enough, in the storage compartment is a jumble of various containers. One or two at a time, I ferry them topside. When I'm down to the last one, I pause for a last feel around the shadowy water. No fyotor. Their weapon must've whirled overboard, same as mine.

My eyes flit back to Zephryk. His olive drab, Zemnan-style tunic would blend in better than my Indianapolis Colts T-shirt—wherever that ended up. I push over to him and start working the tunic loose, being careful not to touch the body more than necessary.

When the tunic slides free, I spot something else—a round, metallic band around his neck, identical to Jakor's. On impulse, I decide to take that too. Maybe Prahv knows how to work it.

Despite my loathing to contact the corpse, I slide my fingers along the band searching for a release. Even after feeling its whole length two or three times, I'm at a loss for how to remove it. The circlet is too tight to slip over his head. Did someone place it there when he was a child, when his head was smaller? In the end, I give up.

Lungs bursting, I break the surface and gulp fresh air. Still no sign of life in the sky or on the lake. I sidestroke back to my samka, where I dry my palm and power up the craft. The tyagils aren't recharged—not by a long shot—but they've regained just enough oomph to lift the craft a couple feet. I hover over to the wrecked samka and transfer the canisters aboard.

Before leaving, I consider the floating wreckage. I don't like the idea of leaving it in plain sight. If I had a fyotor, I could blast a hole and scuttle the thing. But I don't have a weapon. With a shrug, I fly off. What else can I do?

Lake Selador is enormous enough that finding Prahv and Theena takes longer than I expect. I'm twisted around, but by flying along the shoreline, I locate the waterfall where we descended last night. The samka had drifted pretty far out by this morning. Then, there they are—two tiny heads bobbing among the waves. I grin and raise my right hand in greeting as I approach. With large eyes, they wave back.

Even better, Prahv holds my running shoes and tee shirt that blew off the samka in my mad getaway. No sign of my hoodie. I'll miss it, but Zephryk's tunic will be better for blending in.

The moment they're aboard, both Prahv and Theena drop to their knees and bow.

Theena inches closer, eyes down. "Rankin Fithian, please forgive us. We knew you were a chosen messenger of the Light, but we never guessed the extent of your powers."

"We had no idea," Prahv says, awe filling his voice. "To think, I treated you as I would teach any student. But tell us, why did you deceive us?"

I step backward, partly in confusion and partly because it's weird for them to be kneeling before me. "What are you talking about? Deceived you about what?"

Prahv lifts his head. "About aviation. You asked me to teach you, and I did. At least, I thought I did. But I gave only the most rudimentary lesson. You pretended it was your first time. Yet, when the attackers appeared, you piloted the samka as if you'd been flying since birth. From here, we could not see everything you did, but such maneuvers, such staggering speed. You are far more experienced than I, yet you pretended to know nothing. Why did you deceive us?"

"First of all," I say, taking each by an arm and helping them up, "I'm not God. I'm not even an angel. Never bow to me. Second, I haven't deceived you about anything. I've never lied to you. Maybe you're a better instructor than you realize, Prahv."

He shakes his head. "I cannot teach others to do what I cannot."

"Look, I don't understand either. Maybe the guidance helmet merges quicker or deeper with a brain from my world. Or maybe the experiences and training on my world prepared me to figure out the samka extra fast because of the emergency. But I promise you, I did not lie. Today is the first time I've flown one of these."

"Your world," Theena says. "You've told about many events that happened there, but you've never told us your world's name."

"We call it Earth."

Smiles creep onto both their faces. "Dirt?" she says. "You call your planet nothing but 'Dirt'?"

It's my turn to grin. I've never even considered the literal meaning of the word. Earthenware pottery is the closest I've come to that connection. For a Zemnan hearing it in First Tongue, my planet's name must sound goofy.

"We like it. Even if some of my people wanted to change the name, it would be impossible to get everyone worldwide to agree on a new one. Besides, in the beginning of God's Holy Writings, this is the word He used to describe the creation of our planet."

Mentioning God's involvement sobers them up.

"Pardon our smiles." Prahv places a hand on my shoulder. "We did not mean to mock."

"So, what does the name *Zemna* mean?"

My friends look at each other. Prahv sucks in a deep breath. "Those two syllables resonate with more depth and nuances than we could summarize here. For now, let's merely say that Zemna's name hearkens back to the way life once was. To our days of harmony with the Creator. I suppose you could say our planet's name is one of the few remnants of the Before Time."

A tear appears in Theena's eye. She turns away.

10

PARADISE LOST

"So, how do you suppose they followed us?" I ask before popping another of the enemies' lysenes—a strawberry-shaped vegetable with a taste and texture closer to carrot—into my mouth. We're camped within sight of the waterfall we spotted at dawn. The samka is down the hill, camouflaged among the trees and underbrush.

Prahv's eyebrows draw together. "As far as I know, a samka doesn't leave a traceable energy pattern. However, it is possible Lotan's followers installed some sort of beacon that can be monitored. Such a feat probably would not be hard for a mind that delights in such things. Now that I consider it, that tactic would discourage his own overseers from escaping his clutches. I regret saying it, but I believe we'll be safer if we continue on foot as a precaution."

Just my luck. No sooner do I find a skill I can do better than the locals than I have to leave it behind.

"Prahv, you were surprised at my skill with the samka. Would you consider yourself an expert at piloting?"

The question elicits a smile from Theena, who uses a two-pronged fork to stab another cube of meat from a container.

Evidently satisfied with his meal, my friend leans backward, both elbows in the grass. "I'm not a specialist. True, I once flew them as well as most people who care to know how. I understand the basic principles. Yet, that skill is not my special gift. My personal delight is cultivating plants. My area of particular giftedness is the balochia tree."

By this time, I've been on Zemna long enough to recognize balochia as the name of the copper-colored banana things I'd seen on my first day here. We hadn't received many balochias in the quarry, but whenever we did, the succulent fruit was always a welcome treat. Taste-wise, the flavor is close to pineapple, but with a more satisfying tang and texture.

Theena swallows. "A balochia tree planted and cultivated by Prahv becomes a magnificent work of art, both to see and to taste. Friends used to travel from distant wards merely to admire his offspring and to study his ways with them."

"Offspring?"

"Theena's idea of humor," Prahv says. "I never chose a life-long mate. She began referring to my balochias as my offspring, and other friends followed her example." He stands and wipes his hands on his "breeches," as Zemnans call pants. After opening the canvas bag he brought from the samka's sub-floor storage bin—which was a surprise to me—Prahv pulls out an instrument. I can't begin to guess its function. He lays it aside.

"Sounds like you must have made a lot of—" I stop in mid-sentence. My brain can picture American dollars, quarters, dimes, nickels, and pennies. Yet, I can't verbalize a First Tongue word for *money*.

Prahv pauses his inspection of the tool satchel. "A lot of what? Fruit?"

"Uh, I'm not sure what to call it on Zemna. You must've received a lot of whatever people gave you in exchange for your fruits and cultivating lessons."

He brightens, and not merely at the sight of a funky-looking axe, which he withdraws from the kit. "Yes, I did. Many of them. We call them 'compliments.' Of course, our friends and I gave glory to the Creator, both for delicious fruit and for giving me the gift of nurturing them."

I almost laugh but contain myself. The unselfish picture these two are painting of the "Before Time" seems too fantastic to be true.

Prahv studies the blade of the axe then gently touches the cutting edge. "You know, with these tools, we can fashion a raft and cross the lake. If anyone else finds the samka, they would assume we're on foot on this shore, when we would be far across the water."

I sit up straighter. "Wait. Don't change the subject. I want to understand. On Zemna, when one person used his 'giftedness' to raise delicious fruit, or to create a samka, or to construct a dwelling, what physical object did the recipients give that person in exchange?"

"In exchange?" Theena repeats.

Prahv lowers the Zemnan axe and crinkles his brow. Theena gazes at me, waiting for a clue. From their expressions, you'd think I had posed a complex riddle.

Prahv breaks the silence. "The recipients offered nothing, yet everything. In the paradise times before the shadow fell, each person pursued the delight of his or her own giftedness for the benefit of the community and for the glory of God. If friends offered compliments, the Creator received praise. Everything existed as it should. It was the way of life."

He isn't joking.

"So, you're saying, the entire world functioned on the principle, from each according to his ability, to each according to his need?"

Theena brightens. "We never phrased it in those precise words, but your description fits Zemna of the Before Time. Add that we spent our days imbued with the Creator's love and fellowship, and the picture is complete."

Paradise truly existed here—and I've missed it.

Theena sighs. "You never know what you've got until it's gone."

I can't hold back my smile. "Where I come from, those words are part of an old song."

"A song?" Her eyes lock on mine in pleasant surprise. "You appreciate singing, Rankin?"

Prahv continues poking through the tool satchel. "Theena's special gifts are handcrafting and singing. Whenever she visited me in the forest, she sang praise to the Creator. Even birds and woodland creatures crept closer to sit and listen."

"You mean animals here can understand when people talk?"

Both chuckle.

"No," Theena says. "But songs of praise formed a common bond between us humans and lesser creatures. Sadly, that bond is another broken fragment of the past. The harmony has dried up and blown away. Today, most animals fear people. Many have become hostile and harm us if they can."

I absorb these words while sifting memories of the book of Genesis. The Garden of Eden. God's glory on Earth, in harmony with mankind. Even as I listen to personal accounts of the paradise that once existed, my brain struggles to fathom how fantastic, how amazing life must have been in a world untainted by a single vice. Yet, paradise slipped between their fingers.

I shake my head. "Can you sing me a song of Zemna? I'd like to hear one."

Theena's smile radiates like sunshine. "I will enjoy singing for you. However, the experience will not be the same as before. Animals no longer hearken. Also, some other quality has changed, either in my voice, or in our ears, or in our hearts. Human songs no longer ring with the splendor of the Before Time."

I lean back against a tree trunk, my hands in my jean pockets. "Please, sing anyway."

After a moment's reflection, Theena stands and draws a breath.

By the third or fourth word, she has captivated me beyond description. Never have I heard vocal cords produce such refined musical notes. My eyes close on their own and allow her exquisite voice to lift my inner being to some brighter, loftier place. As she sings of God creating the heavens, Theena's lyrics flow up and down the scale. Her voice is smooth as musical silk, sliding along and evoking the most awesome images and emotions. The melody continues, strong and firm, weaving an audible tapestry.

Theena's final note tapers to an end. The tapestry is finished. A hush has fallen over our clearing. I open my eyes, and for an instant the forest—which had impressed me as a miraculous fantasyland—now strikes me as grimy in the wake of her song's exquisite purity.

As predicted, no forest creatures have gathered to sit among us. Still, I notice the birds have stopped twittering and flitting about. Even the wind seems to hold its breath. I've always loved music, but this moment convinces me I've never heard genuine music in its full glory. In contrast, memories of music on Earth suggest cheap echoes of what songs were intended to be. Wow. How much richer and more glorious must be the singing in Heaven?

Theena shrugs. "As I said, songs no longer ring as brightly as they did before the shadow fell. I hope you're not too disappointed." For no particular reason, she hops up and grabs a stout branch that grows almost parallel to the ground. Hauling herself atop it, she leans back against the tree's trunk.

Speechless, I pull my hands from my pockets. Disappointed? The best I can manage is a slow shake of the head.

Prahv sighs and stands up. "Quite a few times, Theena was invited to sing for the whole world through the Unizem. Her voice blessed all of Zemna."

I perk up. "Back in the quarry you talked about this Unizem device. I'd like to hear more about it."

Distracted, Prahv runs his fingertips up and down a young

tree whose leaves I don't recognize. He's already designing a raft in his mind. Hefting the peculiar axe, he swings it once, twice, a third time at his targeted tree, striking at ground level. To my surprise, it tilts and crashes to the forest floor after only three chops. Prahv nods in satisfaction. "The fewer wood chips, the better. By removing trees at ground level, we can cover the stumps with moldering leaves. No evidence that we've been here."

"The Unizem was not a single device," Theena explains. "It was a system that united a number of portals that were constructed around the world."

"Could we go and see one of these Unizem portals?"

Prahv is already hunting the next candidate for a raft. "There's no point. No one activates Unizem anymore. When temptation entered the world, various individuals used Unizem to address Zemna with new messages. Lotan was one of the first. He declared that, yes, the Creator is mighty and influential, but we too could become gods, achieving knowledge and experiencing countless emotions we never dreamed existed. Rankin, it sounded so tantalizing. Imagine the promise of improved vision that will perceive gorgeous new colors. Or picture yourself stumbling across a new, luscious fruit bursting with indescribable flavors no tongue has ever encountered. That's how tempting it sounded. Does that make sense?"

My mind's eye pictures Eve, talking in the Garden of Eden with a conniving snake who promised she could become just like God. "It makes perfect sense."

From her perch, Theena gazes into a nearby meadow. Exotic, bright-colored birds chase one another in playful circles. "I recall that first message from Lotan. His voice had always been so beloved as he sang praises to our Maker. The whole planet recognized his voice whenever the Unizem broadcast it. We trusted his orations. When he claimed he had grown past innocence and become a young god himself, he promised that each of us could achieve the same level as God. All we had to do was forget the Creator and elevate self instead of Him. Prahv and I yielded to that temptation on the third day. We swallowed Lotan's lies. Instead of mastering the universe, we lost everything except the skin we live in." She buries her face in her hands.

Her reminiscing has lured Prahv back from his chopping. As if lost in thought, he picks up the thread of her tale. "For many days, conflicting voices echoed from the Unizem. Some claimed they had tasted Lotan's offer and achieved expanded powers, higher levels of consciousness. Other voices sounded warnings, urging us not to try, to remain faithful to the Creator. Eventually, the clashing voices ended. Probably a third of Zemna followed Lotan's example—to our detriment."

Heartrending though the tale is to my friends, I'm spellbound. I've sometimes wondered what would've happened in Eden had Eve yielded to temptation while Adam stood firm. Something similar had occurred here, with thousands or millions choosing either God or self. "What ended the struggle?"

"One morning, Theena and I woke to find our parents missing. Many townspeople had likewise vanished. We learned that countless friends had disappeared worldwide—always those who had remained faithful to the Creator. By Unizem, Lotan's voice gloated that 'our side' had 'won'—concepts that were new to us. He and his admirers claimed that subjects of the Creator had somehow ceased to exist because they had rejected the New Order."

Tears glisten in Theena's eyes. "My own opinion—and Prahv's—favors the view that God transported His faithful ones to His eternal Realm to protect them from contamination."

Prahv continues while Theena wipes her eyes. "Before the faithful disappeared, someone conceived a new word to describe us, the ones who had succumbed to temptation."

"What word?"

"'Fools.' We had never experienced the tricks we now label as deceit and treachery. Lotan and his type performed the fooling, and we who heeded became the fools."

Prahv tips a water flask to his mouth and swallows. "That was the demise of Unizem. Rather than everyone following Lotan, as he expected, Zemna's population splintered into factions. In each ward, compelling individuals promoted themselves as leaders. The whole concept of world harmony shriveled up and disappeared. So, no more united-Zemna messages."

I hear what they're saying, but I'm unwilling to give up the goal of speaking to the whole planet at once. "Suppose someone were to go to a place where Unizem broadcasts were once made. Could a person like me still use it? Could a Fithian address the whole planet at one time?"

As my friends often do when pondering a fresh question, brother and sister study each other's eyes. They almost appear to communicate telepathically. That's the way some siblings are—so close they understand each other without words.

"A Fithian speaking by Unizem," Theena whispers. "The notion is tantalizing. However . . ."

"However, *what*?" I ease the alien axe from Prahv's fingers. If he can take down a mature tree with only three whacks, can I?

Prahv shrugs. "We're uncertain whether the system has been abandoned, or whether the portals have been dismantled to keep trouble-makers from activating them to ignite rebellion."

"But what if we assume such a portal was not destroyed? Would it be possible to make it function again?" I size up a tree with a trunk about the same diameter as the one that lies on the ground. Slicing it at ground level will be a little awkward, but if Prahv can do it, I can do it.

Theena says, "When I sang in one, an experienced operator regulated it. On the other hand, you bear the Intersection, Rankin. On the first try, you compelled a samka to perform as no Zemnan ever has. If a Unizem portal remains intact, perhaps you and the Intersection could activate it."

My imagination blossoms, picturing myself sharing the

Gospel story with every man, woman, and child on the planet. Surely that would be the fastest way to get seven thousand decisions and return to Earth. Raising the axe, I swing with all my strength, straight at the tree's base.

"Rankin, stop!"

Instead of chopping the tree, the axe bounces back as if I'd strung an iron post. Even the sound reverberates like metal striking metal. The handle telegraphs pain to my hands just before it flies from my fingers.

"Ow!" I shake my stinging hands.

Prahv laughs and picks it up. "My apologies, Rankin. I did not notice your target until too late. I assume stoalock trees do not grow on your home world?"

Astonished, I touch the stoalock's smooth bark, then attempt to bend a lower branch. Not even a smidgen of flexibility. I hop up and grab a limb, which is only an inch wide. It's as if this thing were smelted from cast iron, then painted green to match the forest. "I've never felt such heavy-duty timber."

He laughs again. "Stoalocks grow gradually, but solidly. Their roots imbibe metallic particles from the soil. You could hew all day, and all you would gain is a dull blade. But that was a mighty swing. Your one blow would have felled a hassawood, the variety I cut down."

His praise restores my self-esteem.

Theena returns to the subject. "If you wish, Rankin, we can try to learn the condition of the nearest Unizem. It's not close, but Prahv and I were there during the Before Time."

Prahv sizes up another tree. He hands me the axe and points to its base for a second try. "When my sister says it is not close, take that as an understatement. But I don't recommend we travel straight there. Let's aim first for the dwelling of Arex, the friend who oversaw that Unizem portal. If he survived the purges, he might know whether the system is still functional."

"And if it's not functional?"

"In that case, you must decide. Either we can continue to the next portal—which is a much farther journey—or you can start sharing your message of salvation one on one."

Prahv steps away to give me swinging room. Or maybe in case I lose the axe again?

After eying a spot on the trunk barely an inch above ground, I rear back with the axe and swing. A quick swoosh, and my tree is down.

Theena applauds. "Well done, Rankin. But concerning the Unizem, we should warn you—approaching the nearest one could prove dangerous."

A lead weight drops into my gut. "Let me guess. The nearest Unizem thing is back the direction we came? In Lotan's direction?"

Prahv reaches to take back the axe, a grim smile on his lips. "No. The nearest portal is across Lake Selador in a neighboring ward. Lotan does not rule there."

"No? Who does?"

"His older brother. Entizar."

11

QUEL-TEL-PALARIM

Late that night, still paddling our raft, I peer past Theena and Prahv into the gloom ahead. Are we midway across Selador? Three-quarters of the way? Clouds obscure the sky, so neither of Zemna's moons sheds light on our journey. Good thing Prahv has a great sense of direction.

Our raft is basic, just a long, skinny rectangle of logs lashed together. It's no speedboat, but it floats well. I hate leaving that awesome samka behind, but if Prahv is right about it containing a tracking device—and that seems likely—then we don't dare keep it. I'm just glad Prahv knew about the tool bin under the samka's deck. The trees he selected are the biological opposites of stoalocks—soft wood and light to carry. As Prahv predicted— these things are super buoyant, almost like cork.

Too bad my Intersection doesn't emit a laser beam or some-thing. That would be a cool way to slice down trees. Maybe even melt the stoalock that embarrassed me? On the other hand— Fithian pun—who knows? Maybe this Intersection thing really can shoot lasers. I simply don't know its capabilities nor how to learn them.

Once more, I squint into the darkness ahead but can't make out any details. When I shift to paddle on the opposite side, I accidentally dribble water onto the guidance helmet. Can water short it out? I lean over to pat it dry with my sleeve.

Wait a second. What am I thinking? The helmet.

I'd brought along the samka's pilot helmet to make extra sure no wanderer flies off with our hidden samka. Even if somebody happened to have a spare power disk, he couldn't interface the vehicle without the helmet. I lay the crude paddle across my legs long enough to reach into the canvas sack behind me. My hand locates the helmet resting atop our food canisters. I slip it on.

The world adopts a yellowish hue. Cool—even at night the helmet enables me to see the shoreline, maybe a mile ahead. Looking backward, I can't even glimpse the shore we left behind. How wide is this lake? Wide enough to make my shoulders ache from paddling all night. But Theena hasn't complained. No way I'm going to wimp out while she's going strong. Still wearing the helmet, I dip the paddle and resume the cadence.

I glance down to the water. "Whoa."

Prahv and Theena freeze. "Halt?" Theena whispers from the middle position. "Why should we halt?"

I sigh. "Sorry. I didn't mean 'whoa' as in 'stop.' It's an Earth expression. I just happened to look down. With this guidance helmet on, I can see deep into the water, even at night. Gigantic fish are swimming down there.

Theena giggles, and even Prahv chuckles. He dips his paddle back into the water. "I'd forgotten the first time I looked into a river at night with a guidance helmet. You remind me of when I was a boy."

He doesn't intend the comment as a jab. Still, it makes me feel about five years old.

"But the fish. Some of them look twice my size, and we were swimming in this water." My brain pictures a shark. When no equivalent Zemnan word comes to mind, I say, "On Earth, certain water creatures have sharp teeth and eat people if they get a chance. Are any of your fish, uh, carnivorous?"

They both pause again and cock their heads in my direction.

"How horrible," Theena says. "Fish on Zemna don't harm people. At least, they didn't used to. Most eat small plants from the lakebed."

I look beneath the waves in time to see another finned shape knife through the waters. It rolls sideways and seems to gawk upward as it passes beneath our raft. He doesn't strike me as vegetarian. He does look hungry. With all our paddling, we've probably generated enough commotion to attract fishy attention.

I resume paddling. "You told me that some animals turned aggressive when Zemna changed. If one of those big fish decided to become a meat-eater, how would you know it happened?"

Without missing a stroke, Prahv calls back, "I guess you wouldn't—until it was too late."

Both of them dissolve into laughter. It isn't the first time Zemnan humor has left me scratching my head. I may have received the ability to speak these people's language, but there's a definite difference in thinking.

Mr. Wong had talked about this in tenth-grade World Lit class. "To truly understand a foreign nation, you must do more than translate their words into English. You must study their culture. Get inside their heads and view the world through their eyes, because history, geography, religion, lifestyle, and literature all affect a person's outlook."

If only Mr. Wong could see me now.

The three of us grow quiet as our raft approaches the shoreline. Thanks to the guidance helmet, I can describe some things, but not much. Odd shapes, some taller, some shorter. Hardly a speck of light, though.

Prahv turns toward me and lowers his voice. "Rankin, may I borrow the helmet?"

"Sure." I pull it off and pass it forward. I'm glad. As Fithian, I might be the spiritual leader, but geographically I'm in unknown territory. Let Prahv take the point position.

The raft scrapes into sand. We hop off, and cool water soaks my Nikes all over again. Oh well. They weren't quite dry anyway.

Prahv peers left and right, surveying the scene with whatever advantage the helmet provides. Since he's not yelling or ducking, there must not be immediate danger. Using the short machete—the one tool we've brought along—I slash the vines binding our raft together then shove the logs back into the water. Better for us if we leave no clues of our arrival.

"Come on," Prahv whispers.

In single file, we move out using the same order we sat on the raft—Prahv first, Theena second, and me last. I don't relish being in the rear. This position makes me feel like a follower. But neither do I like the idea of leaving Theena in the more vulnerable rear-guard slot. If anyone gets sneaked-up on from behind, I'd rather it be me than her.

Before long, even in the dark of night, the landscape strikes me as familiar. Silhouettes of broken buildings remind me of the destroyed town I saw the day Jaylel brought me to Zemna.

"Quel-Tel-Palarim," Prahv announces. "Or what's left of it."

Just like my first morning on Zemna, broken rubble crunches under the soles of my Nikes. The street is littered with larger chunks of wrecked buildings, the remains of which loom over us like charred skeletons against the star-studded sky. As we press further, I realize this city was much larger than that first town I'd visited.

A distinct odor of charred flesh assails my nostrils. Fyotors—and maybe other unknown weapons—must have incinerated victims right in their tracks. As if in confirmation, my shoe bumps a pale object. My eyes have adjusted enough to see a skull. The thing seems to leer at me with every tooth showing. I shiver and walk on, sticking close behind my friends.

Why do some bodies disintegrate upon dying, and some don't? Good question, but this isn't the time for idle conversation.

The clouds are breaking up. Even though Eenik must have

set hours ago, Feebia still gleams in the east. By its light we can see the giant, jagged teeth that were once homes for the residents of Quel-Tel-Palarim. Could hostile eyes be watching from gaping windows? My skin crawls at the thought.

Deeper and deeper into the city we tread. Unlike on Earth, instead of erecting square buildings side by side, the residents of Zemna love—or used to love—creating circular structures. Some of these buildings—caloids, Prahv calls them—were broader and only a few stories high, looking like overgrown tree stumps. Others were tall and narrow, towers that stood straight, or else divided into two or three narrower towers near the top. These remind me of a saguaro cactus. And caloids don't stand in tidy rows alongside straight streets with ninety-degree intersections. The remains of the caloids stand here and there in a random way. Best I can judge by moonlight, this arrangement leaves plenty of undeveloped land between them, where grass and trees flourished. Quel-Tel-Palarim must have been half city, half park.

Feebia's beams are too frail to illuminate the color of the walkway—which is as wide as one lane on an American road. Similar walkways bisect it. The whole setup looks ideal for health-minded people who walk or jog everywhere.

Senses alert, we pad along in silence. My ears detect a sniffle. In front of me, Theena wipes her eyes. I'm not positive, but I get the impression Prahv is doing the same. For me, this trek is a fascinating glimpse of an alien planet. For them, being here must hurt as much as discovering the uncovered graves of countless "friends," the word they apply to all Zemnans in their "Before Time."

The odor of putrid meat intensifies. I consider the fact that tiny, airborne particles of rancid human flesh are filtering into my nose, my throat, my lungs. Gross. They're even on my tongue, giving the air a foul taste. With an effort, I hold my nausea at bay. Vomiting won't help. Besides, I dread disturbing the spooky silence. The sooner we reach the far side of this giant cemetery, the better.

Something crackles under my soggy running shoe. When I lift my foot, the skeletal remains of a hand lie there. No other bones, just the hand. An involuntary shudder runs through me. Whatever battle raged here, I'm glad I missed it.

The stench of rotting flesh sparks a new chain of thought. Even though Zemnans may not value keeping count of days, months, and years, Jaylel said the worldwide conflict happened about a decade ago. There was at least one Fithian before me. Yet, such a strong odor can't come from corpses that old. Somebody or something has been killing in recent days. I swallow again, hoping to squelch the queasiness in my stomach.

From time to time, my ears detect a scrape. Is it the wind fluttering a broken door? Then comes a gritty sound, as if a boot stepped on gravel. An icy tingle radiates up my spine. Maybe my imagination is working overtime, but it's hard to shake the feeling we're being watched. In my mind, spooky organ music begins.

Lord, if this planet has flesh-eating zombies, please don't let me find out. Not now.

We tread another fifteen or twenty paces when a voice rings out behind us. "Grab them."

One glance reveals a dozen silhouettes pounding toward us. They grip objects that must be weapons.

"Run!" I shout.

Prahv and Theena are right beside me as I break into a sprint. I drop the sack of supplies. What good are canisters of diced fruit when alien ghouls are licking the brains from your skull?

A moment later, the roadway transforms from solid to fluff. It collapses beneath our feet, dropping us into inky blackness.

12

CAPTURED

Instead of plunging to the cavernous depths of Zemna, my body slams into something rock-hard. Dazed, I feel around in blackness.

"Rankin?" It's Theena's voice. "Are you hurt?"

Great question. The entire right side of my body aches, but no broken bones. "I'm in one piece. How about you two?"

Theena has already found my hand when Prahv says, "Here. I cracked my head so hard the helmet broke. I can't see in the dark anymore."

Above, a flash of light appears, bathing us in its beam. A second later, half a dozen other lights shine down on us.

Harsh laughter echoes from above. "Works every time. Trapped like a pack of weechels."

Weechels. Furless rodents the size of June bugs. Whoever the speaker is, the comparison irks me.

"Korya, are you there?" the voice shouts down.

"Yes, we'll handle them. Good work."

On our own level, ten or twelve men dressed in gray military uniforms stride into the ring of illumination and fan out until we're surrounded.

Adjusting to the light, I find I'm sitting on a tarp-like fabric the same reddish brown as the walkways. Clever way to disguise a mantrap. This isn't just a hole beneath the roadway. A tunnel fades into blackness in both directions.

"Stand up," says a bald man, the one called Korya. In his hands he carries a fyotor, although slimmer than the models used in the quarry. Around his brow is a headband with an extension plugged into one ear. In fact, all of our captors wear identical headbands. But only Korya totes a fyotor. His followers carry smaller weapons I don't recognize. "Keep your hands where we can see them, unless you're tired of living."

We obey. Despite the trap, I'm relieved these are humans rather than gurgling zombies.

"That's it. Now step over here, off that tarp. Give us a look at you."

While those above haul the tarp back up by cords fastened to the edges, our captors activate flashlight gizmos strapped to each one's left wrist then tighten the ring around us.

Most of them ignore Prahv and me. Instead, they leer at Theena and elbow each other, some with winks. One guy even licks his lips.

I despise the look in those eyes and want to punch the lust out of them. Maybe I can't slug these guys, but I can distract them. "So, are you going to take us to Entizar, or what?"

It works. Korya walks up to me, glances back at his gang, then rams his knuckles into my nose. Pain shoots through my face, and I stagger backward until someone stops me. Somehow, I stay on my feet. This Korya might be only an inch taller than me, but he owns a sledgehammer for a fist.

"Insolent weechel. Are you trying to commit suicide? Perhaps you can't help owning a tiny brain, but please don't advertise the fact."

Korya's men break into raucous laughter. I'm still waiting for the punch line, but I'm not about to say anything with the word *punch* in it. This guy doesn't need ideas.

Prahv drops to one knee. "Please. Permission to speak?"

"Ah, a trespasser with better manners. Permission granted, intruder."

"It's not that this friend's brain is small. He's not from here. He doesn't understand—"

"Permission revoked. Stand. I don't care if he comes from Sheema, Taralah, or the islands. Anyone who accuses me of serving Entizar can kiss his life goodbye."

Now Theena drops to a knee. "Please, I implore. Before you react, allow me to explain that our friend isn't even from Zemna—"

With a thrust of his hand, he cuts her off. "Did you not hear me? I don't care if he descended from the Feebian colony. Don't press your fortune, girl, just because you're pleasing to the eyes."

Feebian colony? There's a settlement on the larger moon? How come nobody tells me these things?

"He's a Fithian."

Korya's head jerks up.

In two strides, he's in front of me. He grabs my left arm and nearly wrenches it from the shoulder socket when he jerks my hand up to eye level. By his wrist-light, he studies my palm. His cohorts press closer. Several mutter words I don't catch. From their tone, I'm pretty sure no one said, "Hallelujah."

"So, look at that, men. This time we caught ourselves a living legend. A walking, breathing 'Fithian,' dropped from the sky to pay us a visit."

Should I say something? He wants me to. His eyes convey as much. If I do, he's sure to finish the job of busting my nose. *Lord, I could use some wisdom right now.*

He flings down my hand and bends close enough that his ripe body odor assails my nostrils. "You look human enough to me. I don't know what game you're playing. Maybe someone performed surgery to make your hand look different. But you're not going to play me for a fool. So what if they embedded ink in your skin? What rubbish."

"Let's torch them and be done with it," says one of Korya's troopers.

"They're not ours. Spies from Entizar, that's what I say."

Korya steps back. His set jaw remains fixed as chiseled granite. Yet, he hesitates. What's that in his eyes? Doubt? Curiosity?

Theena drops to one knee a second time. "Permission?"

He sighs. "What now?"

She sucks in a deep breath, closes her eyes and—astonishing to me—begins to sing.

At first I'm horrified. These guys are ticked off enough. They might interpret a song as mockery. Or a diversionary tactic.

Yet, her wonder-gilt words swell and fill the chamber. Listening, I picture a troop of angels glorifying God in the highest. Again, the unbelievable notes this girl conjures up blow me away. I long for the next verse, but she halts.

In a voice more soothing than a moonbeam, Theena says, "Please believe me. We are not spies from Entizar, nor from anyone else. We escaped from Lotan's ward. We were passing through Quel-Tel-Palarim and did not realize anyone still dwells here."

Korya strokes his chin. The flame in his eyes has subsided to embers. "Your face isn't familiar, but the voice is. Have we met?"

"The Unizem," someone says. "That's where we've heard that voice."

"I'm called Theena. It's true. Several times I was invited to sing for Zemna."

Korya's chin lifts. "Yes. I recall. A whole world ago that was —and yet not."

A dour man with a fyotor steps to Korya's side. "So, she's gifted in song. Who cares? Isn't a pretty package the most cunning way to deceive? Let's just melt them and not take any risks."

Another figure disagrees. "Silence a voice like that? I don't know about her companions, but no one who sings like that can be a servant of Entizar. Spare her, at least."

Korya backs up. Hopefully not to stand clear of the line of fire. "Speak, any of you three. Whom do you serve? You travel toward Entizar yet disavow Entizar."

Since he gave permission, I don't do the one-knee thing. I say, "We three serve no man—only the Creator."

A moment of disbelief on their faces yields to laughter. Korya shakes his head, this time with the patronizing smile you might give a misguided kindergartner. "Your giftedness is no doubt hilarity, imitation 'Fithian.' Don't try my patience. Even humor can spark an explosive death."

Prahv turns to me. "Show him the Writings, Rankin. Show him the Book."

"Of course. I should have thought of that."

However—to my dismay—my jeans pockets are flat to the touch. No New Testament. "I don't understand. It's got to be here. I haven't taken it out to read since—"

My hoodie. The New Testament lay secure in its pocket before I jumped into Lake Selador. It was still there when I gunned the samka out of the water. That's the last time I saw either one. I could kick myself.

"It's gone. Probably at the bottom of the lake." I could cry. I'm exhausted from lack of sleep, my arms ache from paddling all night, a bunch of suspicious aliens want to torch us with fyotors, and the only New Testament on this whole planet is gone forever. What else could go wrong?

Prahv must interpret the consternation on my face. To Korya he says, "It's a long story."

"Oh, I love a good story. Try me."

I'm not certain it's a great idea to tell all of Korya's commandos about our search for a Unizem portal. I hedge. "A story such as ours isn't for all ears. Could we speak to you alone?"

He considers. "Alone without my men? I can arrange that. Alone without a fyotor, no. Your pretty companion sings a glowing tune, but it will take more than a wisp of antique music to make me trust you. Maybe I'm just not the note-worthy type."

It takes a moment for my brain to register I've just heard a Zemnan pun. "Fair enough."

He squints. "Tell me, does any part of your story include that fancy symbol on your left palm?"

"Yes."

He spits. "I was afraid of that. Let me warn you. I don't believe the Fithian legends. Your tale had better shine like no other I've heard, or you won't live to regret it."

13

BENLATHIM'S OFFER

Hours later, I wake and bump my head on something metal. Unfortunately, I'm still face down in the coffin-sized holding pen built into a wall, somewhere beneath the ruins of Quel-Tel-Palarim.

I've been dreaming about a colony up on Feebia. Was Korya joking about one? I'm intrigued, but that's a puzzle piece that can wait. Feebia's orbit is thousands of miles away, which makes it the least of my worries.

Bars at my head guarantee I can't slide out of the pen. An electric lantern sits on the floor of the chamber beyond, providing a solitary light. At least, I assume it works off electricity. I have to crane my neck to see more. One of Korya's minions sits, tilted back in a chair against the far wall. Another guarantee we three aren't going anywhere without permission.

Sigh.

What exactly these little prison cells originally held is unclear. I doubt they were intended for human contents. They weren't designed for comfort either. Although big enough to confine an adult, they're more like overgrown file cabinet drawers, slid into the wall until they lock shut.

"Prahv? Theena? You two awake?"

Simultaneous yeses sound from identical holding pens farther along the wall. In a flash, the guard thumps to his feet. "No communicating between prisoners. Korya's orders."

I twist my neck to see him better. "All right, I'll talk to you instead. I was just wondering what happened to Korya? When he forced us to climb into these little prisons, he said he'd be back soon."

"That's correct. He'll be back soon."

"But he's already been gone a long time. Soon is past. We're getting hungry."

A shrug. "Now is now, but soon? Anyone can debate when soon will be. Maybe for Korya, his soon lasts longer than your soon."

Terrific. Maybe this is a sample of the profound mysteries this guy ponders while pulling guard duty.

"Any chance of getting some breakfast?"

A smirk. "Soon."

Double great. Not just a philosopher, but a moonlighting comedian, too. "Don't quit your day job, my friend."

"What?"

"Never mind. I'll explain sometime. Soon."

I roll onto my back and close my eyes even though I'm no longer sleepy. I've lost my sole copy of the Word of God. That stinks. Sure, I can recite some Bible verses from memory, but nowhere near the whole New Testament.

Grab this opportunity to pray?

Flat on my back, I talk to God in my head. *Lord, I feel so unworthy for this job You've given me. Every day I'm frustrated because I'm surrounded by things I don't understand. I need wisdom beyond my own. I couldn't even hold onto my New Testament. I don't see how I could possibly fulfill my mission and earn that trip back to Earth.*

That last thought sends a twinge of guilt through me. If I could disappear this instant and appear back on Earth, I'd be safe—but at the expense of leaving my two friends locked up as prisoners.

Thank You, Lord, for Prahv and Theena, for their loyalty, their help, and friendship. Without them, I'd be a mighty lonely Fithian. They're great. I really don't deserve them.

Bless all three of us. And please help me to think, speak, and act in ways that are pleasing to You.

Despite the prayer, foreboding creeps into my mind. Am I squandering opportunities on Zemna? Should I be doing something I'm not?

Jaylel's parting instructions drift back to me: "The same as on Earth. Live for God. Share His Good News of salvation to everyone willing to listen."

I decide to share the Gospel with this guard. "As long as we're not busy, would it be all right if I tell you a story?"

"No."

"It won't take long. Promise."

"No. Stories are a waste of time. Besides, you might be attempting some type of trickery. Keep your chronicle to yourself." Well, that's one pair of ears not willing to listen. Maybe later.

"Okay, let's forget breakfast and the true story I wanted to share. How about something to drink? A little water, maybe?"

He's tilting his chair against the wall again. "Water? Sure. Soon."

Sheesh. This jerk's vocabulary begs for an upgrade. I guess it's just as well. A cup of water might make me need a restroom —what Zemnans call a "biology break"—and I can predict the one word that Einstein will pronounce if I ask for a bathroom.

Within a few moments, however, the sound of booted feet enters the chamber. I roll over to look.

"Anything suspicious from our intruders?" Korya asks.

"No tricks. Mostly they slept."

"I also held a stimulating conversation with your man there," I say. "His special area of giftedness must be the art of dialogue."

Korya looks from me to the guard. He shrugs. "Let's get them out."

When my prison drawer is extracted, I hop off and rub my shoulders. Being cooped up a few hours didn't hurt. In fact, it provided valuable rest. But my shoulders are still stiff from last night's paddling marathon on the raft. Plus, my right side aches from tumbling into their mantrap. Luckily, no ribs feel cracked.

Prahv and Theena also stretch and twist, working the kinks out of their muscles. I catch Prahv's gaze, hoping for some sort of clue or guidance on how to respond. All he offers are raised eyebrows and a slight shrug.

"Story time," Korya says. "But I won't be alone. Let's go see Benlathim."

"Benlathim?"

Korya shoots me a withering look, but how am I to know? We follow his men out the chamber and along a dark corridor. Like in the holding area, two of the guards carry lanterns. My guess is that underground tunnels once provided access to the city's water, power, and whatever public utilities they had. The lighting system must be offline. Or maybe they need to conserve resources?

In a low voice, Prahv says, "Benlathim is the friend who served as chief counselor of Quel-Tel-Palarim."

"There are no more friends," Korya calls from the rear, demonstrating an excellent sense of hearing. "Allies and enemies, that's all. Benlathim is curious to learn which category you fit."

We continue straight through some junctions. At others, they guide us left or right. If there are road signs, I don't see them. The place is a labyrinth.

A brightness up the tunnel reveals we're approaching something different. Sure enough, we enter a large chamber furnished with tables, chairs, and a giant-sized monitor split into a dozen smaller images, like security cameras. Against the left wall, both men and women wearing uniforms and headphones operate a string of consoles—a communication center? At the largest table, half a dozen men lean over a map.

"Here are the intruders," Korya says.

Hard metal that must be a weapon pushes between my shoulder blades, driving me forward a couple extra steps. If that's a fyotor, I hope he doesn't slip and depress the trigger button.

"This is the one making wild claims about himself."

All the men at the table study me, but only one steps closer. Benlathim, no doubt. I struggle to guess anyone's age on this planet, but Benlathim's eyes reveal a bottomless well of experience. His skin is smooth, and he has no beard, but he's old. I sense it. Maybe ancient, like Methuselah.

"Welcome. It's not every day Quel-Tel-Palarim is privileged to receive a Fithian descended from Heaven."

His men's laughter echoes off the chamber walls. He scored the point he wanted.

"I never claimed I'm from Heaven. I've never been there. I'm only from a different world."

"Oh, merely from a different planet? My mistake."

Sarcasm drips from Benlathim's words. Three seconds, and already the interview is turning sour.

"Korya recommends I glance at one of your hands. Perhaps listen to an anecdote?"

I extend my left arm, palm up. Benlathim picks up a lantern and steps directly in front of me. He stares at the Intersection of All Things, which glitters with multicolored iridescence in the glare of his lantern. In lighting like this, the symbol can appear almost like electronic circuitry. His eyes flick to mine, then back to the Intersection.

One of his generals—or whoever they are—joins him. He spits onto my hand, then rubs his sleeve back and forth across it. The Intersection is cleaner now, but of course not smudged. "It's not ink, whatever it is. I can't tell if it's on the surface, beneath the surface, or both."

Another minion walks over. He pulls a long, narrow knife from a scabbard and, hoisting my hand just inches from his eyes, presses the tip into the middle of the Intersection. Instantly, white-hot pain zips from my palm all the way to my spine.

"Ow!" I yank my hand away. For the first time, I realize the symbol isn't merely part of my hand. The Intersection seems hardwired right into my nervous system. I hope this guy didn't short-circuit something.

He slides the knife back into the scabbard. "The symbol reacts like real skin, but it's different."

Benlathim's gaze bores into me. He sits back on the table and crosses his arms, his eyes locked on mine. "Suppose you tell us the true nature of that mark? What's it made of, and how you applied it?"

"As far as its composition, I don't have a clue. It feels no different from my own skin. The first time someone pointed to it, I was shocked. I hadn't realized it was there."

"So, you claim no knowledge of how or when that thing came to be?"

"I was living my own life on my home world, where I became a follower of the Creator. An angel named Jaylel appeared and transported me to this world, where he said the Creator wants me to bear His message of peace and reconciliation to everyone willing to hear it. Sometime during that conversation, the symbol must have appeared. As I said, I never even noticed it until someone in Lotan's ward spotted it. They called it 'the Intersection of All Things.' I'd never heard that expression on my world."

At the name Lotan, angry murmurs rippled through the men.

Arms crossed, Benlathim drums his fingers on the opposite bicep. "I see. And your one purpose in life is to wander the countryside talking about the Creator who abandoned us? I assume you'll also claim your hand can activate power systems. At least, in the children's tales that's what happens."

Before I decide which argument to address, Theena says,

"The Intersection works. We escaped from Lotan in one of his own samkas. Prahv piloted, but Rankin's hand provided the activation."

If Benlathim buys any of Theena's words, he isn't letting on. To the contrary, he expels a deep breath then rubs a hand over his eyes. By all appearances, he's a leader with troubles. The three of us create complications.

"I'll prove it. Take me to the nearest device that activates by control disk. I'll power it up."

His mouth curving downward, Benlathim looks to Korya.

"A convenient offer," Korya says. "You know perfectly well Entizar has obliterated or stolen all such equipment. Quel-Tel-Palarim is a dead shell, thanks to him. Or, it would be if we were to abandon it. You make your proposal knowing full well it's an empty gesture."

"No. I didn't realize—"

He silences me with a slash of his hand. "All right, 'friend.' What did she call you? Rankin? I'll give you another chance to prove you're what you claim. In the Fithian stories, the Intersection can do more than access power grids. Give us a demonstration. Do something wondrous."

In other words, perform a miracle. I picture the glow that developed under my fingers just before Gorlic's head snapped backward. "It doesn't work like that. I can't just turn it on and off. Since I'm still a new Fithian—"

"Bah. Enough already." Fuming, Benlathim turns and stalks back to his chair at the far side of the table. "So, you stole a samka from Lotan, did you? Where is the samka now? I could use one. You three could use one, too, judging by how fast my men trapped you."

"We left it on the western shore of Selador," Prahv says. "Near the waterfall. We had reason to believe Lotan's overseers were tracking it. We didn't dare keep it."

Benlathim isn't even looking anymore. He leans on the table

and fixes his eyes on the map. "Another handy excuse. Your trio seems well stocked with them."

Everyone's eyes rest on Benlathim, waiting for a decision.

Lord, please help him make a good one for us.

"Korya, what's your opinion? You're the one who suggested we hear them out. What do you think now?"

"I'm undecided. I don't believe in fables any more than you do. The old times are gone. Still, these three have a different feel from Entizar's typical spies. If, indeed, they are enemies of Lotan, then that's one tally mark in their favor."

In my personal opinion, the Intersection should be a second tally mark in our favor. I bite my tongue.

"Suggestions?" Benlathim says.

Korya studies us. "Would you be willing to aid us in occupying the city? Join us in opposing Entizar? Quel-Tel-Palarim could use more allies."

I choose my words with caution. "We have no love or loyalty for Entizar. We were passing through this district so I could share my message about the Creator with others. Staying here with you wouldn't be our first choice."

"And if the alternative is death?" Benlathim says.

I clear my throat. "In that case, we would be delighted to accept your offer."

14

WRIST CUFFS

Okay, so we're in the army now? Problem is, Benlathim, Korya, and the other occupiers of Quel-Tel-Palarim don't trust us.

"Each of you, take a comm-band," says Myek, the female lieutenant or whatever she is who received Benlathim's order to "take care of them." Myek's uniform is the same style as the others we've seen here. Only hers is light brown as opposed to the darker gray, with a trace of fraying here and there. Trimmed just above the shoulders, the cut of her brunette hair strikes me as mainly practical, yet still attractive. Lean and confident, she moves like a tigress.

I slip on the inch-wide headband. It automatically cinches itself snugly around my forehead but feels crooked. I try to straighten it.

Myek's business-like tone softens. "Not like that. Here, let me show you." She adjusts the comm-band until it's straight. "Does that feel comfortable?"

I twist my head. "I guess so. Not too tight, not too loose."

"Now the earpiece." She bends the wire extension to my left ear, and I catch the end of a conversation. Something about reconnoitering a perimeter, followed by, "Yes, sir."

After watching her example, Prahv and Theena adjust their own comm-bands.

"Wear those during all waking hours. Touch the small node once to speak, then again to deactivate speech function. Never use it for idle chatter. If you have something to report, state the recipient's name first, then whatever you have to say, unless you're answering a question directed to you. This is how Defenders keep each other updated on important details."

I immediately like Myek, partly because she talks with a kinder tone than most people in this subterranean complex. Also, her name reminds me of the English name "Mike." Plus, I'm learning to appreciate any person who doesn't talk about torching me with a fyotor.

The comm-bands distributed, Myek turns to me. "Raise your right hand,"

I obey, assuming we have to recite some sort of oath of allegiance to Quel-Tel-Palarim.

"Not so high. What are you doing?" She grabs my forearm and lowers my hand to waist level. Next thing I know, she lifts a short, snakelike thing of flexible gray-black metal from a tray and wraps it around my wrist. All by itself, the ends meld together, and the thing constricts right to my skin. It doesn't bind, but there's no wiggle room. I look closer. There's no joint or seam. Just tiny, scale-like patterns running all around it. Weird. Almost like wearing a metal serpent that has swallowed its own tail.

Myek motions Theena forward. "Next."

"So, what's with the fancy jewelry?"

When Myek flashes a wry smile, dimples appear in her cheeks. She applies Theena's band and motions Prahv into place. "No jewelry. That cuff guarantees Benlathim and Korya and any other admins who take an interest can monitor your life force at all times. By the way, don't even think about removing it. If you try, they'll know. You'd be vaporized before you cut halfway through."

Her spiel reminds me of words from the kiddie Christmas song, "He sees you when you're sleeping. He knows when you're awake."

"As long as we wear these, we better watch out, we better not pout? How do we know that's true and not just a fabrication to pacify the gullible?"

Myek raises her own right arm and tugs down the sleeve of her tunic. Glinting in the lantern's light, an identical band clings to her wrist. "I'm not from Quel-Tel-Palarim either. Seven of us made our way here from my home village of Lith. As they do everywhere, Entizar's warriors had been raiding Lith. They stole our fruit, our clothing, any useful tools—and our citizens. To escape becoming slargs, we seven hid high in the hollow cores of willafin trees, then made our way here by night in search of something to eat."

"For that, Benlathim cuffed you?" Prahv asks.

"Not for that. And not at first. But one of our group—Vahn was his name—was a bitter man. He was angry about Entizar, angry about hunger, angry at Benlathim's style of leadership, angry at the whole world. Vahn persuaded three others from Lith to join him in raiding the Quel-Telans' food lockers and then setting out for uninhabited territory to live independently. Benlathim's men caught them and brought them back. However, all seven of us from Lith received cuffs until such time Benlathim decided we are trustworthy."

"And this Vahn accepted that?" Theena asks.

"Unfortunately, no. He concocted another scheme for stealing supplies and escaping. I tried to discourage him and his followers. Told them we're better off here. But Vahn's anger blinded him. Before they reached the end of the corridor, the four of them simply vaporized. Saw it myself. All that was left was the lantern Vahn carried. In fact, this is the very lantern. Before long, my probation will be over. I've earned Benlathim's trust."

"Is cutting the only way to remove one of these?"

"Better not to talk about that." But then she lowers her voice to a whisper. "Each one responds to a code. Only the person who configures a cuff knows that particular sequence."

Aha. Like a combination lock.

Prahv lowers his voice to the same conspiratorial whisper. "Who is the person who configured our cuffs?"

Myek steps backward. Her louder, emboldened answer seems tailored for more than our ears. "Your lives will be simpler if you ask fewer questions. Too much curiosity can brand a person in a negative way. You don't want that."

I shrug and shift mental gears. After the story of Vahn, the lone source of soft light in the chamber has gained a deeper significance.

I catch Prahv's eyes. Since I still haven't figured it out, I might as well give in and ask. "Somebody please explain vaporizing. Where I come from, nobody gets vaporized."

Prahv is examining his wrist cuff, but says, "In the Before Time, it was never practiced here, either. Of course, back then, everything was goodwill and harmony. No one raised an angry voice or fist. When vicious rulers like Lotan, Entizar, and others began desecrating the remains of dead victims, some people began vaporizing loved ones to protect their images after death."

Myek stands with folded arms, listening and observing without comment.

"But how does it work?"

"'Vaporize' is an inaccurate expression. Basically, the protons, neutrons, and electrons of all matter are bound together and form molecules. The act of vaporizing neutralizes the atomic bonds, releasing particles to flash-disintegrate."

A missing piece of my Zemnan puzzle just clicked into place. "I've seen several lifeless bodies vanish—or 'vaporize'—all by themselves. No family or friends were nearby to do it."

Prahv nods. "Some people wear a bracelet or neckband set to auto-vaporize when it senses the life force has departed. Other times, a slarg is forced to wear one. His master or whoever monitors the cuff can initiate vaporization for disobedience, even from a great distance."

Okay, that makes sense. Amazing how much I can learn when I'm willing to admit my ignorance and simply ask.

"Who are you?" Myek says. "Everyone knows about vaporizing."

I'm no poker player, but this is the time to show my hand. Literally. I hold out my left palm. "You heard everything I told Benlathim. I'm your next Fithian. This is no game."

She squints with suspicion. "Forgive me if I withhold judgment."

In other words, "I'll believe it when I see it." She and these others have endured plenty of misery. Must be tough to believe a loving and merciful God still cares. Didn't I struggle with the same issue when I got word of what happened to Mom and Dad in Nigeria? And they were missionaries. The wound in my heart cracks open again, but I shove personal feelings from my mind. How can I convince these people God sent me?

"I'll pray for you, Myek."

She emits a bitter chuckle. "Go ahead, say a prayer. Although I don't know why yours would get through when so many others don't."

* * *

In the underground dining hall, the lights are low. Evidently these people ration their energy. Prahv, Theena, and I receive a small loaf of leather-smelling bread and a mug of strong tea with an aroma reminiscent of cinnamon.

"You won't receive fyotors or any other weapons," Myek says between bites. "Until further notice, you will be under observation and receive duties to perform, same as me. Probation."

I didn't expect a weapon. In the eyes of Benlathim and the underground survivors of Quel-Tel-Palarim, the three of us are human question marks. Especially me. News concerning the symbol on my palm must have spread fast. Quel-Telans in the corridor and dining hall stare at me, trying to check out my left hand despite the meager light.

"Ready to learn your way around?" Myek says after a final swallow of tea. "Follow me."

We trail her through the half-lit corridor. Could we be Benlathim's final exam for Myek? Train us well, not try to recruit us for any devious purpose of her own, and she gets rid of her wrist cuff? She doesn't say that, but it seems like a reasonable guess.

"Up here." Myek motions us to a ramp sloping to the surface. In daylight, the crumbling city remains a depressing sight, but now it looks less like a horror movie. As a newcomer, I find it fascinating. The main thing that hasn't changed by daylight is the odor of dust and ashes. The reek of charred flesh lingers in certain neighborhoods we pass through—evidence of clashes between the airborne warriors of Entizar and the Quel-Telans. Blackened bones jutting from burnt corpses prove the effect of a fyotor on a human being is gruesome. The stench encourages us to pick up the pace until the air resumes its normal, ashen odor.

"The only bodies left to rot are enemies," Myek says. "A stinking warning to invaders sent by Entizar. We treat our own fallen with dignity."

"They don't vaporize?"

Myek throws a sideways glance. Probably still trying to figure out whether I really don't know or am playing dumb. "Not always. If a fyotor blast hits a warrior's wrist cuff or neck-band, it melts instantly. No time to initiate." Her tone isn't hostile, more like impatient.

I nod and step over more scattered rubble.

Myek changes the subject. "There are many ways to get

around the city, but these paths I show you during orientation have the least rubble and the easiest walking. They're safe, too. Many vacant caloids are so damaged I don't advise poking your noses in them."

Even amidst the devastation, a glimmer of Quel-Tel-Palarim's former beauty peeks through. The construction method baffles me. As I pick my way alongside blasted walls, I detect no trace of individual bricks or cinderblocks. In fact, when I pause in the breach of a broken wall long enough to touch it, the coarse texture reminds me of petrified wood. My fingertips detect a grain to it. If I owned a magnifying glass, I bet a close-up would resemble fossilized fibers, almost as if the Quel-Telans had somehow "grown" round, soaring dwellings—caloids—with their sweeping extensions that protrude here and there. Imagining the city as it was before its destruction imprints one word in my mind—*Awesome.*

Like me, Prahv and Theena study the war-blasted caloids with curious eyes. The primary emotion I read in them is grief. As she did last night, Theena sniffs and wipes away a tear in a way that strikes me as endearing. She and Prahv must have fond memories of what once existed here. Memories of friends, now either slaughtered or in slavery.

Later, near the city's edge, Myek leads our trio into one of the less damaged towers. On the left, just inside the circular wall, instead of steps or an elevator, we come to a curving ramp. Myek leads us up it.

"I'll show you a typical periphery outpost. Most likely, you'll assist with sentinel duty in the future."

The ramp—which has a soft feel the consistency of a pencil eraser—provides my feet with welcome relief from the rubble-strewn ground. The gentle incline hugs the inside of the tower's wall. Here and there, a round window allows an elevated view, either of the decayed city on one side, or of open fields and a distant forest on another, or of enormous Lake Selador on yet another side. On our right, doorways provide access to each darkened level as we troop up the ramp. We're five or six stories up when the ramp comes to one of the hollow "branches" that reach in the direction of the lake.

"This way," Myek says, turning into it.

Overhead, round skylights aid the double row of glassy portholes in providing natural lighting. At the far end, the corridor widens into a rounded enclosure that's totally clear, except for the floor. Standing there is almost like being inside a giant version of an old-fashioned light bulb. Beyond and below lies a breath-taking panorama of Selador, glinting beneath Zemna's lavender sky.

"Myek, greetings."

Two men and a woman who had been sitting and facing outward in an arc of three directions turn to greet us as we enter. The woman stands and embraces Myek.

"Good to see you all." Myek nods toward the two men. "All quiet on the lakeside today?"

"All quiet. Which, of course, is all the more reason to pay close attention. What better direction for Entizar to attack from than the route that is normally calm?" The female sentinel studies us. "Newcomers?"

"Yes. Three new recruits. We're on their orientation tour. This is Theena, Prahv, and Rankin."

"You are most welcome. Myek and I were neighbors in our home village of Lith. Thank you for giving her a good excuse to visit us."

Before I can so much as open my mouth to say, "Nice to meet you," a single, stretched-out electronic note sounds, quiet at first but then growing in volume until it trails off again. Only one note, but its timbre is unique. The Zemnans' eyes go wide. Myek's face actually pales.

"People of Zemna," says a disembodied voice. "Greetings. Lotan, Administrator of the Ward of Hezkiel, bids me to give you a beneficial warning and an offer. Recently an ungrateful and treacherous resident of Hezkiel did ignominiously and unfaithfully reveal his devious heart by stealing a samka under the jurisdiction of Lotan and—along with one male and one female companion of like deceit—did exit the Ward of Hezkiel to escape prosecution for multiple crimes. The ringleader of this foul trio goes by the odd name of Rankin."

The Quel-Telans' heads swivel in our direction.

"People of Zemna, be warned. The conniving nature of these three—particularly of the one named Rankin—cannot be under-estimated. They have murdered many innocents. They portray themselves as refugees and travelers, while their true intent is to kill and steal. Do not trust them. Moreover, Lotan offers a personal reward for the individual or group who can deliver to him the scum Rankin—who masquerades in the laughable guise of a Fithian. Whoever can deliver this murderous Rankin, whether alive or dead, to Lotan will receive honor, protection, and everlasting meals with comfortable lodging in the new Citadel of Lotan. Behold—an image of the traitorous one."

Theena gasps.

A three-dimensional image of myself, bare-chested in drip-ping blue jeans, magically appears in mid-air. I've heard of holo-graph images but have never seen one—especially not of me. How can they project this without a receiver on our end? I'm stumped, but it obviously works.

"Study the face well. Memorize every feature. Do not be lulled by the schemer. He preys upon the immature and the naïve. Reject him. Return him to Hezkiel to face justice, and great will be your reward. That is all."

My image lingers a moment, then fades away.

So that's a Unizem broadcast? Entizar must have permitted a messenger from his brother into the broadcast portal. I'm glad for proof that the system still functions, but I'm shaken at being the main news story. In some high-tech way, Lotan has plastered a virtual wanted poster of me in front of every being on this planet.

I clear my throat. "I hope no one believes all that garbage about deceiving and killing innocent people."

Myek sizes me up with wonder. "If nothing else, you certainly know how to impress with the size of your enemies."

15

"YEAH"

In the following days, as I learn my new duties among the defenders of Quel-Tel-Palarim, I'm uncertain whether Lotan's Unizem warning has helped or hurt my mission. Although Benlathim and Korya don't speak of it—at least, not in my hearing—the respect they show me has shot upward several notches. Others exhibit mixed attitudes. Occasionally I overhear bits of debate as I pass a doorway or arrive at a post for sentinel duty.

"He's a liability. He's going to draw dangerous attention."

"How can he be good? Haven't you seen that mark on his hand? What kind of fool masquerades as something fictional?"

"I don't trust him. Not for an instant."

On the other hand, positive opinions also emerge.

"I've talked with him. There's an honest feel about the man."

"Anyone who is an enemy of Entizar's brother has my support."

"Forget about his hand and that eccentric Fithian stuff. Everyone is peculiar in his own way. We need allies, and those three are willing to support us."

Intuition tells me a Unizem broadcast—which in bygone days served as a trusted source of joy—carries a potent subliminal impact for Zemnans. Even the musical note that signals a broadcast resonates to their core. Sure, the survivors of Quel-Tel-Palarim know better than to believe either Lotan or Entizar. Still, it's hard for them to brush aside a Unizem message as pure propaganda. Something unfathomable inside them yearns to accept a communication delivered this way, even when they detest the messenger.

Sneaky, Lotan. Cunning.

The most positive outcome from Lotan's message is curiosity. Even those who declare, "I don't believe in Fithians," will some-times clear their throat and ask to hear the message I shared in the Ward of Hezkiel. Some Quel-Telans become pensive as they listen to my account of the life, death, and resurrection of the Son of God. My heart rejoices when they pose follow-up questions: "How did the Creator manifest Himself in flesh in the first place?" "If He was the Son of God, how would the follower you call Judas dare to betray Him?" "Do all residents in every ward of your 'Earth' embrace the sacrifice committed by the Son of the Creator? And why would the Creator's plan for your world mean anything on ours?" During the tedious hours of sentinel duty, these questions spark fascinating conversations.

My days in Quel-Tel-Palarim give me ample time to observe a wide variety of Zemnans. Just like humans on Earth, Zemnans come in a variety of skin tones. Here, however, ethnicities seem much more blended. In addition, no one seems to display any particular favoritism or prejudice based on the shape of people's eyes or the amount of pigment in their skin. It's similar to every-one's attitude concerning their age—no one seems to pay atten-tion to such things. So, Zemna got at least one thing right. That much is refreshing.

On the occasions when a meal or other chance encounter lets me chat with Prahv and Theena, they mention how Quel-Telans pepper them with questions, too. Partly about life in the Ward of Hezkiel, but even more about me and my message.

I wrestle with this snail's pace of sharing with people.

Wouldn't I be a million times more effective if I could sneak off and find that Unizem place, power it up, and share the Good News worldwide? In fact, by using the Unizem, I could tug at the same emotional chords Lotan manipulated, but this time with God's Truth.

Of course, I can't. My wrist cuff prohibits it. Whoever is monitoring the wrist cuffs would vaporize me immediately. They wouldn't risk letting me blab everything I know about the city defenses to Entizar.

When I share these warring thoughts with Theena over a loaf of leather-smelling tahbot bread the next day, she takes her time chewing while pondering how to respond. After a sip of bartel-berry tea, she says. "I agree about how exciting it would be to speak the Good News to the whole population. I think your desire would please the Creator."

I swirl my own mug of tea. "But?"

"In my opinion, we can keep that goal in mind, especially since at least one Unizem is functional. The 'but' here is the Creator Himself. Rankin, sometimes at night I lie awake and try to recall how it felt having a relationship with Him in the Before Time." She gazes upward, even raises her hands, as if trying to recapture the full memory of that blessed existence. With a sigh, she shrugs and gives up. "When I try to imagine how it was to live in daily touch with the Creator, specific memories have disappeared. It's like stretching to touch a cloud—it's real, yet beyond my reach."

"What's that got to do with Unizem?"

"In those days, all who were alive trusted and obeyed God without shadow of doubt. The will of God lay in our hearts. I might not recall how it felt, but I know it's a fact. Now here's my main point: The Creator knows where we are. He knows where *you* are. He must have a reason for confining you to Quel-Tel-Palarim even when our personal plan seems so much better. Perhaps He wants us to speak with scores or hundreds face to face instead of hundreds of thousands by broadcast. Shouldn't we trust His omniscience as much as His love, Rankin?"

Her childlike faith pricks my conscience. First-century believers sometimes testified before large crowds, but other times to small groups, or even one Philippian jailer. Jesus taught one woman at a well as sincerely as thousands on a mountainside. Yet, the slow approach will never get me seven thousand decisions and a trip back to Earth within a year. That's one nugget of information I can't bring myself to mention.

"Maybe you're right. Probably I should accept my limited opportunities here and be content. On the other hand, what if this is a test?"

"A test?"

"Long ago on my planet, a believer who loved the Creator left some advice. He said, 'Expect great things from God. Attempt great things for God.' If our Creator placed me on Zemna so that I could attempt great things for Him, won't I fall short if I sit here, ministering in one little corner?"

She swallows another bite of bread. "For every up, there is a down. For every inside, there is an outside. You are the Fithian. I can give advice about our culture and our people. As for your mission, that's between you and God. Have you prayed about it?"

I sigh. "Every day."

"Then, if His response is to leave you in Quel-Tel-Palarim, is that not His answer for this phase of your assignment?"

Wow. Sometimes Theena's faith puts me to shame. Deep inside, part of me already understood this truth, but something in my brain still chafes—those seven thousand decisions within a year. Like a cross country runner, I yearn to reach that finish line. But I can't confess it to Theena.

"Let's change the subject. I've never seen a baby on Zemna. No children at all. Don't Zemnans have babies anymore?"

She laughs in her musical way. "Of course, they do. Your

experiences have revolved around quarries and battlefields. Not the best of seasons for seeing children."

I spot an opportunity to tease. "You mean there's an official mating season on Zemna?"

Again, her tinkling laughter gladdens my heart. Too bad she doesn't have reason to laugh more often.

"I didn't mean that. You make Zemnans sound like beasts of the field. If anything, more babies are being born nowadays than in the past."

"Oh, why is that?"

For the first time in my presence, a blush tinges Theena's cheeks. Her eyes lock on the remaining half loaf of tahbot. "It's embarrassing to explain. In the Before Time, lifetime companions sometimes ... You know, had offspring. The birth of a baby provided an occasion to celebrate life to the glory of our Creator. Back then, only lifetime companions engaged in such activities. But when people turned away from the Creator ..."

Her blush deepens. She inhales and lowers her voice even as she pulls apart her morsel of bread, breaking it into tinier crumbs than necessary. "The world changed. Now, even people with no lifetime companion sometimes, um, struggle. With strong desires, I mean."

"Desires to have a baby?"

Her cheeks glowing, Theena shakes her head. "I mean, touching. Intimacy. Um ..."

Oops. I've accidentally backed her into a corner. Now my own cheeks and ears are warming up.

"Women too, but men especially seem driven to engage in—" With a sigh, she gives up. "A Fithian wouldn't understand normal people."

"Theena, don't say another word. I might be a Fithian, but I'm more normal than you realize. I do understand."

"Truly?"

"Completely. The same situation exists on Earth. Except I

wasn't alive in our 'Before Times.' My world was already that way long, long before I was born."

Her gaze penetrates deeply into my eyes, as if trying to view Earth through me. "How horrible. Does that mean even you are"—she examines the crust between her fingers—"affected?" She pronounces this final word with such tender compassion I don't even consider laughing.

"Yeah. I'm affected. This is one way the demon enemies fight against God's will. They tempt us humans to focus on personal, physical pleasure and temporary things instead of pleasing God and eternal things. It's a type of spiritual warfare."

"I've listened many times as you've spoken about God, but you've never gone into details about spiritual warfare."

"Yeah. Maybe I should. It's a tough subject."

She looks up from the morsel between her fingers, a mischievous smile on her lips. "I like how you sometimes pronounce 'yes.' *Yeah.* It contains enough of *yes* to let us know what you mean, but then you soften the ending in a unique way."

I laugh. All this time I've simply talked and assumed that if I can say something on Zemna, then it must be a genuine Zemnan word. Jaylel didn't mention that I could fake slang in First Tongue.

She places one hand atop mine. "Would you mind if I sometimes do that, too? Or is *yeah* an expression reserved only for Fithians?"

This time I laugh hard enough to attract stares from other diners. Sometimes Theena is too cute for words. "I will count it a privilege to share my pronunciation with you."

She beams. "Yeah?"

I smile back. "Yeah."

Ting.

End of break time. What rotten timing. I resent the electronic tone that concludes the most interesting one-on-one conversation I've had since leaving Earth.

She stands and slides her pack onto her back. "I must hurry. I'm scheduled for duty in the Kahlyn post."

"Kahlyn? That's quite a hike from here. I'd walk you part way, except I've received a summons to a meeting with Benlathim."

"With Benlathim? What about?"

I shrug. "I'll rejoice if he wants to talk about God. More likely, he needs somebody to shovel out a clog in the sewage conduit."

She doesn't laugh, but her smile is the widest I've ever received from her. "You'll clean up this planet one way or another, Rankin."

"See you later?" I call as she hurries toward the main tunnel.

She pauses at the doorway and throws me a wink. "Yeah." Then she's gone.

I chuckle. It's the first time I've ever seen a Zemnan wink. Did she learn that from me, too?

I drain my cup then hustle out of the dining area, activating my wrist light as I do. By now I've learned to navigate most of the tunnels beneath the central district of Quel-Tel-Palarim without a guide. Still, it sure would be great if the engineers could get the lighting system down here back online.

Within fifteen minutes, I approach the two guards outside Benlathim's workstation. "Rankin reporting. Benlathim summoned me." I lift my arms for the security pat down.

"Proceed," says the one who checks me for weapons. "Benlathim is expecting you."

For the first time, I find Benlathim alone. Various maps still cover his table, and he's measuring something on one as I approach. "You sent for me?"

"Yes. We need food. Our supplies are dwindling too low." He looks up from his computations. "I've ordered a gathering team for this afternoon. You're going with them. All you have to do is pick fruit. If you get a chance to herd any stray unilox toward the team, all the better. Fresh meat is always a bonus."

"I understand." My tone is official, the way everyone talks to

Benlathim. Inside, though, my heart leaps at the news. Soon I'll be outside this shattered hulk of a city and soaking up the beauty of nature.

"I can't stress enough the seriousness of this operation. Attackers from Entizar sometimes pounce on our gathering teams. They know that food supply is a critical weakness."

"I understand. I'm glad to help."

"There's more. Rankin, you probably realize not everyone wants you among us. Some Quel-Telans view you as a hazard at best, and a possible spy at worst."

"Right, but I'm not sure how to prove I'm no threat."

"I'm taking a risk by sending you on this work detail. But we're short on hands, and you own two of them. Even if one of them is rather peculiar."

"Sir, you have my promise I'm no one's puppet and no spy."

"Personally, I believe you. But before you leave the city, I want to give you fair warning."

"Sir?"

"One, while you're out there, don't say anything about this faith of yours. With a constant chance of attack from Entizar's warriors, I don't want my people distracted by your stories."

"Understood, sir. No problem."

"Second, keep your hands busy with the assignment. Don't say or do anything that might give anyone reason to question your loyalty."

"I beg your pardon?"

"What I'm saying, Rankin, is that some of our defenders are fatigued. They're jumpy, even more so above ground and outside the city. If you make even one questionable move, you just might get melted from behind. Be on your best behavior."

I swallow. "Thank you for trusting me, sir. I'll remember your advice."

16

RAIDERS

Before long, about forty of us—both male and female defenders —depart north out of the city. Four single-horned uniloxen haul large, empty wagons. This method isn't how Quel-Telans gathered the harvest in their Before Times, but this is how survivors do it nowadays.

Étan, the leader of our expedition, glances back at me and scowls. He's never voiced his opinion to my face, but I've overheard him griping to others that I never should've been spared. According to him, I'm worthless. A pest. Worse, he declares I'll be a magnet for trouble since Lotan has singled me out for revenge.

I'd hoped Benlathim would assign Korya to lead this expedition. Korya might not be fond of me, but he's less judgmental than Étan and treats everyone with justice. No such luck. I'm stuck with Étan. The one similarity he bears to Korya is his baldness. Maybe that's the style among some defenders?

A wet mass of dribbling tongue slurps against my face, filling one ear with slobber.

"Oh, yuck. Stop!" I step aside just as the foot-long tongue uncurls toward me a second time. Chuckles erupt as I wipe a tunic sleeve across my cheek and neck.

Yalp, yalp, yalp. By now I've been around long enough to recognize the mating chant of a unilox in heat. I widen the gap between me and the creature to keep it from trying anything disgusting.

More chuckles. None from Étan, though. If his eyeballs were fyotors, I'd already be charbroiled. He's not even giving me a chance. Something inside me bristles. That guy despises me, and even though I'm supposed to be a good Fithian, my opinion of him is lower than a snake's belly. The fact that I've spotted him eyeballing Theena from head to toe irritates me even more.

Unbidden, a Bible verse comes to mind. "Love your enemies and pray for those who persecute you, so that you may be sons of your Father who is in heaven."

Love Étan? Yeah, right. It's challenging enough sitting in the same dining hall with that clown. I'd rather kiss this unilox than be anywhere near him.

Once again, doubt floods my mind. How can I be the right Fithian for this job? Sometimes I want to ram my fist into Étan's face, to blacken his lust-filled eyes. On the other hand, I'm pretty sure none of the apostles ever punched out a jerk. Sure, Peter once chopped off a guy's ear with a sword, but Jesus told him to knock it off then reattached the ear.

On the other hand, didn't the apostle Paul once strike a sorcerer with blindness? I suppose that doesn't count. The sorcerer—what was his name? Elymas?—wasn't just irritating Paul. Elymas stood in the way of people coming to God, so Paul zapped him.

I'd never given that chapter of Acts much thought. The Bible doesn't say so, but could it be the early apostles also received one of these Intersection symbols to work miracles?

That mental picture stops my feet. What a wild idea, that I might actually have something in common with a miracle-working apostle. They probably didn't, though. Surely the Bible would mention it. Still, my self-doubt suddenly seems ridiculous. After all, if God does the equipping, does it matter whether you're a fisherman, or a tax collector, or a high school senior? Feeling bolder, I resume walking.

Étan jogs forward and plays traffic cop, motioning our caravan off the road. Here, a line of trees angles away from the road and toward the forest. In a line beneath the trees, something has pressed the green turf flat. I get it. To disguise their movements, earlier teams have walked in shadow, beneath the spreading limbs of the tree line. This way, no samka-riding spy in the sky can spot us.

Would it be better strategy to gather fruit at night? I suppose not. To do that, each of us would need wrist-lights. At midnight, forty flickering lights could be seen for miles. A gathering team might as well shout, "Entizar, look over here!"

"Eyes up, you. Be alert." Étan falls into march beside me. "At least act like a useful member of the team."

For a moment, I consider telling him to grow up. But he would love a fight. Instead, my calm reply is, "Whatever you say."

"Whatever I say?" He spits, and some of the spittle hits one of my Nikes. "You wouldn't enjoy what I'd like to say, little lord Fithian."

Oh, brother. A jerk and a drama king rolled into one. Only by forcing myself to remember that Jesus died for guys just like Étan keeps a civil tone in my voice. "Maybe not. But that's all right. Benlathim put you in charge. Our job is to follow your instructions."

A grunt. "Be sure you do." He quickens his pace and hustles forward again.

I glance Heavenward. *Thanks, Lord. I couldn't have done that without You.*

Peace flows into my heart for not letting Étan ignite my anger. He's still a jerk, but now my footsteps become lighter, and not simply because of the green grass.

Quel-Telans within earshot cast glances my way. New, respectful glances.

When we reach the forest outskirts, no fruit is in sight. Earlier missions have picked it. We'll have to penetrate farther. At least walking is easy, since no rotting logs or thick underbrush hinders our feet. Just like the other Zemnan woods I've seen, local residents once manicured this place to perfection. Not enough time has passed for it to fall into complete disarray.

Finally, we find fruit dangling from branches.

"We'll start here," Étan says. "All those assigned as defenders, set up a standard perimeter. The rest of you, start picking."

Some of these trees bear kinds of fruit I still don't recognize. Are they all edible, or no? Rather than ask and risk looking like an idiot, I decide to specialize in balochias. Not only are the copper-colored banana things delicious, but according to Prahv the harvested fruit retains freshness longer than most others. I snatch a basket from the nearest wagon and start picking.

"You—stay where I can see you," Étan calls to me.

"I'm picking right here. If you don't go anywhere, you'll see me just fine."

His eyes smolder, but he stalks away without comment. Étan doesn't help gather, but he doesn't guard the perimeter either. He struts around, brandishing a fyotor that's polished to a glossy sheen. Must be his idea of supervising. I ignore him.

At the end of the clearing, I spot a patch of the same black flowers that knocked me unconscious my first day on Zemna. Like the other harvesters, I matter-of-factly step around the lyra blossoms. Although I'm a relative newbie to this planet, it's comforting to see I've learned a few things about life on Zemna.

I haven't picked for long when I realize the most bountiful clusters of balochias hang high overhead, where earlier teams couldn't reach them.

When I notice a coil of lightweight rope in one of the wagons, inspiration strikes. Why stay down here when the best pickings are up high? Without requesting permission, I grab the rope and tie one end around the handle of my basket. The other end I secure to my belt. I begin climbing a stout-trunked balochia, with plans to haul up the basket once I'm high enough to reach better fruit. In sixth grade, I'd been a champion tree climber. The knack hasn't left me.

"What do you think you're doing? I ordered you to stay where I can see you." Étan isn't aiming his fyotor my way, but his upturned face radiates rage.

"The best fruit is up here. I'm not going anywhere you can't see me. Besides, even if I entertained some crazy notion of running away—which I don't—that would be impossible to do up a tree, now wouldn't it?"

Étan fumes but says nothing.

I climb higher. Forty or fifty feet up, I come to branches heavy laden with some of the largest balochias I've ever seen. I haul up the basket, and within seconds it's heaped.

"Ishtaniel," I call to a man on the ground as I lower the basket by the rope. "Will you dump these so I can refill it?"

Ishtaniel waves and pours my load onto an empty wagon. Moments later, I have the basket wedged between two branches once again and proceed with picking.

Étan's glower remains darker than a thundercloud, but he holds his peace. Even a jerk can see I'm gathering fruit five or six times faster than anybody on the ground. Within a minute, the smooth rope slides through my fingers as I ease my next load down to Ishtaniel. Following my example, a strawberry blonde named Salexa ties a rope to the handle of her basket then scampers up a balochia across the clearing. Impressive. A monkey would have trouble racing this girl up a tree.

"Want to compete?" Salexa calls across the gap between our trees. Her mischievous smile strikes a pleasant chord.

"You're on. The person who fills the most baskets wins. Ishtaniel, keep track for us."

"Go," she calls, fingers already flying.

Baskets slide up, down, up, down as Salexa and I pluck, fill, lower, then haul our empty baskets back up. I soon lose count. From her tree, infectious laughter rings out. She's enjoying the sport as much as I am. In fact, my fleeting peeks show the rest of the team often glancing up to marvel at our progress.

"Faster, Salexa," calls a woman. "You may have met your match."

What do you know? Smiles all around. Nothing like a friendly race to lift a person's spirits. With the exception of Étan, a new mood of goodwill seems to energize the group.

Slimmer and lighter than I, Salexa has an advantage. She can teeter farther out on slender branches than I dare to try. Still, no way I'm going to let this girl show me up.

Just as my fingers close around a plump balochia at the extreme end of my reach—*Blam!* A detonation startles the fruit from my fingers, letting it plummet.

"Raiders!" someone shouts.

Enemy fyotor blasts explode two more tree trunks into a hailstorm of fiery bits, sending the harvesters on the ground scurrying.

Étan and other fyotor-bearing defenders begin shouting, shooting upward. But at what? On my lofty perch, I'm surrounded by foliage. So many leaves block my view that—

Blam!

This time I spot the fyotor blast. The superheated wood explodes as if by cannon fire. Four—no five—black samkas whirl into sight. Must be Entizar's men, sent to torch us. But our guys are firing back. Defenders on the ground dive for cover behind trees, lean out to shoot, then dash to a new hiding spot. It's a fast-action firefight that leaves me struggling to keep track of which trees conceal a Quel-Telan.

And here I sit. Up a tree. I feel like a useless coward, but what can I do? Tie my rope to a branch and slide down? But what then? I'm unarmed.

Down below, Étan is pressed against the base of my own tree. He grips the fyotor vertically to his chest, minimizing risk of detection. No sooner do I conclude our leader has turned chicken than he leaps out, raises his fyotor, and fires.

The samka he targeted explodes into a fireball. I duck my head to avoid the shower of debris, but that does nothing to halt the wave of stench from roasted tyagil cells. On the ground, Étan sprints across the clearing to take position behind another tree.

Incredible. Étan might be a prize-winning jerk, but he's Rambo with that fyotor. Now I understand why Benlathim entrusted the team to him. What the nut lacks in social skills he makes up with guts and marksmanship.

Our harvesters are unarmed, and the raiders seem to know it. Quel-Tel-Palarim doesn't have enough weapons for every citizen. Fyotors rotate from defender to defender with every change of work shift. The raiders pay no heed to fleeing Quel-Telans with empty hands. Those who shoot back draw their main fire.

If only I could do something. But what?

17

QUICK THINKING

For the third time, an enemy craft zips between my hiding spot and the balochia tree where Salexa crouches, attempting to hide her strawberry blond braids behind the leaves. Our eyes lock. Fear. The feeling is mutual. If those invaders spot us, she and I are sitting ducks. In fact, if we make a move toward the ground, we'll still be dangling ducks—easy to see and shoot all the way down.

Another black samka flashes between us. I hide behind the tree trunk in time to avoid detection. More than ever, I'm glad for my olive-drab tunic, which provides good camouflage. What I can't conceal is the big basket of balochia fruit still wedged between two limbs not three feet away.

Wait. The basket. The rope! Maybe there's something I can do after all.

I slip from my hiding place and—with trembling fingers—try to work the rope loose. The weight of repeated loads has tightened my knot around the handle. I resort to teeth. The knot loosens, then slides apart. Perfect.

Another enemy craft swoops past, right at eye level. This is becoming a regular freeway up here. No wonder. Because fyotors must recharge between shots, the raiders swoop in close, fire a shot, then throttle away before a Quel-Telan on the ground nails them. Hit and run. The gap between Salexa's tree and mine is the widest corridor for zipping in and out.

My ears catch a new threat—*Pop, pop, pop.*

One of those gunners is shooting something that reacts like an old-fashioned pistol, only bulkier, longer, and worn right over his hand like a glove. Whatever it is, that weapon needs no time recharge.

"Argh!"

Down below, a defender crumples, face down. The sight of blood spreading across his back convulses my stomach. This is no video game. It's life and death. No matter how much I feel like puking, there's no time. I've gotta try to help.

The next time I look to Salexa, her keen eyes follow my movements as I tie my line to an oversized balochia fruit. She must guess I have a scheme up my sleeve.

That done, I glance left and right. The airway is clear. "Salexa, catch!"

I reposition my body to clear the surrounding branches then throw the fruit like a football, rope trailing behind it. The balochia sails just above Salexa and snags a branch. "Wrap the rope around the tree trunk and tie it. Nothing fancy, just a solid knot. I'll do the rest."

She follows my instructions, pulling the knot tight with all her weight.

Attagirl. We're in business!

I run this end of the rope around my own tree, cinching it tight as a guitar string then tie it off. A tightrope walker could stroll from here to Salexa without the least bit of sag.

God, please let this work.

I climb higher and motion for Salexa to do the same. If that line does happen to snap, I don't want it catching us in the face like a bullwhip.

A samka whizzes past. Too low. He misses my trap. The positive note is that the pilot doesn't react to the new obstacle. His focus must be on the forest floor.

As I listen to the angry pops, hissing, and explosions around us, I do a mental count. Five attacking samkas. Minus the one Étan fried leaves four, assuming no reinforcements arrive. If I can snag one out of commission, would the remaining three back off?

Another samka soars through the clearing, zipping under my line with no trouble at all. What gives? They were flying at this height earlier.

A split second later, that last samka rushes back, maybe to retreat and recharge.

Then—"Yes!"

The taut line catches both pilot and gunner at chest height. Better yet, they strike the rope with such force that it pops their safety harnesses and tumbles both occupants forty feet to the ground. The empty craft hurtles straight into a monstrous stoalock. The metallic tree shudders but remains rigid. The unpiloted samka flips then crashes to the stoalock's roots. Bull's eye!

Across the way, Salexa's grin shows every brilliant tooth. She raises an upright fist. Ecstatic, I return the salute. Unfortunately, the rope has snapped in the middle, but my spirit soars anyway.

Another invader swishes into the clearing. It brakes then backs up and hovers over the spot where the bodies of their two comrades sprawl in the grass, motionless but not scorched. The pilot must be trying to fathom what happened since no fyotor torched his comrades. With both halves of the rope hanging alongside our tree trunks, no clues remain.

The enemy samka floats about fifteen feet below my hiding place. Should I—?

A flash of movement on the ground. The gunner aboard the samka spots it, too. It's Étan, leaping from behind a bush, whipping his fyotor to shooting position.

The enemy gunner—the one wearing a sci-fi pistol glove—points at Étan.

Pop. Pop. Pop.

Étan's weapon flies from his grasp. A crimson splotch blossoms on his midsection. His knees buckle.

"No!" Without thinking, I launch from my perch and crash, feet first, onto the gunner just as he looks up. My momentum sends both me and the gunner under me thudding to the samka's deck. In a flash, I'm on my feet. Despite his surprise, the gunman swings his gun-glove my way.

I lunge. Grab his forearm. Try to pull the weapon from his hand. It won't budge.

Pop. The mini-missile discharges over my shoulder.

Pop. Heat sears my cheek.

The thing won't separate from his hand. Desperate, I slam the gun hand against his chest. Once. Twice. Three times.

Pop.

Scarlet drops explode into my face. I jump back in shock. A red splotch covers the front of my dead enemy's tunic. I meant to remove the weapon, not fire it!

He slumps to the deck, vaporizing immediately.

Before I can be sick, an inhuman snarl of rage sounds behind me. I whirl in time to see the pilot pulling on a glove-gun of his own. Unlike me, he uses an activation disk to power the samka, not his palm. Both his hands are free to fight while the samka hovers around the clearing.

I'm no martial-arts expert. Never took a class in karate or even boxing. But I spot one quick way to stop this fight before it starts—darting forward, I grab the guidance helmet, yank it from his head, and pitch it overboard.

Ha! The pilot's face is like that of a deer caught in headlights. The samka's anti-grav clicks off. It drops like a cinder block—but taking us with it.

Reacting on sheer instinct, I fling myself into the branches flashing past. I flail. Claw. Twist in every direction for a handhold. Bark and tree limbs scratch and bite as I plummet through them. I glimpse a chance—there! When I grab a branch, both my shoulders nearly wrench out of their sockets, but my fall has stopped.

Thank you, God.

The pilot of the samka isn't so fortunate. He's still aboard when it pancakes onto the forest floor with a mighty whomp. Even as I stare at the smoking hulk, the pilot vaporizes into nothingness.

Three out of five enemy samkas are history. The remaining two shoot sky high then bug out, racing eastward.

Aching as if I've just crawled out of a giant rock tumbler, I work my way down, branch by branch, and rejoice when my Nikes finally touch solid ground. Bent over, I gulp deep breaths of air, trying to calm my runaway heart. A robust aroma like campfire smoke lingers in the air.

"He's still alive."

A cluster of Quel-Telans gathers in the spot where Étan fell. He's alive? How can that be? I'm glad, though. Étan might be a jerk face, but I don't wish him dead. I jog over. When I push through the ring, my joy deflates. Whatever projectile they shot at Étan has entered his stomach. He's unconscious. His clothing and the patch of moss beneath him glisten with blood.

"He can't survive," says one.

"He's lost too much blood," another agrees.

A woman I don't know kneels beside him. Instead of trying to help him, she says, "The most merciful thing we can do is to release his atomic bonds. Are we agreed?" She reaches for the black band around Étan's neck.

Release his atomic bonds? I pull back her arm. "No, don't vaporize him. Quel-Tel-Palarim needs defenders. Maybe we can save him."

Recalling basic First Aid, I clap a hand over Étan's bleeding stomach wound.

"Rankin, it's too late."

"It's not too late. He's alive. The first thing is direct pressure to stop the bleeding. Lift him up. Put him on a wagon. If we can get him back to the city in time, the medics—"

"It's pointless, Rankin. If we were closer to home, we might hope. But the city is too far. Most of his life force has drained away. Stand back so we can release him from his misery."

Face after face gazes down on me with sadness and pity. No one believes Étan has a chance. Even Salexa, my partner in victory, shakes her head.

I lean in, pushing down harder to staunch the blood flow. "He fought to keep all of us alive. The city needs men like him. Let's not give up too soon." I'm resolved not to budge, but how can I convince them to try?

"What's he doing to him?"

Salexa sinks to a crouch beside me. Her blue eyes are wide. "Rankin. That light. What is it?"

I follow her gaze. An orange-red glow emanates from beneath my left hand. The Intersection. It's doing something.

The memory of Gorlic's head snapping backward after a similar glow comes to mind. For a split second, I fear a repeat performance, which would kill Étan for sure. But no—the Intersection is trying to disburse healing, not hostility. There's an impression of controlled energy oozing from my palm into Étan's inert form. Staring, I begin to "hear" some sort of biological process inside my brain. There's disharmony that practically begs me to engage and smooth it out. Yet, something hinders the Intersection's effectiveness.

Someone's fingers touch my shoulder. Ishtaniel's voice says, "Rankin, that's enough. There's no reason to torture Étan in his dying moments. Whatever you're doing, stop. Let us release him."

"Wait," Salexa urges. "Something is happening. Something good."

An odd intuition persuades me that *I* am what's hindering the Intersection's potential to heal. It demands genuine ministry from me. Not intellectual arguments for Christianity. Not dry repetitions of the Gospel to get myself home. To save Étan, I must truly *care* about this loudmouth who has irritated me since the day I met him.

It's a tall order. Taking a deep breath, I force myself to cast aside all distain for Étan. He's misguided, sure, but he's a person. He deserves better than a meaningless death.

I close my eyes. *Dear God, help. Let Étan live. Please spare his life —and his soul.*

Voices continue to mutter around me, but I tune them out. Crazy as it sounds, the Intersection inexplicably urges me to concentrate more deeply on the wound. To "touch" it in my thoughts. No, not simply touch it—to merge my mind with the cell damage and intervene. I don't quite understand what's happening, but as I make the attempt, the sensation of healing grows stronger, faster.

Étan's chest rises a fraction. Falls. It rises higher. Falls. Then higher yet, stronger and stronger with each breath. With my physical eyes I stare at my "patient," but part of my consciousness remains down there, inside him, seeking and reharmonizing each note of biological discord. Amazingly, I seem to get better at it as I practice.

All whispering ceases. No doubt, everyone is staring at the spectacle of a lethal wound healing before their eyes. None of them can be more astonished than I am.

Then—Étan's eyes pop open.

18
———

A MIRACLE

To the accompaniment of gasps, Étan blinks. At first, he stares vaguely into the leafy canopy overhead but soon shifts his eyes to fixate on me. Instantly Étan lurches to a sitting position and shoves my hand from his stomach.

"What do you think you're doing? Back away!"

In no time, he's on his feet. "That outlander was trying to murder me. You're all witnesses."

Salexa steps in front of his accusing finger. "No, Étan. Rankin saved your life. You took a hit from Entizar's men. The rest of us surrendered you for dead. Your body would be vapor by now if Rankin had not stopped us. You owe him your life."

"You're insane. Look at the blood on him. He's already slaughtered somebody. He tried to snuff me out, too."

One of the more muscular defenders steps forward. "Just the opposite, sir. He's a miracle worker." The man kneels before me, head bowed. Before I recover from surprise, several others drop to their knees beside him, all bowing toward me. This scenario is unfolding all wrong.

"Everybody, please stop. Don't bow to me. I'm human, just like you."

The muscle-bound guy shakes his head. "Not like us. You

bring down samkas with your bare hands. You restore life to the dead with those same hands."

"Étan wasn't dead. And his healing wasn't mine. Give God the glory. Our Creator healed Étan."

Étan's eyes smolder. "Nobody healed me. I got the wind knocked out of me. I lay unconscious a few moments. That's all. Don't praise this charlatan for a miracle that never happened."

"His tunic. Even the hole has disappeared."

I stare, hardly believing my eyes. Red stains remain in the fabric, but sure enough, the hole in his tunic has closed. The Intersection even repaired the fibers.

Étan fumes. "If Rankin has any power, it's to create mass delusion. He's mesmerized the lot of you."

Muscle man ignores him. "Rankin, what would you have us to do?"

"I'm not in charge of this gathering team. Étan is. The raiders are gone, but they could return with reinforcements. Étan, what are your orders?"

His eyes flick from me to the destroyed samkas behind me then to the empty sky. He might believe the wind got knocked out of him, but his eyes show bewilderment. He has no clue what's happened here.

I suppress my smile.

"They know we're here. Time to retreat. We'll take the harvest and head back." As he speaks, he regains his military composure. "Standard procedure. Count the missing. Check for salvageable weapons. Wounded ride the wagons. Those bearing arms take the front and rear. Let's go."

The crowd hesitates. Take orders from a man they considered dead?

"You heard him," I say. "Let's do our jobs, people."

With dubious glances at Étan, the team obeys.

I trudge back into the clearing and locate the guidance helmet I'd pitched off the samka. Cracked and useless, it's taken on a dull gray shade. I let it drop.

Salexa appears beside me. "What are you doing?"

I walk toward the wrecked samkas. "Scrounging to see if there's anything worth salvaging. Doesn't look like it. Just two heaps of crumpled metal."

With Salexa tagging along, I head back to the others. The column is moving out.

"Rankin, I don't care what Étan says. I saw what happened. Whatever you say, we will follow you."

"If I hold a meeting to share the story of the Creator, will you come?"

"No force in the world could keep me away." Without warning, she throws her arms around me and plants a kiss on my cheek. "You must be the most remarkable man I've ever met." Before I recover, she hurries to take her place with the others.

Where did that come from? Not that any normal guy minds a hug and kiss from a cute girl, but Salexa isn't Theena. The girl I care about shows me nothing but friendship. Another girl I've barely noticed before displays open affection. Is this a sign I'm paying attention to the wrong girl? Then again, Salexa doesn't admire the real me. She's admiring what God did through me.

"Coming?" Sarcasm drips from Étan's single word, but his eyes flick once more to the wreckage in my wake. He's trying to puzzle through what happened.

Good. Let somebody else on this planet take a turn being baffled. "I'll be right there. I, uh, need to step behind a tree for a moment."

"Go ahead. Take your biology break. Just know that I'll be standing over there with a fyotor."

When Étan strolls away, the image of the dead warrior once again floods my mind. No longer able to distract myself, I drop to my knees and vomit.

* * *

Back in Quel-Tel-Palarim, Benlathim convenes the mandatory debriefing.

"How many did we lose?"

"Nine," Étan says. "The enemy came in fast and low. Jumped us before we realized they were there."

Benlathim winces. The fact that losing lives grieves him raises him in my estimation. "Were you able to eliminate any of Entizar's men?"

"We believe we took out six warriors. Three of their samkas are now scrap."

Benlathim's eyebrows rise. "Three samkas downed? Excellent. Either Entizar's men are losing their skill, or else ours are getting better. Which of you took out the samkas?"

I break my silence. "Étan blew up the first one. Saw it myself. Fantastic shot from the hip." No reason not to give credit where credit is due.

"Congratulations, Étan. And which of you heroes are responsible for the other two?"

Salexa points at me. "Score those to Rankin's credit. He destroyed both."

Benlathim's smile falters. "Rankin? Étan, I sent Rankin as a harvester. Who gave him a fyotor against my orders?"

Étan hesitates. What can he say? He didn't witness either victory.

"Nobody gave him one," says Ishtaniel, the man who'd been emptying our fruit baskets into the wagon. "Rankin brought them down with his bare hands." His gaze slides to Étan, then lower, to his midriff. "It seems Rankin can accomplish a lot of things with bare hands."

Multiple voices overlap. "Ishtaniel speaks truth." "I saw Rankin do it." "More of us would be dead if not for Rankin. Including Étan."

When those nearest me pat my back, confusion spreads over Benlathim's face. I'm not the team leader. In fact, I'm the lowest-ranking person here. He sticks to protocol. "Étan?"

With all the embarrassment of a night watchman caught dozing, Étan says, "I got knocked unconscious toward the end. I didn't witness everything that happened."

No fool, Benlathim holds his peace while weighing what he's just heard. "Very well. Get me a list of the dead. We'll hold a memorial service. I'll meet with each of you later to discuss your individual recollections of the day's events."

Like the others, I turn and file from the command post. As I do, I can practically feel Benlathim's eyes watching me leave.

19

BURIED ALIVE

Theena's song climbs to a final, triumphant note. She opens her eyes and steps from the platform.

"Praise God," I say. "That concludes our service for today. Thank you all for coming."

With smiles and well wishes, the crowd disperses from the shattered building and heads to their various duty stations.

Prahv's face radiates joy when he walks over and claps me on the shoulder. "Nearly one hundred people today. The Creator is working in our midst."

"He is. Even though there's joy in Heaven over even one person who repents, I'm excited to see how many people have accepted Him these past few weeks. My main regret is losing the Book in Lake Selador. I could teach so much more if I had the Book."

"You're doing a wonderful job," Theena says. "You were wise to memorize so many passages while you had it. Objects decay. What's tucked into your heart is yours forever."

A touch on my arm. I turn and find Salexa smiling.

"Thank you, Rankin. I look forward to hearing you next time." When Salexa's eyes collide with Theena's, her lips transform into a tight, straight line. She pulls the strap of her satchel over one shoulder and pads out the door, but not without glancing back at me before she rounds the corner.

Theena looks away.

Prahv shoulders his own duty satchel. "What's hard to understand is why the whole city doesn't accept the Creator's message. Who wouldn't trade misery and emptiness for joy and renewed reason for living? Especially when so many witnesses saw you heal a mortal wound. Twenty days, and you're still the main topic of conversation."

"Remember what Jesus taught, Prahv. Narrow is the gate that leads to eternal life. Most people love themselves and sin too much to follow Him. They're blind to what they're missing, and they don't want to change."

Theena nods. "It would help if Étan could overcome his pride and admit you saved his life. His talk about your deceiving the team has soured many opinions."

"I know. All we can do is pray for Étan."

"Want me to talk to him one on one? Maybe I can reason with him?"

The mental image of Theena chatting with Étan disturbs me. "No. Just pray for him. In fact, let's pray every day for everybody in Quel-Tel-Palarim to come to the Savior."

Prahv grins as he backs to the door. "Pray for the city? I pray every day for all of Zemna."

Theena hoists her own satchel. "I need to run, too. I'm back on the Kahlyn post today."

"Again? I wonder why they're making you specialize in that particular post? Sure would be nice if they would assign you and Prahv and me to the same station once in a while."

"Not likely, and you know it. Probation until Benlathim decides otherwise."

"Yeah. I know."

"Yeah. Bye." Flashing her signature smile, Theena strolls to the exit. There, she pauses and looks back, one hand on the doorway.

"Forget something?"

A pause for thought, then she shakes her head before slipping around the corner.

Alone in the round audience hall where Quel-Telans gather to hear me teach about the Creator and His Son, I replay her parting words. Funny how her simple "Yeah" can boost a good mood even higher.

My spirits droop, though, when I step outdoors and begin the hike to my own post for the day—Salabas district on the south side, the exact opposite of Theena's direction. Sunshine erases the eeriness from Quel-Tel-Palarim, but not the gloominess. A blasted and dying city is ugly. Seeing it is bad enough. Smelling it is worse. When the wind blows—which is often—it stirs up ash and grit, depositing them on my tongue. I spit to rid myself of the taste of death.

As I walk, an image of Indianapolis in a similar state of destruction comes to mind. Would I have abandoned Indy if something similar had happened back home? Or would I dig in like the Quel-Telans and thumb my nose at the barbarous invaders? I shrug. What does it matter? I'm stuck here until Jaylel comes back to offer me a trip home. For the first time, the notion of returning to Earth troubles me.

I kick a fist-sized chunk of rock. There's a whole lot of Zemna out there, just waiting for me to explore it. Not to mention the colony up on Feebia. I look heavenward, but it's Eenik—the smaller, oblong moon that's more of an asteroid—I see at this time of day. Yet, here I am, practically quarantined from most of Zemna by Benlathim.

Is it God's will that I hang around this destroyed city? Or is it possible I've missed the boat? Maybe Prahv and Theena and I should have flown in some other direction when we escaped from Hezkiel Ward?

Since arriving in the city, I've discovered shortcuts over piles of debris. As I sometimes do, I duck into a tilting structure that once served as a Zemnan version of a school. I pause and soak in the sight of pint-sized benches arranged in a circle—what else?—around a teacher's adult-sized chair. If you could ignore the omnipresent grit and cracks in the walls, the scene spoke of innocence. Of happier times.

As I continue down the corridor, a closed door catches my eye. Curious, I decide to explore. You never know when you might find a cool tool or other artifact.

The door is stuck or locked. Not to be daunted, I step back and give it a hard kick with my sole. In the feeble light of the interior, swarms of squeaking little weechels scuttle in and around kiddie-sized skeletons, crawling through the eyeballs of tiny skulls.

Shocked, revulsed, and on the verge of throwing up, I charge the rest of the way down the corridor and through a gaping hole in the exterior wall. The glaring sunshine makes me blink, but it doesn't erase the hideous image printed in my brain. Those poor kids—innocent little victims of a war they didn't start.

If Entizar's henchmen can deal out such brutality to little kids, what sordid garbage must rot inside his heart? And to think that back in Hezkiel Ward I concluded Lotan was a scumbag. Compared to big brother, he's angelic.

Halting, I half turn to look back. Should I suggest to Benlathim that we recover the children's bones for a decent burial? Even though I never knew those kids, they were still someone's—

An explosion directly in front of me shatters the silence and hurtles me backward, toward the school. My back thuds into the caloid wall, and I tumble to the ground faster than my brain can process what's happening.

In quick succession, two more detonations sound in the exact direction I was walking.

With ears ringing, spine aching, and my brain bouncing inside my skull, I can't think. When I open my eyes, my first impression is that the abandoned caloid above me is swaying, bending, trying to reach me with its fractured arms.

Fear and confusion energize me. Like a madman, I crawl, scramble, and slither over rubble. Gotta put distance between me and the hideous building come alive.

Next thing I know, a rumbling louder than Niagara Falls roars at me from behind. Without even looking up, I dive into a depression in the rubble, where I cover my head with my arms. The noise crescendos, and I hunker lower, urging my body into the ground for protection as bits and pieces of chaos pelt me from behind. Unseen chunks roll across me, attack me, pin me, gloating at the pain they cause. More broken pieces of building jump atop me. Then more. When I inhale, grit and dust invade my throat, seeking my lungs. They're burying me alive.

* * *

Voices. Although muffled, voices repeat my name, along with other words. Have I been asleep? Then the sense of weight crushing my backside returns. My lungs. So hard to breathe. I inhale, only to spasm into coughing as dust and grime funnel down my windpipe. With an effort, I force myself onto my elbows then work my way from the debris like an ant climbing from a collapsed mound.

Another voice in my ear, answering the first via the comm-band around my head, says, "Understood. All we heard was a series of explosions. Possibly biomines. You sure he's alive? It's not like Rankin to disregard direct questions."

Korya's voice replies, "His bio signature registers green. It's on him, and he's alive, somewhere in your sector."

"Understood. I'll send out patrols. Should be easy enough. All they have to look for is something in the city that looks like it's been blown up."

I don't recognize the voice, but the speaker's morbid humor is typical for a Quel-Telan. Is there anything in this wasted city that doesn't look blown up?

A few more coughs, and I struggle to sit up. Powdery chunks

of rubble slide off me. Grit filters down my neck and into my tunic. I run my fingers along the band around my forehead until my fingers detect the comm-nodes. "Korya, Rankin reporting. I've been unconscious. Part of a caloid collapsed on top of me." More coughs force me to clear my air passages before continuing.

Korya's voice crackles back. "Rankin, do you require medical assistance?"

Do I? With an effort, I rise to my feet. As I do, the back of my head throbs. When my fingers touch the spot, they come away tinged with clotted blood and dust.

"Rankin?"

"Something bloodied up the back of my head. Standing now, but wobbly. Any chance somebody else can handle my sentinel duty?"

"We dispatched a substitute a long time ago. What's your location?"

A long time ago? "I'm on the south side of the school caloid in district 29." I turn and look into empty sky. "Correction. I'm standing south of where the school used to be. It's gone. Guess that's what nearly crushed me."

"We're on our way."

I sink to the pavement and ease back against a broken heap. "So, what would be better, dying from a fyotor blast or dying under tons of collapsed caloid?"

The throbbing in my head increases.

"Oh, stop it. Why do you have to ask yourself dumb questions?" For once, I resolve to do nothing except the most important thing. I gaze into the pastel purple sky. "Thank You, Lord. I don't know what happened, but You were with me."

* * *

Before long, Korya and three other men lug me and my stretcher into the underground Medical Section. To my surprise, the overhead lights actually shine. Must be the one division in the underground complex not dependent on portable lanterns.

"Set him on the exam table," says a man garbed all in green. Probably a doctor.

After they do, Korya tells his helpers, "You're dismissed."

Two female assistants in pale green outfits join the doctor, who glances me over then frowns. "Sit up, please, if you can. No broken bones?"

"No. My body took a hammering, and something conked my head pretty hard, but seems that no bones are broken."

"Hmm."

He's poking through my hair. Meanwhile, I survey my surroundings. Lots of futuristic-looking equipment. On the opposite side of transparent double doors stand rows of cots, most of them occupied by patients.

The doctor's fingers reach the knot on the rear of my head.

"Ow!"

"Aide, take a note. This head wound must be radiated with antiseptic beams. Then apply Atteron cream. Gently."

"Yes, doctor."

"We should check everything while we're at it."

Before I realize what he means, his two female aides step closer. One unties the cloth belt securing my tunic and tugs it from my body. The other pulls off my Nikes and then the socks. So glad I rinsed and dried those socks last night.

Before I can object, the aides are twisting and tugging the belt loops of my Levi's.

"Hey, wait. Doctor, is this really necessary?"

"Your body has undergone a traumatic experience. A full examination is imperative."

"Well, okay, but let's do this my way." Even if the nurses are medical professionals, I'm not. I slip behind a neck-high machine of some kind and pull off the jeans.

The doctor tosses me a folded towel. "You can tie this around your waist."

When I return to the examining table, the two nurses pay more attention to my Levi's than to me. While the doc runs some sort of scope over my skin and peeks into my ears, one of the women says, "Ingenious." The two take turns running the zipper of my jeans up and down and peering at it through their magnifying scopes. I've never seen anyone scrutinize a common zipper. How ironic. These people have futuristic weapons and anti-gravity vehicles, but they've never seen a zipper? One looks me in the eye. "Such a fascinating design. Did you devise this apparatus personally?"

I can't help laughing even though it hurts my ribs. "No, that was invented by ..." Come to think of it, I have no clue who invented zippers. I wonder—have these people ever seen Velcro?

"And how do you explain this?" The doc lifts my left palm and studies the Intersection through his magnifying scope. "I had heard of this emblem. Fascinating."

"Now isn't the best time, but someday I'd like to tell you the story behind that symbol."

The doctor addresses Korya. "Countless abrasions. Contusions. Bits of shrapnel embedded in his skin. It's a wonder he's not in a coma with that head injury. I prescribe the usual ointments and bed rest. I want to keep him for observation, possibly several days."

Korya nods. "From now on, Rankin, you'd better be careful of unoccupied structures. It's a miracle the wind doesn't bring down more of them."

"It wasn't the wind that brought this one down. Something blew up. I recall at least three distinct explosions. In fact, if I hadn't paused to think about something, I would've been right in the thick of them."

"Biomines, perhaps? Maybe leftover from an assault when Entizar—"

"Korya, I've cut through that building and the courtyard plenty of times. No biomines ever went off before."

He gazes into my eyes. "I'll look into it. Meanwhile, take care of yourself, Rankin."

* * *

That night, the overhead lights glow only dimly in the Medical Section. Heavy breathing from forty or fifty male and female patients surrounds me. An occasional groan. No doctors or aides in sight. Here's the chance to try my experiment.

I slip out of bed dressed in the white wraparound issued to me by Medical. The floor chills my bare feet as I step close to the nearest patient, a man who has been unconscious since I arrived. Thick gauze covers his head from the eyebrows up. If there's any corner of Quel-Tel-Palarim where I can practice using the Intersection, this is it. Can I heal these patients the same way I healed Étan?

I place my left palm over the man's bandages. By focusing my thoughts on my palm—or rather, by letting the Intersection of All Things detect the degree of injury—I'm amazed when my mind begins to "feel" the brain damage right down to the cellular level. Not that I experience his pain. Rather, in a biological link I can't fathom, the stream of impressions flowing through my thoughts is like listening to a biological orchestra, except many musicians play out-of-tune, while others simply sit there with broken valves and strings, their instruments not functioning at all.

"Lord, I believe You gave me this emblem to do good. This man needs a touch from You. In the name of Jesus, please help him."

A pulse of orange light emanates from beneath my palm. As happened with Étan, a pleasant tingle of healing virtue seeps downward from the Intersection into the bandages. When the glow fades to nothing, his biological symphony is restored. His sleeping face now appears relaxed. I move to the next bed.

A woman. The right side of her face is horribly burned. So are her neck and bare shoulder. I can't tell how far the damage extends under the blanket. Looks like a near miss from a fyotor. I don't wipe away the doc's ointment. I simply place my palm alongside her cheek. Right away, my mind picks up the tune of biological music playing inside her being. Once again, quite a few instruments screech out of tune, but in a far different way from the previous patient.

I pray.

This time, when the glow starts, it doesn't confine itself to the area beneath my hand. The healing gleam filters down the scarred tissue of her neck to the shoulder, then extends under the coverlet. When the light fades, I straighten. Awesome! No more burn marks. As a bonus, her earlier fitful sleep has eased into sweet-looking peace with steady breathing.

Gazing down the rows of remaining cots, I can't resist the smile that springs to my lips. Too bad Mom isn't alive to see. She always hoped I would become a missionary doctor in some foreign land, and you can't get more foreign than Planet Zemna. What I'm about to do would've blown her away.

The knot on the back of my head throbs from the effort of standing, but I can tolerate it. These people have been suffering longer than I have. Time to get busy.

20

DIVERSE DANGERS

Days later, the sun—alias Aena—dips below the horizon. I've come off sentinel duty and am hoofing it back to the central district when a figure steps from a darkened doorway and grabs my arm.

"Stay."

My heart lurches before I recognize my best friend. "Prahv, what's the big idea? With everybody talking about how the city is overdue for one of Entizar's surprise attacks—"

"We need to talk. In private."

His serious tone tells me this is no prank. Besides, Prahv never jokes.

"Quick. Duck in here."

I follow him through the archway, where we blend into the deeper shadows. Prahv motions me against the inner wall and holds a warning finger to his lips. Seconds later, the unmistakable sound of boots on rubble crunches closer. The unseen feet halt. They scrape once. Twice. Whoever is out there, he's turning in different directions. The crunching resumes, faster this time as the mystery person breaks into a trot.

With a gesture of his hand, Prahv leads me up the debris-strewn ramp to the second floor. I've never been inside this particular caloid. Most of Quel-Tel-Palarim is a wreck, but this place is a genuine shambles. A battle must have raged here. Large, ragged holes gape in both interior and exterior walls. On the second level, Prahv enters a chamber that may once have served as a dining area. He picks up an overturned chair, wipes the dust from it, and pushes it toward the table. "For you." He picks up another for himself and settles onto it.

"What's this all about?"

"We have to get you out of Quel-Tel-Palarim."

"That's the same tone of voice you used for getting me out of Lotan's quarry."

"Exactly. Slargs there wanted to kill you. Now someone here does too. Maybe more than one."

"Who?" Étan's leering face appears in my mind.

"I'm not positive. But ever since the morning they released you—and everybody else—from the Medical Section, I've been watching you from a distance. Know what I discovered?"

"What?"

"That I'm not the only one shadowing you. Do you realize you are being observed?"

I tilt back in my chair. "That's nothing new. People stare at me all the time. Even more since the night every patient in Medical healed overnight. Maybe the Quel-Telans hope to witness a miracle?"

"I'm not talking about harmless curiosity. Without fail, whenever you leave the dining hall, someone waits a few moments and then follows you. Same thing when you walk to or from your duty stations. Those footsteps we heard outside just now—that was one of five different men I've caught spying on you. All of them high-ranking. That fact, combined with your near brush with death last week, tells me someone wants Rankin Fithian eliminated. They're contemplating the best time and place for you to experience another accident."

"I seem to have that effect on people wherever I go." My half-hearted attempt at humor isn't funny, even in my own ears. After all these months, people are finally showing interest in the way of salvation, and I'm beginning to see purpose in being here. Suddenly—boom—I need to leave or else die. I'd kick the wall if I weren't afraid of bringing down half the caloid.

"Perhaps the Unizem message from Lotan is tempting a few who are weary of dwelling in ashes and hope for an easier life. Or perhaps some Creator-haters don't appreciate your quick rise in esteem. I counted over three hundred people at yesterday's meeting. That's a lot of Quel-Telans. It's possible someone is jealous."

Despite the nearby window, the shadows of dusk deepen inside this condemned structure. I lean forward to see Prahv better. "What do you suggest? Last time, we confiscated a samka for a getaway. Even if there were a samka here"—I hold up my cuffed wrist—"the three of us can't get far as long as we wear these."

"Right. That's the major complication."

"Maybe I should raise the matter with Benlathim? If my neck is in danger, he could investigate, find out why these men are spying on me. Maybe he would even let me leave the city if we find evidence of a conspiracy to kill me."

Prahv's hand descends to my forearm. "Rankin, what makes you assume Benlathim isn't the one plotting against you? If he is, tipping him off that you're aware could destroy all hope of escape."

Benlathim? My brain recoils. "I'm no threat to Benlathim. In fact, he had a chance to kill all three of us when we first arrived. He spared us."

"Don't think like Rankin. Imagine yourself inside Benlathim's brain. As leader, you rule a discouraged band of survivors in the shell of a semi-dead city. The survivors follow you. One day, a handsome new face arrives. He defeats armed enemies with bare hands. He heals the wounded by the power of his touch. In fact, the newcomer claims to represent the Creator

Himself. Might not a man in Benlathim's position feel his leadership challenged?"

"But I'm not in competition with Benlathim."

"Perhaps not intentionally. But merely being here and being a Fithian—whether he admits it or not—might be enough for him to wish you gone."

"If so, he could escort me to the edge of the city and order me out, never to return."

"He cannot do that. You possess sensitive information about Quel-Tel-Palarim. The details a person carries in his brain can be tortured out of him. Benlathim doesn't dare allow you to fall into Entizar's clutches."

"Sounds like you're confident Benlathim is the bad guy."

"Not at all. My point is this: trust no one. A smile can be sincere—or it can mask envy, greed, or malice."

Prahv sure knows how to give a guy something to think about.

"Those explosions happened when I walked alone. If everything you say is true, then whoever planted the bombs wants to make my death look like an accident. He probably won't strike again soon. That would look suspicious."

"Agreed. Meanwhile, let's you and me and Theena stay alert and brainstorm for a way out."

"All right. Sounds like a plan." I stand to go.

"One last thing. There is a sixth person paying special attention to you."

The weight of his statement pushes me back into my chair. "A sixth person?"

"This one is a woman. Salexa."

Her strawberry blond hair and quick smile come to mind. She attends every meeting. "Salexa is trailing me? Why?"

Prahv chuckles. "Not trailing. But attentive whenever you are near. Extremely fixated, in my opinion."

"Well, she was in the forest the day I healed Étan. She seemed quite impressed." I stop short, not mentioning her tight hug and kiss on the cheek.

"Impressed? A better word might be 'infatuated.' She talks about you. A lot."

I clear my throat. "What does she say?"

"Compliments. Words of praise. Requests for changes in the duty roster so she can work the same sentinel post as you."

Despite the failing light, Prahv's grin is unmistakable. He's enjoying this and, being Prahv, probably even guesses how warm my cheeks feel right now. Still, the news flatters me. Who couldn't notice Salexa's beauty and bouncy personality? On the other hand, Theena is the girl who's captured my own interest. Too bad she doesn't act a bit more like Salexa.

"The way I hear it, some Quel-Telans request changes to *avoid* doing duty with me. Either I unnerve them, or else they feel uncomfortable when I talk about God. Do you believe Salexa poses any danger?"

He laughs and strolls toward the doorway. "Definitely. But not the life-threatening kind."

I sigh. "Do you suppose Theena has noticed her interest?"

His silhouette pauses in the gloom. "Absolutely. In fact, she is the one who—how do you phrase it?—'tipped me off.' Come on. Let's get moving, or else we will miss supper."

* * *

Over the course of the following days, I almost wish Prahv hadn't warned me. I jump at every unexpected noise. Even now, as I lie in the darkness of my cubicle, footsteps in the corridor draw closer. My gut tightens. Is that person armed? Will my door burst in? When the footsteps pass and fade, I breathe easier.

Of course, I've prayed about the situation and asked for God's protection and peace. Yet, in the dark of night, I can't shake the knowledge that the Fithian before me was murdered.

Where? How? Who killed him?

I flip from my stomach onto my back. Still not satisfied, I seize my pillow and fluff it before mashing it underneath me again. No position is comfortable.

"You're getting paranoid," I mutter to myself. Then again, is it paranoia when somebody wants to snuff you out? A calculating human mind caused those explosions. I'm convinced the guilty party waited a certain number of seconds after I ducked through that hole in the school wall, then detonated the explosives. They knew my routine.

Do you trust God, or not?

Is that my own question, or did someone supernatural craft it and slide it into my brain? I consider. Yeah, sure, I trust God. If He works to fulfill His plans through my life, that's awesome. On the other hand, when Jaylel dropped me on Zemna, I assumed I'd get a little angelic direction for this Fithian mission. So far, zilch.

I speak aloud to the ceiling. "You know, Jaylel, a support team of angels would be handy. Or maybe a guiding voice once in a while. Hey, I'd even be satisfied with a little yellow Post-It note with a few lines of encouragement jotted in ball-point pen."

No reply.

I halfway recall a Bible verse about the apostle Paul saying he was ready to glorify God by his life *or* by his death. Were both options equally okay with Paul? I mean, really truly?

"How could I be so careless and let my New Testament fall in the lake? I bet that other Fithian never lost his."

As if shocked by electricity, I jolt upright. "Of course! Why didn't I think of that before?"

Jaylel. When he transported me here, he explained I could read my English-language New Testament in Zemnan *because I would need it.* Jaylel wouldn't have brought me here if I didn't have God's Word with me. I bet that dead Fithian had a New Testament, too. Maybe even a whole Bible. Is it possible somebody saved it as a souvenir? Even if not, were there earlier Fithians before him? Who knows, I could be the fifth, sixth, or tenth Fithian. There might be several Bibles on this planet, just waiting for me to locate one.

I settle back onto my pillow and draw the velvety blanket to my chin. Did I jump to that thought on my own, or did God steer my brain toward it? Just that fast, my mood has shifted from self-centered fear to God-centered excitement. Is there any chance I can sneak out of Quel-Tel-Palarim without getting vaporized? If so, by finding out where on Zemna the previous Fithian lived, I just might be able to recover his Bible.

Still, in the back of my mind is the previous goal of operating a Unizem portal. Isn't that the quicker way back to Earth? I can't just drop that goal in hope of locating a Bible.

Then, in the blackness of my cubicle, two words drop into my brain. *Side quest.*

Once more, I sit up to think more clearly. Sure, a side quest! In video games, sometimes the game forces you to detour away from your main quest. You can't pursue the primary goal until you complete the side quest. During the side quest, you might feel like you're squandering time, but once you complete it, you power up. The side quest provides exactly what you need to achieve the primary quest. If God opens a way to get my hands on an actual Bible to quote from, that will definitely power up my message, regardless of reaching a Unizem.

I lie back down. My thoughts grow sluggish, my eyelids heavy. At last. Diverting my mind from assassins has helped. I could use a deep sleep. Counting sheep is stupid, but reciting Psalm 23 might help. I begin at verse one. "The Lord is my shepherd; I shall not want. . . ."

21

PRACTICING WITH THE INTERSECTION

Over the following days, I go about my normal routine, with the exception that I try to stick with groups as much as possible. Before I walk from the central district to my sentinel post for the day, I check the roster to see who else is assigned to that location. If possible, I walk with one of them there and back. If an unknown person wants to kill me, there's no way to stop a blindside attack. But I can make sure there are witnesses.

Meanwhile, every seven days our group of believers holds a service—no longer called mere meetings—where we sing praises to our Creator, take turns sharing how He's working in our lives, and acknowledge Him as the Author of all creation.

The House of Prayer, as we call it, is a large, round chamber in the central district. Benlathim's engineers have checked it out and consider it stable enough for gatherings. We use only the ground floor. The roof and most walls of the second floor got shot up long ago. In the meeting room, benches radiate in half circles from the front. The only other furnishings are banners that some of the more artistic believers created to display portions of God's Word I recited from memory. The Lord's Prayer. John 3:16. Plus others.

"Prahv, how about if you lead the service today?" I say one morning.

"Why? Are you ill?"

"I feel fine. But we need to show our brothers and sisters in faith they don't need a Fithian organizing everything to worship God. You can lead this one. So can the more mature ones from time to time. If my ministry here is to have lasting effect, then it must continue whether I live or die, whether I stay in Quel-Tel-Palarim or not."

"Wise. All right. It would be my privilege."

So, when everyone has gathered, I face the assembly and say, "I've asked Prahv to direct our time together this day." Then I take a spot on the front bench. They expect me to lead, as usual. However, when I murmur an occasional "Praise God" in support of Prahv's words or someone else's personal testimony of God's grace in their life, they relax. They see that a normal person— that is, someone without an iridescent emblem on his palm—can lead a worship service just fine. Good. They need to understand that in case I ever do leave.

At Prahv's request, I conclude with a prayer for God to draw each of them closer to Himself in personal fellowship. A second request is that He will open the understanding of Quel-Telans who shy away from hearing about God. I don't mention Benlathim by name, but I picture his face.

As the believers disperse, I'm surprised to spot Étan in the rear. Before I can greet him, he casts a longing look at Theena and then slips out. A cloud settles over my heart. I'm glad he was here, but he still churns mixed emotions inside me.

"Rankin, would it be possible for me to lead a service one day?" I turn to find Ishtaniel regarding me. We've grown much closer since the day he was emptying my basket of fruit in the forest. His faith in the Savior has grown so much since he saw me take down two enemy samkas, followed by healing Étan.

"Ishtaniel, I'm thrilled you would like to do that. But let's wait a while. You're new in the faith. For now, let's allow those who have been walking with the Lord longer to conduct. Your time will come. When it does, remember that the main goal is to point people's hearts and minds to the Creator, not to ourselves."

He grins and places his upraised palm to mine, the Zemnan version of shaking hands. "I will wait. I wish blessings on your day."

"And I on yours."

As she always does, Salexa catches my eye and smiles on her way out. It's not exactly flirting. That pleased expression generates conflicting emotions in me. On the one hand, Salexa is both sweet and attractive. Plus, she expresses sincere love for God. More than once I've noticed her praying over the meager meals we receive in the dining hall. On the other hand, Theena is the girl who's always in my thoughts, the face that appears in my dreams. Yet, despite my growing fondness, Theena treats me the way she treats Prahv. I sense affection, but it feels like sisterly devotion. If she harbors the least glimmer of wanting to be "more than friends," she keeps it well hidden.

Then again, so do I toward her. Should I demonstrate how much she means to me? Let her know I have feelings for her? Or would that alarm her and drive a wedge between us? I sigh. How can a guy who was a star athlete on the varsity track and cross-country teams be so awkward when it comes to girls? Besides, maybe earthling Fithians aren't even supposed to get mixed up with Zemnan females? In fact, what if—

"You're deep in thought. Praying with your eyes open?"

I blink back to reality.

Prahv grins. "Sorry to interrupt your meditation."

I must've zoned out. Everyone else is gone, including Theena, who didn't even say goodbye. I kick myself for not talking to her. Did she witness that endearing glance from Salexa? Or, worse, is Étan escorting Theena right now?

"No problem. I was just thinking." No way I can tell Prahv I have a thing for his little sister. He might spill the beans—or whatever Zemnan veggie resembles beans. I'd rather break that news myself.

Although I long to hurry after Theena, Prahv continues talking. "I'm eager to hear about your experiment last night."

My eyes sweep the room. Even emptied of human ears, it's possible the place is bugged. "Let's go upstairs and enjoy the shine from Aena."

Prahv catches my meaning. We exit the auditorium and walk up the ramp to the second floor. Like many rooftops in Quel-Tel-Palarim, because the damaged top level lies open to the sky, the surviving residents have covered it with a layer of fertile loam and created a garden to supplement food rations. Atop this one they've planted lorshas—pink, strawberry-like berries that grow on knee-high stalks. Whenever I need a patch of green nature where I can pray or relax, this rooftop is my first choice. Or it was, until Prahv's warning that men are shadowing me.

"You were planning to probe your wrist cuff with the Intersection. Did you find a way to release it?"

I can't contain my grin. "I'm sure of it. It's amazing I never thought of it sooner. Not until I reconsidered that night of healing in the Medical Section did the idea even come to me."

"I prayed God would show you a way. Can you describe the experience?"

The mental image provided by the Intersection comes back to my mind. "Not in details I can explain. Basically, I pressed the Intersection against the wrist cuff, same way I did to those wounded patients. The Intersection automatically 'knew' this object wasn't a wound in need of healing. My thoughts could probe right down to the molecular level, or I could zoom out to a higher level and visualize the functioning components. You know how we can't see the seam where the two ends meld? Through the Intersection, I can tell the exact spot where it joins."

"Similar to the way a guidance helmet links a pilot's mind to a samka?"

"A little similar. Aboard a samka, you can scan through all

the operational systems, but you can't zoom right down to individual molecules. Still, that's a helpful comparison."

"But the release? Could you decipher the passcode?"

"Sure did. In fact, when I stumbled onto it, my brain nearly unlocked the cuff by accident. I had to pull out fast for fear of popping the thing off. Here, hold up your wrist. Now that I know where to probe, I want to see if yours uses the same passcode."

Prahv complies, and I place the Intersection over his wrist cuff. With eyes closed, I lower my psyche into it faster than I did my own. The quicker, the better. I don't want any Quel-Telans to wander up here in search of lorsha berries and catch Prahv and me standing in the garden, my hand around his wrist and my eyes shut. They might jump to any number of odd conclusions.

"Well?"

"Almost there." I navigate my thoughts to the release data with caution. Tripping it prematurely could be bad. Then—there it is. Sure enough, the exact sequence as mine. Theena's must be identical since we all received cuffs on the same day. Someone got lazy, relying on a common denominator. Then again, that someone couldn't guess the abilities of a Fithian.

I open my eyes. "Yes, yours is configured the same as mine. That simplifies things for the escape. If you and I were to hold our right wrists side by side, I could release both cuffs with the same mental command. Theena's, too, if hers is configured the same."

"Excellent."

"Halfway excellent. The bad news is that the release mechanism is double rigged. The original programming of the cuff was to initiate vaporization if someone tampers with it. That's dangerous enough. But within the last week, the program has been upgraded from some central control unit. Now someone has added an alarm feature. The exact instant I deliver a release code, the cuffs will release *and* signal their controller before vaporizing."

"Then we do not dare remove them before we are ready to flee the city."

"Exactly. The controller who updated the programming must worry that we'll try to get them off. You and Theena and I arrived here together. All of Quel-Tel-Palarim knows we're friends. If one cuff signals it's off, I'm thinking the controller might panic and hit the sequence to vaporize the other two, no questions asked. In fact, that reaction might be preprogrammed."

Prahv's eyebrows knit together. "Diabolical, but rational in its own way. Someone owns a cunning mind."

"But who designed and monitors these? Benlathim?"

Prahv cocks his head sideways in doubt. "Benlathim gave orders for us to receive the cuffs, but if you ask me, he's too preoccupied with higher-level concerns to be the designer. He might not even know about that alarm. I would assume he relegates that duty to a trusted officer who is gifted in this type of science."

My mind discards face after face, all of the higher-level figures in the defenders' hierarchy. I even consider Korya, who has softened toward me and seems sociable enough in his own way. None of them strikes me as the brainiac type who could engineer a complex device like this. But if not them, then who? I shrug.

"Myek might know."

"Don't ask her. She comes to our worship services but hasn't made a profession of faith. She might think we're using her if we press her for information."

"Agreed. I'm curious, but I suppose knowing wouldn't make a difference anyway."

I almost hate to leave the beautiful lorsha garden but, as every day, Prahv and I have duty assignments.

Prahv is talking, saying something about his co-sentinels for the morning, but my attention wanders. The odd sensation is almost as if the Intersection is calling to my brain, summoning me to think through the most recent session. Glimpses of other, untried techniques appear in my thoughts. I sense possible ways to probe even deeper.

Prahv halts in mid-sentence. "Something wrong?"

Thoughts of the Intersection vanish. He observes me with concern.

"Not wrong exactly. This is hard to explain, but it's almost as if the Intersection is a textbook shrouded by multiple layers of translucent veils. Lately, every time I activate the power in my palm, another veil slides off, allowing a clearer understanding of how to accomplish the procedures I've already tried—and providing hints of applications I haven't yet guessed."

What I don't try to verbalize for Prahv is the intense feeling of satisfaction that accompanies each new success with my emblem. Almost like one of my computer games back home— every level you master endows you with new powers. Except life on Zemna is no game. If I bomb out here, I'm dead. No respawning.

22

PALAGEIST

Next morning, I emerge from an exit arch of Quel-Tel-Palarim's subterranean network with a shovel—my gear for the day. Billows of fog enshroud the ruins of the city. Not just any fog, either. Maybe as a trick of refracted light, the murk hangs as a lavender mist, impenetrable more than thirty feet away down here on ground level. Higher up, the crumbling upper stories of caloid towers jut skyward as ugly islands amidst the vapor. It's as if the fog is trying to soothe and nurse the wounds of the devastated city. The pale purple sky is overcast, making it hard to see where fog ends and sky begins.

So bizarre. Like standing inside a snow globe filled with mist instead of snow. Who would've thought that even water droplets suspended in air could appear so alien? Of course, the lavender fog isn't alien. I am.

"Palageist. Horrible, isn't it?" Theena waits outside the archway, leaning on her own shovel. Instead of the adorable little Theena smile that warms my soul, her lips curve downward. Her eyebrows, likewise, droop lower than usual. Her eyes with their purple irises strike me as deeper pools of the same phenomenon.

"Palageist? The word I know is 'fog.'"

She shakes her head. "Fog is nothing. A flimsy little sheet that kisses the ground until Aena evaporates it. Sometimes we had fog in the hill country of Hezkiel Ward. But palageist is different. Thicker. Heavier. It lies only in lowlands around large bodies of water, like Selador. A true palageist can last for days if no wind drives it away. So sinister."

"Sinister?"

She shivers. "Can't you feel the otherworldliness of it? Almost as if we're observing the amassed atoms of every person who has ever been vaporized returning to haunt us, to suffocate us and bury us beneath their mingled essences."

I'm tempted to chuckle, but she's dead serious. "Theena, you conjure up the most vivid word images. You could be a poet."

"I enjoy word craft. Yet, on this morning morbid descriptions are the only ones that come to mind. Makes me want to lock myself in my quarters until it goes away."

"Try a fresh viewpoint. Instead of watching with dread, admire it as a work of beauty. A temporary gift of artwork from the Creator. One that paints over this defiled city with gentle, feathery strokes."

Her eyes flood with doubt, but she graces me with a feeble smile.

I lower my voice. Swathed in fog—or palageist—I can't be sure how close my spy for today might be. "Did Prahv get a chance to share what he and I discussed?"

"Yeah."

There. She said it again. One syllable, and only whispered, but how Theena charms my heart when she pronounces the word she learned from me.

"You nervous?"

She considered. "In a way. Still, I have peace. If the Creator wants us to stay alive, He can control that. I'm ready to die, if that is part of His plan, but I cringe at the idea of agonizing pain."

"I know what you mean. Come on, let's get started."

Shovels over our shoulders, we set out for the southern rim of Quel-Tel-Palarim. Although the powers that be never assign us to the same sentry post, all week Theena and I have been scheduled for community work teams. In this project, we clear rubble and remove the crumbling remains of rooftops, transforming the exposed upper floors into additional gardens. Because foraging trips into the woods come under increasing attacks, Benlathim has ordered an expansion of the city's farming efforts.

As we march along, stepping over and around the ever-present wreckage, the sea of palageist muffles sounds. Only our own footsteps disturb the quiet. Twice, Theena jerks her head around as if she's detected something too subtle for my Earth ears. Both times she resumes walking, but not with an air of calm. She wasn't exaggerating about not liking palageist. She's really freaked.

Or maybe she hears the feet of whoever is stalking me. Might that person decide such a fog is the perfect cover for deleting me —or us—without witnesses? The hairs rise on the back of my neck. Maybe I'm a little freaked myself.

Out of the silence, Theena says, "Are you getting enough to eat? I imagine our rations are much less than what you enjoyed on your world." It's an awkward sort of question, the kind people toss out when they want to make conversation but don't know what to say.

"Less, yes, but I'm surviving all right. Thank goodness for your tahbot bread. I still haven't figured out where the grain comes from to make it, but I'm getting addicted to the stuff."

She replies with tinkling laughter. "Rankin, are you teasing, or do you truly not know? Tahbot isn't grain. Tahbot is a water plant. Large beds of tahbot grow on the bottom of Lake Selador. Teekla fish love to make their homes among the fronds. The droppings from the teekla fertilize the tahbot roots, making the plants grow thick and tall, almost to the surface."

"You're serious? Bread made out of fish dung and seaweed?"

More laughter. "Haven't you heard mention of the boats? Crews go out to harvest tahbot by night."

I swallow to cleanse my throat. If ignorance is bliss, I could use a big dose of ignorance. The principle is no worse than fertilizing with cow manure, like people do back home. Still, it's a shock to learn I've been enjoying bread grown in fish dung.

She changes the subject. "Do you know you're becoming a source of grumbling?"

"Uh-oh. What sort of grumbling?"

"Nice grumbling. Some people murmur that in light of your 'extraordinary skills' and 'proven loyalty' the higher-ups ought to promote you to leader status with access to a fyotor."

It's my turn to laugh. "I hadn't heard that. I'm happy to accept menial jobs."

"That is another trait people admire. You balance great ability with immense humility."

I shrug. "They can keep their fyotors. I'm not here to kill people. Both sides need to hear about the Savior and the opportunity of new life."

"I hope Benlathim has not heard the grumbling."

"Oh?"

"He might conclude you instigated such ideas. There's talk that some superiors want to put a halt to our worship services."

An icy arrow pierces my heart. "Stop our services? Why?"

"The argument is that any above-ground gathering presents a danger. They claim one well-placed bombardment during a surprise attack could collapse a building on hundreds at once."

I vent my anger in a savage kick to a hunk of blackened rubble. "That's crazy. The odds are totally against anything like that happening. Who could make such an idiotic proposal?"

"If the rumor is true, Benlathim himself."

Her words freeze me in my tracks. "That makes no sense. Benlathim is the one who granted permission to use that vacant caloid, provided we cleaned and repaired it during off-duty hours. We did even more than he demanded by planting the lorsha garden on top."

She nudges me forward with a light touch in the small of my back. "That was before, Rankin. Things have changed."

Under other circumstances, I'd rejoice at any contact from Theena, but not this time. "What's changed?"

"Politics."

They were bad enough on Earth. Even here I can't escape political maneuvers.

On impulse I growl and swing my shovel at the gray skeleton of a sapling that once grew alongside the walkway. The blade decapitates it at neck level.

Theena says nothing, just keeps walking. I hope my display of temper hasn't spoiled her impression of Fithians. Too late to worry about it. I've suffered enough at the hands of people willing to kill an idea just because they can't control it for their own selfish goals. The smiling photo of my missionary parents materializes in my thoughts. The image dissolves into one of their twin gravestones.

Gone. Murdered by fanatics.

Theena sniffs the air. "That's odd. For a moment I thought I smelled something burning."

Now my nose catches a whiff. Something smells like campfire smoke. As I put the shovel back over my shoulder, I notice the source. Circling the shovel's handle is a scorch mark the width of my left palm.

23

BATTLEGROUND

I pause in my shoveling to stand straight. Twisting left and right does nothing for the kink in my spine. It refuses to leave.

"Hard toil, isn't it?"

A few feet away, Salexa smoothes a mound of dark topsoil, then likewise leans on her shovel. Her brilliant smile flashes right through the palageist. Lost in my own thoughts, I hadn't realized Salexa was working nearby. But where's Theena? I don't spot her among the thirty or so people performing garden duty. Maybe she's on a water break.

"I wouldn't want to do this every day for the rest of my life. I'm sure there must be an easier way."

She giggles. "Of course, there was. But most of that equipment is gone. At least, gone from Quel-Tel-Palarim. But perhaps there are peaceful wards where they can still do this kind of work with levitation?"

Her eyes lock onto mine and won't let go. What does she think I am, all-knowing?

"I can't say, Salexa."

Her eyes hold mine. "Oh. I understand. You don't have permission to speak of it to regular people."

"Salexa, you misunderstand. Fithians don't know everything.

Our special knowledge is about God and His love. For instance, I don't even know how you lived before the dark times came." Not wanting to be a lazy example for the crew, I resume spreading topsoil.

"You don't? Then I'll tell you. My favorite way to exercise my personal giftedness was in phloeming."

By this juncture of my stay on Zemna, I've learned tons of new vocabulary but am still puzzling out other expressions. I'm positive this is the first time I've heard the term *phloeming*. Salexa nonchalantly returns to working her shovel as if any child would understand. Pride kicks in, and I decide not to confess that my brain is as foggy as today's palageist.

"So, what part of phloeming did you enjoy most?"

"What part was there not to like? At least, for a person blessed with the ability and inclination. If I had to name one favorite slice of the experience, I would say the climbing. It was a blessing to exercise my limbs in the beauty of outdoors—especially as I clung to the side of a tall caloid—that was always exhilarating!"

Climbing? My brain clicks back to the first day I met Salexa. In the forest, she had scampered up a balochia as if she'd been born in one. Does phloeming have something to do with construction? That would explain Salexa's compact, gymnast figure. I'm dying to ask, but this is one Fithian who feels dumb far too often. Nope, I won't admit my ignorance. In time, I'll piece things together.

Another glance around fails to locate Theena. An undefinable weight settles in my gut. I hope she didn't come back and see me chatting with Salexa. The last thing I want Theena to believe is that I harbor interest in another girl.

An earsplitting wail drowns out my thoughts. Like everyone else, I stop working and gaze upward. What *is* that racket?

Overlapping shouts ring out. "An attack!" "Raiders!" "Run!"

Pandemonium breaks out. Every person flings down their tools and bolts toward the ramp to the ground. A few agile souls scramble over the wall to beat the rush. Hissing, explosions, and distant screams burst through the mist.

"Rankin, we can't stay up here." It's Salexa, tugging my elbow.

We race down the ramp to ground level. Of course, attackers from Entizar would strike today. With such a palageist, their samkas and other craft must have swooped in low to the ground, unseen. It's Pearl Harbor with a sci-fi twist. Or H.G. Wells's *War of the Worlds* come alive, right over my head.

By the time my Nikes hit street level, explosions reverberate from all directions. Fyotor beams lance through the haze with blinding intensity, vapor literally crackling from the intense heat. The gardening crew scatters for underground shelters.

"Rankin!" Parting the mist in a sprint, Theena appears. She spares one hasty glance at Salexa, then looks me in the eye. "It's time. The opportunity."

"Right." An attack provides the ideal diversion Prahv, Theena, and I have been waiting for. Now to meet Prahv at our rendezvous point.

Theena and I are running full tilt when Salexa's voice catches up. "Wait, where are we going? The shelter is back that way."

No good. Salexa is right behind us, and with her athletic build, I doubt we can outrun her. I slide to a halt in loose grit. "Salexa, please go back. Save yourself."

"Why? Where are you going? I want to help."

"No time to explain. Please stay here. Help lead the services."

Her eyes shoot wide, more at the realization I'm leaving Quel-Tel-Palarim than at the crisscrossing fyotor blasts overhead. "You can't leave. You'll be vaporized."

"No, I won't. Trust me."

"You mean Fithians are impervious to vaporization?"

Theena grabs my hand. "We don't have time for chatter. We can't predict how long the raid will last."

"Salexa, for the last time, please take shelter. My mission as a

Fithian is calling me elsewhere." Without waiting for her reply, Theena and I turn and break into a run.

Part of my inner self feels like a coward, running when disaster strikes. On the other hand, what good could I accomplish by cringing underground? Defenders with fyotors will repel the attack. Both sides will suffer losses, but the city's protectors will beat back the invaders as they always do. Life will go on but without me.

As Theena and I pound around a caloid, a hanging terrace explodes overhead.

"Theena, look out!" I yank her backward, just as a smoking chunk of debris whomps into the spot where she'd been.

For protection, we scramble behind the trunks of dead trees lining the walkway. Even as more rubble from the tower pelts the ground around us, a scream pierces the air. It's Salexa, behind us and caught in the open.

The second the rain of rubble ceases, I bolt to where she lies. I roll her over. She moans and opens her eyes.

"I told you to save yourself."

"I want to help you."

"Lie still. Let me see how bad it is."

Theena kneels beside me. "Is she all right?"

Salexa groans. "My stomach. A big chunk bounced off the ground. Slammed into me."

As gently as possible, I lower the Intersection until it touches her tunic over the spot. With eyes closed, I "hear" the dissonance of battered biology. Cracked ribs. Cell damage. Nerve endings pleading for help. I suck in my breath and allow the Intersection to merge with the injury, warming and restoring every cell.

When I open my eyes, Theena stares at me in a way she hasn't done since my first day in the quarry. Her gaze shifts from Salexa to me, and then to my left hand. She dares to touch the back of my Intersection hand. "Your hand—it's so much warmer than usual."

The clamor of explosions continues, some of them quite near.

When the damage is healed, I say, "We can't stay here. Salexa, follow at your own risk, but Prahv and Theena and I are leaving the city."

She stands, completely healed. "Let me come, too. There's nothing for me here."

Theena shrugs, but in the gesture, I glimpse more than resignation. An unspoken irritation. Jealousy?

"Let's go then. Everyone, keep your eyes open."

Again, we set off at a sprint. Theena and I lead the way, always angling north and east, to the rendezvous point with Prahv. All the while, raiding samkas swish overhead blasting rooftop gardens and returning fire at any windows where defenders dare to shoot back. The battle rages nearer, then farther, but everywhere a tremendous amount of airborne dust and smoke mingles with the palageist. Running with one sleeve over my mouth is a pain, but I'm glad for the filter.

Salexa puts on a burst of speed to draw parallel with us. "Where are we going? Maybe I know a shorter route."

"To what's left of that big fountain on the northeast edge."

"In Flotessa Greenway? I used to live near it. There's a quicker path if we leave the main walkway."

Although I've been in the city long enough to find my way wherever I need to go, my routes aren't the straightest. Theena offers a terse nod.

"Okay, lead us there. Wait. I nearly forgot." I pull the comm-band from my head and toss it away. From here on, we can't risk being tracked. Theena pulls hers off, and after a moment's hesitation Salexa drops hers as well.

"Okay, Flotessa Greenway. Let's go."

Salexa points to a grassy gap between two caloids.

Sprinting around towers and flitting across streets and plazas I've never encountered, I'm disoriented. Yet, Salexa is true to her word. It's clear we're covering ground faster than Theena and I could've done on our own. For the first time, I'm glad Salexa followed us.

Are any authorities in Quel-Tel-Palarim aware of our mad dash toward the city limits? I'd hate to work up all this sweat and then puff out of existence at the last moment.

And Prahv—will he make it? I didn't ask about his work assignment for the day. He could get struck in the battle. I won't forgive myself if he gets killed while running to help me escape.

Slightly paranoid, I glance backward. There's a blur of a shadow in the mist. Is someone chasing us? I spare another fleeting glance. This time, though, I spot nothing but swirling murkiness.

Theena shouts, "No!"

A hundred feet up, a huge armor-clad bolsamka bristling with fyotor muzzles comes swooping into the plaza, heading straight toward us. We're caught in the open. No place to hide.

Before I can put on a burst of speed, double fyotor beams flash from windows several stories up on opposite sides of the plaza. Caught between the two, the invading bolsamka super-novas with blinding radiance and heat.

In an eye blink, my fear morphs into relief then terror. The blazing wreck is hurtling toward us, spewing greenish smoke as it drops. Grabbing both girls by the sleeves, I veer right, half dragging them. Just as searing heat prickles the back of my neck, I haul them through the arched doorway of a tower.

The careening, molten explosion rips the air behind us. Searing globs of metal pepper the plaza, and some spatter through the same archway we just entered, embedding them-selves in the inner wall. On either side of me, Theena and Salexa burrow their faces into me as we hunker down, but what protec-tion can I offer? My body can sizzle to a crisp as quick as the next. Will this damaged caloid hold up, or will it collapse and crush us?

A secondary explosion sends us pressing even lower. I want to burrow right into the floor. A foul stench pours into our sanc-tuary. I can't hold my breath fast enough to avoid the disgusting odor invading my nostrils. It's as if a mountain of pig manure got half incinerated, then left to smolder. Can't these people invent anti-grav cells that don't reek when fried?

When nothing else explodes and the roar dies down, I stand and peer from the archway. Burning wreckage of the bolsamka churns black and green acrid smoke into the air. Every speck of palageist has been roasted from the plaza. Even this far away, intense heat from the inferno radiates into our archway.

"Salexa, the defenders who brought down that bolsamka are hiding in windows up above. I would prefer they not get a clear look at us. Is there an alternate route to Flotessa Greenway that will avoid the plaza?"

Salexa blinks, then leaps to her feet. "I'll find out." She darts deeper into the building but returns moments later. "The rear exit is blocked. This is the only way out."

Not what I want to hear. "All right. No choice then. Are you both up for another run?"

They nod.

"Okay. But if the boys above mistake us for the enemy and start blasting with fyotors—separate. Keep running and dodging, no matter what. They might hit one of us, but not all of us. Let's go."

I leap through the arch and break into a full sprint, zigzagging across the plaza to avoid bits of flame and puddles of molten metal. I've used similar footwork in paintball battles, but knowing you might get killed for real pumps up the adrenaline.

In case defenders of Quel-Tel-Palarim overhead are pointing weapons at us, I grin the toothiest smile I can muster and wave a hand of thanks toward the upper stories. Let them think they saved three Quel-Telans. At the minimum, they'll wonder where in the world we're dashing. They might report us. Not good, but better than torching us in our tracks.

When we're a safe distance away and back into palageist, I slow the pace. "Which way, Salexa?"

"Follow me."

Unlike me, Salexa isn't even perspiring. I struggle to keep

pace. My feelings toward Theena haven't lessened, but it's tough not to admire a pretty girl in such terrific physical condition. Salexa is outclassing the captain of a cross country team.

We sprint down a lane, around a tower, then clamber over a huge mound of crumbling debris Salexa hadn't anticipated. Then, there it is—Flotessa Greenway.

We enter the grounds of what must have been a beautiful park-like district. The broadleaf grass is now sparse, and in this mist, the majority of trees stand like blackened remnants of a forest fire.

"Rankin. Theena." Prahv rises from behind the demolished remains of the fountain then runs to us. His face registers surprise at Salexa. "Change of plan?"

"She helped us get here quicker."

The background noise of battle has grown fainter. The fight could end any moment. We need to get out of the city—and fast.

I raise my right hand and yank up the sleeve to reveal the flexible metal cuff. "Prahv, Theena, quick. Hold your wrists alongside mine."

I waste no time placing the Intersection over all three at once. I have the passcode memorized. I've mentally rehearsed this moment so many times I could disengage these things in my sleep. The background clamor is distracting, but within seconds the circular images of three metal cuffs appear in my mind. In triumph, I issue the mental order to release the cuffs.

At once, two of the three images in my thoughts release their grip and drop out of the mental picture. However, one cuff remains in place, unaffected.

Huh? My eyes shoot open to find Prahv's and my wrists bare.

Theena's cuff holds tight. Her wide eyes reflect pure fear. "R-Rankin?"

We don't need to say it—the two open cuffs have just emitted signals that they're off. Will the controller vaporize Theena?

24

REVELATIONS

In terror, Theena sinks to her knees.

Prahv finds his voice. "Rankin, do something."

"Her passcode. It's not the same as ours." When I checked Prahv's cuff in the lorsha garden, I assumed all three codes must be identical. How stupid!

I drop to both knees beside her and wrap my left hand around Theena's cuff. If the controller triggers vaporization, both of us will wink out of existence before we know it's happened.

Like a safecracker, I have to compute her code from scratch. My thoughts barely begin the descent into her cuff when Salexa's voice cuts in. "What's he doing? Rankin, how can we—"

"Shh!"

Eyes closed, I restart the melding process. At first, distant explosions tug for my attention. I tune them out. Explosions contain no words, no meaning. I must shrink my whole universe to this one band of flexible metal and the secrets inside it.

Now the focal point of my thought drifts closer, closer to the release data. I crave speed, but hurrying will end in disaster. One mental bump into a data pod, and this thing will zap us out of existence.

Digit by digit, the veil slides away until I can visualize the complete sequence. I cradle the code in one mental thought then issue the order. "Release." Like a fat rubber band snapping, the cuff arcs into the air. Just before hitting the ground, it puffs out of existence. Gone.

"Not a moment too soon." I heave a sigh of relief.

"I nearly vaporized." Theena's arms fly around me, wrapping me in a colossal hug and pressing her face to my chest.

My muscles tremble. The sounds of war still echo in the background. But if possible, I'd stay in this position with Theena forever.

"You saved my life."

I want to express how much I care about her, how scared I was she would evaporate. But my mind is still returning from the meld with the Intersection. I grope for words, but none materialize. All I can do is hug her back until Prahv interrupts.

"We will have time later for hugs and thanks. Now we have no choice—we must get out of Quel Tel Palarim."

A new voice breaks in. "Rankin, that was astounding. How did you do it?"

I whirl and spot Myek. She stands, barely visible against the palageist, a fyotor resting in the crook of her arm. The sight bewilders me. When did Myek get promoted to defender? And if she's truly a defender, what's she doing here, on foot, in a park? Shouldn't she be positioned up high to zap Entizar's forces?

"Myek, what are you doing here?"

"I came to see what you all are doing. Tell me how you removed those wrist cuffs. I've never heard of anyone getting one off without help."

Busted. As the person who placed them on us, Myek knows we don't have permission to remove them. "It's too complicated to explain. Now isn't the time."

Another explosion, this time nearby. The attackers must be headed this way.

Myek holds her ground. "You're right. This isn't the time or place. Come on, we're going underground."

Was that a suggestion—or a command?

Prahv gambles on her sympathies. "Myek, you of all people know what it's like to be wrist-cuffed. Rankin has an important mission beyond Quel-Tel-Palarim, and we're going to help him. If you want to leave the city, you can. Rankin can remove your cuff, same as ours."

Myek confuses me even more by bursting into laughter. She tugs the sleeve of her tunic high enough to reveal a bare wrist. She's a full citizen?

"Did you truly swallow my fable about trekking here from Lith? And the poor soul named Vahn, who got vaporized for trying to sneak away? I concocted the whole story. Did you not once suspect all of that was a trick, invented to keep you in line?"

My blood pressure is rising. "All right. You fooled us. We trusted you. Now what?"

"Now what? Is that not obvious? A minute ago, I gave you a final chance to come underground with me. Until that moment, Benlathim and I weren't sure whether you had become a loyal member of our society. You refused. Now the game is over."

"Over?" Theena echoes.

"Rankin is dangerous—to the city in general and to Benlathim in particular."

My mind races. Gotta stall for time. "What's Benlathim to you? Leave him and this ash heap behind. Join us."

Again, she laughs. "I must be better at role-playing than I thought. Benlathim is my lover, you idiot. I won't desert him for the likes of your motley little crew. He and I make a great duo. He, the powerful commander. Me, his roving eyes and ears."

She raises the fyotor, aiming straight at us. "Ironic, is it not? You must have been waiting for an attack so you could escape. We've been waiting for an attack, too. Partly to test your loyalty, and partly to torch you if you're disloyal. This way, the Quel-Telans will heap blame for your death on Entizar. You'll be a hero, Rankin, but dead heroes pose no threat to living leaders."

The moment of death. Why hadn't I shouted "Run" when I had the chance?

The brilliant flash of a fyotor blast, then—Myek bursts into flames. Her corpse slumps into a sickening heap. It's one of those gruesome sights you immediately wish you could unsee.

Despite the heat, a chill sweeps through my body. I stumble backward on legs that suddenly go wobbly. What happened?

My answer strides out of the palageist until I can see his features. Étan, wielding a fyotor of his own.

"Is everybody all right?" He addresses the group, but Étan's eyes alight on Theena.

"We're fine," Prahv says.

I need to say something, if nothing else, to pull his gawking eyes off Theena. "We're grateful. But I have to confess, we're surprised to see you."

"I was surprised to see you three, too. Along with other defenders, I blasted a battle bolsamka. My jaw hit the floor when you three dashed across the plaza, running through the wreckage and waving like maniacs."

"Then you and your fyotor have saved us twice," Salexa says.

I'm still trying to see the logic of his action. "But why save us from Myek, Étan? According to what she said—"

"I heard every grimy word, Rankin. I haven't decided who or what you are, but one thing I know. I owed you. If what everyone says is true, you saved my life in the forest. I repay my debts. I'm not convinced, but if your talk about the Creator is even halfway true, then I had to stop her from executing you. Myek had it coming anyway. She's killed more Quel-Telans than you could guess. Always made it look like an accident, or as if invaders did it."

The city has lapsed into silence, as if listening to us and the crackling of Myek's flames.

"All right. I saved your life. Now you've saved mine. Our plan is to leave the city and share my ministry in other parts of Zemna. What do you say to that?"

"I say we continue your plan. Let's go."

"We?"

"You heard me. Look, like I said, I'm still not convinced about all this Fithian tale, but if it's true, I should help. If it's not true, I need to find out. Besides, there are people in this city I care about. You're heading into hazardous territory, and I won't risk letting Entizar get his claws on you. If for no reason but protecting my friends here, I need to guard you."

Impressive. Who would've thought this guy could muster so much integrity?

"Besides, if you disappear and I stay, Benlathim will guess who held the fyotor that melted his woman. I don't have a choice. It's either stay here and die, or else go with you and hopefully live."

"I see your point."

So now we're up to five? Bringing Étan and Salexa wouldn't have been my first choice, but a chain reaction of events has begun. Is God doing something?

Voices call from a distance. "Hello?" "Is anyone there?" "Étan, are you here?"

Étan rips off his comm-band and flings it onto the flaming lump that used to be Myek. How I detest the stench of burning hair and flesh.

I nod. "Agreed then. No time to waste. We leave Quel-Tel-Palarim together." I raise my right palm toward Étan. After a second's hesitation, he touches his to mine. No high five. Just a gentlemen's agreement.

I cast a parting glance at Myek's remains. Even though she wanted to kill me, the sight pains my heart. "Let's move out."

25

A SHAKY ALLIANCE

"Let's take a short rest," I call when the five of us crest a tree-clad knoll. "If anyone needs a biology break, men go to the right, women to the left."

Everyone but Étan and me heads in their designated direction. With the fyotor slung over his shoulder, he gazes back over the thinning palageist. The ruined towers of Quel-Tel-Palarim resemble tombstones in a distant graveyard. The cracked burial markers of a giant race long perished. Standing here, no one would guess that a community still thrives among those ashes. A community that refuses to bow to Entizar, but obeys a lesser leader named Benlathim.

"Too bad we couldn't say goodbye to our believers."

Étan grunts. "From what I observed, you did a fair job preparing your people to carry on without you." Even without the comm-band circling his forehead, Étan talks like a soldier. "So, have you slept with her?"

I step back, as thunderstruck as if he'd whacked me across the face with an iron bar. "Slept with who? Theena?"

A grin. "Either one of them. But I meant Theena."

"Of course not. How could you even think such a thing?"

Sure, Étan can be a jerk, but I never expected such blunt crudeness.

Another shrug, but the same oily grin. "Just wondered."

"For a man and woman to be intimate without becoming life partners is wrong, Étan. You attended at least one of our meetings. You've heard me talk about repenting from sin, living pure lives as God wants."

He settles on his haunches in the deep grass. "Sure, I heard it. But who gets to define what sin is? Besides, how am I to know you don't say one thing and do another? Hypocrites abound. Benlathim is one. Why not you?"

"Sin is basically anything we say, think, or do that God doesn't like. When the created one rejects the will of his Creator and goes his own rebellious way, it's a heartache for God."

"Perhaps. But how can a person know what is a heartache to the Creator—if He truly exists? When I think of the Before Times, much of it seems like a dream. I never hear His voice."

"That's part of my mission here. To make people aware of sin. To call them back into fellowship with their Maker. Search your inner self. Isn't there some spark inside that tells you certain actions are evil, while other actions are good?"

He plucks a blade of grass and pops it into his mouth. "So, you've never slept with any female?"

"I haven't."

"You've never even considered it? Not tempted whatsoever?"

Sheesh. If no one has ever slugged Étan for rude questions, it's a miracle. I squelch my ire. "Let me explain it like this. The spirit wars against the flesh, and the flesh against the spirit. I'm nowhere near perfect, but my goal is to do what's right in His eyes."

"But you're still human, regardless of your fancy hand. Are you never tempted toward anything wrong?"

"Of course, I'm tempted. Temptations come into my brain, same as yours or anyone else's. Sin begins when we play with the temptation in our mind. Picture it in military terms. When a child of God wears his armor and stands his ground and wages war against temptation, God is pleased. Then the Creator's Holy Spirit provides reinforcement in that battle."

He laughs. "Message understood. You pass the test. Still, part of me can't help wondering whether *she* has ever relaxed her defenses and played with temptation. Even for a little while?" Again, his oily grin.

The image of Étan and Theena together in the way he imagines is so repulsive my fingers curl before I can stop them. It's been years since my last playground fight, but the old impulse is still there, just beneath the surface. Would it be so wrong to teach this guy some manners with my fist?

Prahv trudges back up from his side of the hill. "Getting better acquainted?"

My fist relaxes, but not my stomach. "Yes, that sums it up. Just discussing life."

A trace of Étan's smirk lingers. It grates my nerves, but I remind myself he's not a believer. Not yet anyway. I can't expect him to think pure thoughts or even care about them.

Theena and Salexa reappear, too.

"Prahv, you know the territory. You take the lead."

Étan's face swings from me to Prahv. "What's our destination, anyway?"

A line from my favorite World War II novel, *Gunner's Run*, pops into my head. "Can you keep a secret, Étan?"

"Of course."

"So can I. Let's go."

Our group sets off, Prahv first, then me, Theena, and Salexa, with Étan bringing up the rear. I don't mind if he guesses we're headed to the nearest Unizem portal. At least, that's my plan unless God opens the way for a side quest to a replacement Bible. Eventually I'll fill in the details for Étan. But not yet. His slimy way of asking questions hasn't left me feeling generous with information. Let him stew awhile.

Meanwhile, against my will, the residue of Étan's curiosity

continues to grate inside me. What I really want is for him to keep his shameless eyes off Theena. But maybe that's not realistic. Such a gorgeous girl with such a shapely figure must have attracted more lustful desires than just Étan's.

Well, how do you know she has a shapely figure? Have your eyes been roving the same territory as Étan's?

That's different, I tell myself. I've made a vow never to touch a girl in an improper way until my wedding day.

Oh? Have your eyes made the same vow?

I clench my teeth. Now I'm mad at Étan, but I'm also annoyed with myself.

Does Étan really need to be with us? If I had a way to beam him back to Quel-Tel-Palarim, he'd be there already.

A shadow flits overhead. Then another.

Prahv freezes. "Samkas. Take cover!"

We scramble to the shade of nearby trees. Beside me, Étan unslings his weapon and points it toward a gap between branches.

I place a hand on the fyotor. "Hold your fire unless they spot us."

His eyes betray irritation. "Instincts. Spend enough days fighting those animals, and you react automatically. I would not have fired, though."

I'm not so sure.

When the sky clears of shadows, I wave to attract Salexa's attention. She crouches under a massive stoalock with Theena. "Climb up. See where they're going."

With a confident grin, Salexa scampers upward. At one point she actually leaps from one branch to an upper one that grows too high to reach by stretching. I haven't seen actual squirrels on Zemna, but if this planet has any, Salexa could chase them through the treetops.

I turn and find Étan studying me. "Right now, are you being tempted, or merely supervising?" This time the smirk is absent.

His voice carries the same neutral tone a guy might use to ask about the weather.

"Just admiring her agility. I could never climb a tree like that."

He merely grunts, whatever that means.

Salexa descends again. She drops to the grass with the lightest thump of her half-boots. "All clear, everyone. Not so back home. It's a second wave, cruising straight to Quel-Tel-Palarim."

The pain in Theena's heart shows on her face. She tucks a strand of hair behind her ear. "Can we pray for our friends left behind?"

"Go ahead, Theena. Lead us in prayer."

In Zemnan style, four of us lift our faces to the heavens and close our eyes. After Theena begins, I can't resist cracking one eyelid. Étan doesn't join in tilting his face upward. He stands apart, observing. Good. Let him hear Theena lifting sincere prayers to the Creator. Maybe a holy moment will help him to see her in a less carnal way.

As for me, I silently pray for God to work in the heart of this team member I can't stand.

26

REFUGEES

From the rear, Étan calls, "Prahv, we're losing our daylight. I suggest we plan our bivouac for the evening. This is a proper site. Soft moss for sleeping and sufficient trees to provide cover."

Prahv's eyes connect with mine. Without words, we understand—Étan wants to lead the group. As the only fyotor-toting defender among us, he must consider himself the natural captain. To us, though, he's a self-appointed tagalong.

I evaluate our surroundings. Not thick forest, but enough scattered trees to offer concealment. "I'm not opposed. We could march a little farther, but we're in less hurry now that we're far from the city."

Étan unslings his fyotor and leans it against a tree trunk. "March farther? Unwise with Aena sinking toward the horizon."

Must he always have the final word? I can't tell whether Étan is putting on a show to impress the girls or just full to the brim with himself. Prahv actually rolls his eyes.

Salexa stretches her leg muscles, pulling one foot up behind her by the toes and then the other. "Theena and I can search for food. My stomach is rumbling."

Étan jumps on her statement. "But not any food that requires cooking. You never know who or what a fire might attract. Stealth is our best protection."

I force myself to turn away and take a calming breath. What does he think we are, idiots? Can't we just skip the torture and kill me now?

"Hear something, Rankin? Samkas?"

"Yes, Étan, I heard something, but nothing dangerous. Only wind."

Prahv must be reading my mind. He nearly chokes trying not to laugh. "I'll be back shortly. I want to scout out our surroundings."

"Smart idea. Want me to come with you?" Étan offers.

Please do.

But Prahv shakes his head. "No, you had better not. Rankin is our only Fithian, and you have the only weapon. It is better for you to stay here and protect him."

Prahv strolls away, flashing me a mischievous grin.

Hmm. Could the Intersection of All Things zap him with a hundred playful volts of electricity?

In no time, I'm alone with Étan for the second time today. Coincidence? Or is it my destiny to spend time with him? Of course, he might feel the same about me. He's the one person here who doesn't know the Savior. I need to man up enough to overlook his gritty personality and start a conversation. Besides, if I don't pipe up first, he's bound to pose embarrassing questions I'm too tired to answer.

I pick out a sapling across from where Étan sits cradling his beloved fyotor. My narrow tree isn't much wider than my wrist, but the leaves indicate it's a stoalock. Although skinny, this thing won't bend if I sit and rest against it.

"Étan, I don't know you as well as I do the others. But I do know you haven't had a high opinion of me ever since the day I arrived in Quel-Tel-Palarim. Since you've joined us, I need to trust you with some information."

From some hidden pocket he procures a square of white cloth

and begins polishing his weapon. Now I understand why Étan's fyotor sparkles while others in Quel-Tel-Palarim are often dull from fingerprints and other grime. "I'm listening."

"As a Fithian, my task is to share the message of God's grace with as many people as possible, so—"

"Pause right there. That touches a big question of mine. If the Creator is all-powerful, and if He wants as many people as possible to hear this story about manifesting Himself in a human body, then why doesn't the Creator just tell it Himself? I mean, why not pen it across the sky in majestic, glowing letters? Or why doesn't He speak in a booming voice? Either of those methods would be quick and efficient. Why should He dump the job into the lap of flesh-and-blood messengers?"

"I'm glad you wonder. Those are thoughtful questions."

He shakes the dust from his cloth and resumes polishing. "Don't patronize me. I wouldn't be here if you didn't force me to wonder such things. Is there an answer?"

"The general answer is that we people can drive ourselves crazy if we try to figure out every motive of an infinite God powerful enough to speak whole planets and stars into existence."

"A smokescreen answer if ever I heard one."

"Hear me out. Sometimes I've figured God ought to find a better way. Or at least a more impressive messenger. Yes, God is mighty enough to achieve whatever He wishes all by Himself. He doesn't need me or anyone else to accomplish His will. However, He didn't create us to be lazy creatures who simply sit and occupy space. It pleases Him to work in us and through us. In a sense, we become living tools in His hands."

"So, you picture the Creator as a supreme commander who delegates duty assignments?"

His military imagery stops me cold. "Not at all. Jesus taught that the Creator is a Heavenly Father. I pray to Him as a loving Father, not as a military commander. Although I'm amazed that

He's willing to use an imperfect guy like me, it's my privilege to serve Him."

Étan chews on that thought. Meanwhile, the question provides insight into his mind. Étan interprets the world—maybe the whole universe—like a military conflict. Kill, or be killed. Receive orders or give orders. It's a minor miracle he broke away from his commander to follow me into the wild unknown.

Since he doesn't reply, I continue. "What I wanted to tell you concerns our destination. You might as well know. We're heading to a Unizem portal."

Étan stops polishing and pins me to the stoalock with furious eyes. "A Unizem? Have you ever been inside one? Ever calibrated one to establish the all-Zemna link?"

The sudden resentment catches me by surprise. "I've never even seen a Unizem. But Prahv and Theena have been in one. They tell me Theena used to sing for the whole world."

Eyebrows huddled like thunder clouds, Étan rams the scrap of cloth inside his tunic and stands. He paces first one way, then the opposite direction. Clenching the fyotor, his knuckles turn white.

I rise, too. "Is there a problem?"

"A problem? If that's your goal, we're swimming in water infested with problems. I assumed your mission was to wander the world and share your message with anyone who would listen. But a Unizem portal!"

"That's different?"

"Of course, that's different. For starters, all we have is a single fyotor. Listen, all told, six Unizem portals were created. By coincidence, one of them is within reach by foot, although it's still a long journey. One portal was definitely destroyed. But if any Unizem still functions, expect a legion of armed guards. And don't believe for one instant that opening the worldwide connection is as simple as strutting in and pressing a button. It's not. The whole process is complex beyond words. The specific brainwaves of the individual inside the portal must be taken into account, and then there's the hard part—adjusting the sensors to teleport the broadcast to the proximity of all human life forms. To sing or speak a message—that's child's play. Getting those words to echo worldwide for the minds of the entire population —that's where genius combines with magic."

"Magic?"

He erases the word with a wave of his hand. "A figure of speech. The point is, this quest of yours is foolish. Men have been killed just for knowing how to synchronize a Unizem. Those places are guarded."

"You seem to know a lot. Have you ever spoken by Unizem?"

"Me? That's a laugh."

"With all your knowledge on the subject, I thought maybe you—"

He whirls. "You thought I might have a hidden gift of song? Or for uttering flowery phrases? Hardly."

"So, you're just guessing then? About the Unizems, I mean."

Étan glares. He strides right to me and plants a forefinger on my chest. "Listen, I know exactly what I'm talking about."

Maybe he does, but his attitude is perturbing. I shove the finger away. "I know what I'm talking about, too. The Creator brought me to Zemna to deliver a message. I need to follow my mission the best way I can—or die trying."

"Go ahead and die, then. But don't drag the rest of us into your grave." He turns and faces away. How can I wriggle loose more information without sparking his powder-keg temper?

I allow him a few moments of silence then say, "You seem to have more information than Prahv and Theena. They told me six Unizems had been built, but they didn't say anything about one of them being destroyed."

"They couldn't know. They weren't there."

My heart lurches. "And you were?"

When he turns to meet my gaze, his eyes fairly smolder. "I was more than there. You're looking at the man who blew it up."

Jaw clamped, he stalks away.

* * *

Later, the five of us sit in a ring with Feebia gleaming overhead for light. We munch on a variety of carrot-shaped tubers the girls have collected from the soft soil near a stream. This is the first time I've camped without a campfire. However, secrecy demands we blend with the darkness, especially tonight.

Étan is uncharacteristically silent. While the rest of us discuss the day's battle in Quel-Tel-Palarim and speculate on the damage, his head remains lowered. Judging from their glances in his direction, the others notice the change, too. Earlier I would've given anything to make Étan shut his mouth. How can we get him talking again?

I catch Theena's eye and motion toward Étan with my chin. A trait I noticed in the city is that Étan tolerates more questions from women than from men. Maybe Theena can grease the wheels for conversation.

She nods. "Étan, I never heard what brought you to Quel-Tel-Palarim. Had you lived there long?"

The very question provides a minor revelation for me. I figured he'd always lived in the city.

For once, Étan doesn't look at Theena. "I arrived as a refugee." He punctuates the statement by biting off a mouthful of tuber.

Theena continues. "I visited Ketaron once. But only the one time. Our family didn't travel much."

Her statement just hangs there.

"Ketaron?" I've heard the word in passing conversation before, but like most geography on Zemna, I know nothing about the place.

My one word draws a disdainful stare from Étan. "You didn't even know I'm from Ketaron?" He points to his bare scalp. "Doesn't this mean anything to you?"

Prahv leans toward me and drops his voice. "Ketaron is a large island in the Palatien Ocean. No one born there has hair. Neither males nor females. Korya came from there, too."

I mentally kick myself. Just when Étan's temper was cooling, I had to dribble gasoline on the fire.

"Forgive my lack of knowledge. Not so long ago I'd never even heard of this planet. Newcomers need time to learn geography."

He grunts. It's not much, but he hasn't melted me, so maybe he's accepted the apology.

"We're all refugees now," Salexa adds.

Étan shakes his head. "It's not the same."

Salexa scoots closer and places a calming hand on his shoulder. "We want to know you better, Étan. All we have now is each other. Won't you share a little about your life?"

"My story is not a happy one. At least, not anymore."

Moonlight reveals Salexa's fingers massaging his shoulder. It seems to pacify him. She must have the magic touch.

Étan relaxes and emits a long breath. "All right. Nobody invited me on this expedition of yours, but if your plan is to put our Fithian in a Unizem, then I should explain a few things."

If there had been a seat handy, I'd be perched on the edge of it. Not only is Étan about to clear up some mysteries, but it's the first time he's called me a genuine Fithian.

27

THE STORY OF UNIZEM

Feebia's wan light illuminates our group, but Étan doesn't look at us. Instead, he gazes at the ground in front of him and speaks in a monotone. "My father was one of the talented individuals who designed and implemented the Unizem concept."

My jaw drops open.

"Don't misunderstand. I'm not claiming the system was Father's initiative or that he was the main visionary. But when the others invited him to assist in creating a method for uniting all of Zemna in praise to God, he accepted."

I'm speechless. Evidently, Étan's father and his cohorts were brilliant in applications of science even other Zemnans could scarcely imagine.

"Unfortunately, I didn't inherit Father's mental skill in such things. Oh, I have a knack for devices. I can tear down and rebuild a fyotor blindfolded. I once repaired a malfunctioning samka that friends considered hopeless. But the Unizem? My brain can't begin to comprehend the complexities of its inner workings. Once the prototype was functioning to everyone's joy, the team volunteered to create others, so that any friend gifted in word or song need not travel far to enter one."

Prahv and the girls hang on Étan's words with obvious

hunger to hear more. It's fascinating how Zemnans can each remember the "Before Times," but not clearly, as if watching their own history through fogged glass. Did that happen to Adam and Eve after they violated God's one taboo?

Theena leans forward, her eyes practically sparkling with interest. "Did you ever watch how they carried out the broadcasts?"

"I did more than observe. I volunteered for training. The Unizem Team, as we called them, couldn't be everywhere. Plus, they were already dreaming up other marvels to design. They inducted a select group for training. Because of my aptitude with devices, Father put my name forward. Calibrating all the variables is tricky, but I coordinated quite a few full-planet links without any of the Unizem Team assisting."

Dumbfounded, all I can do is swallow and marvel at God's working. The one guy I wanted to beam back to Quel-Tel-Palarim had personally operated the system I hope to access. Does the Lord know what He's doing, or what?

Étan draws a big breath, as if summoning fresh strength for his story. "As you all know, the world changed. We changed. Trying to recall everything is impossible, like trying to grab a handful of mist. But I do recall how one charismatic personality —a man named Jarrel—persuaded a mass of Ketarons to follow him. But governing one island wasn't enough. Jarrel decided the Unizem was an ideal way to offer his leadership to all Zemnans."

Prahv snaps a twig he's been fiddling with and tosses the pieces away. "Greed and the desire for power are never satisfied. Once they take root in a heart, they grow."

"Indeed. But Father refused. He saw through Jarrel's charming veneer. Beneath the façade, the man's heart was rotten, self-centered. When Jarrel dropped all pretense of friendliness and ordered Father to obey, he still refused. For that, they lopped off my father's head."

For a fleeting instant, moonlight twinkles from a tear on

Étan's cheek. For once, my heart goes out to him, this fellow human who lost his father in a way not so different from the way I lost my parents.

"Next, Jarrel and his followers demanded I perform the link or suffer the consequences."

"You didn't agree, did you?" Salexa says.

"Actually, I did agree. But only to get revenge. The moment Jarrel entered the Unizem portal, I ramped up the energy, overloaded the circuits, then ran for my life before the place exploded. I fled to Tel-Quel-Palarim to begin a new existence. Little did I realize that life in Entizar's ward was no better."

Étan fell silent. For a long moment his only motion is to flatten and comb the grass in front of him with his fingers. At last, he says, "I vowed never to help anyone access a Unizem again. This is why I despised you, Rankin, from the start. I saw your image broadcast by Unizem, heard Lotan's slimy words, and my whole hatred of people using Father's grand work for selfish purposes resurfaced."

"But that wasn't Rankin's doing," Theena counters. "He was the victim, not the perpetrator."

Étan ruffles the grass he had smoothed. "My logical side understood that. But it's hard to be logical about the death of a father. A Unizem showed me Rankin. Something deep down resented him for bringing back painful memories."

Before I could utter anything in my defense, Étan stands. "Let us sleep. It's been a long day."

* * *

Hours later, I lie sunken into a thick bed of silky-soft matta moss and watch twinkling stars through branches overhead. Feebia has already set behind the eastern horizon. Little Eenik provides feeble illumination. My mind can't stop replaying the story Étan poured out. Nor can I overcome my awe at God's working. The person I least wanted along, Étan might prove the companion I need most.

I roll over in the soft matta. How can I condemn Étan's rage? I've been there. The image of the Johnson Family missionary prayer card, complete with our three smiling faces, appears in my thoughts. When fanatics beheaded Mom and Dad in Nigeria, didn't I vow revenge on the culprits? To this day, my cheeks burn as I recall the night when I shook my fist at a crescent moon. Three years, and to this day I have to quell the rage that rises inside when I think about my parents' murders. Digging out the roots of hatred isn't easy. Yes, I can definitely relate to Étan.

The question is, will Étan reverse his vow and help me? I don't think even he can answer that. For now, the most he will promise is to accompany us in the general direction of Perlessa, the location of the nearest Unizem portal. Meanwhile, Étan needs prayer. Sure, he can be a royal pain in the neck, but Jesus came to save jerks, too. Probably, I'd be just like him if I didn't have God in my life.

Next, the thought of my missing New Testament comes to mind. I'd sure like to have a replacement before I even try to use a Unizem. If there is one on this planet, will God show me where to find it?

A whispery breeze rustles the treetops.

The Unizem. Somehow, everything swirling around my new life points to it. Is God funneling me in that direction? Or maybe my personal hopes are blinding me to reality? After all, even if Étan were willing to help me, gaining access sounds impossible. The fact that a messenger from Lotan got to use one means noth-ing. Entizar did his brother-ruler a favor. But me? I'm Public Enemy #1 in Lotan's eyes. His brother Entizar won't look on me with kindness.

Again, the flimsiest of breezes rustles leaves high overhead. For a moment, the sound tugs at my memory. What does it remind me of? My sluggish brain doesn't care. I'm thirsty but unwilling to walk the three hundred yards to the stream for a drink. Simply thinking is a chore. Sleep beckons. I snuggle deeper into the moss. This matta is terrific stuff—as soft and warm as a thick comforter. Even more awesome, matta is a natural insect-repellant. Praise God, Zemna has no mosquitoes.

Wait. My mind perks up. The one thing Lotan's Unizem message about me proves is that either he or Entizar has at least one technician who knows how to key in the system. From what Étan shared, calibrating the thing for a broadcast is no piece of cake. Only a bright mind trained to operate a Unizem can pull it off. Yet, one of those two rulers does have such a technician, either a slarg or a loyal follower. If Étan refuses to fire up the mechanism, is there a chance—even a razor-thin one—that this other guy could be persuaded to aid me?

Tomorrow I'll talk to Prahv. He remembers the "friend" who operated the Unizem when Theena sang. I want that name.

As my last shred of consciousness fades away, I thank God for getting us out of Quel-Tel-Palarim alive, ask Him to protect His followers back in the city, commit my future path into His care, and tell Him goodnight.

I don't know how long I've been asleep when a blast of pain to my ribs shocks me awake. "Wake up. All of you, on your knees!"

Darkness reigns over our campsite. A dozen or so silhouettes stand around us.

"Now!" Two shadows nearly wrench my arms from their sockets when they haul me out of the matta. When they drop me, the hard ground slams pain to my knees.

"Who are you?" I shout.

In reply, a metal-glove slaps me across the mouth.

"Freeze!" The rough voice comes from the spot where Étan lay beneath a tree. The sickening thuds of kicks and punches accompany a flurry of shadows in that direction. Étan must have made a grab for his fyotor.

"Let's check them out."

Overhead, unseen leaves in the treetops rustle. Spotlights pop on, illuminating the area as five samkas settle on the perimeter. Sure enough, the newcomers wear high-tech visors—night vision—which they flip upward. Not a familiar face in the bunch. My gaze drops to their hands. Half of them grip slender, foot-long knives that glitter like icy death in the harsh beams of the samkas.

"Don't resist," I say to my friends. "Don't get yourself killed."

That was no wind rustling through the trees earlier. If I'd been more alert, I might've recognized the faint whisper of samkas in flight. What has my drowsiness cost us?

Among the samkas touching down is a smaller, one-person vehicle. At first glance, it appears to be a flying motorcycle. But no—instead of tires its base is a flat platform, pointed in the front. From it steps a figure with the build and confident bearing of a Marine Corps drill sergeant. Still visored, he strides into the ring and—one at a time—studies each of our faces. First Salexa. Then Theena. Next Prahv. Étan earns extra attention since blood dribbles from both nostrils. The fact that his bald scalp marks him as a native of distant Ketaron must raise questions, too.

A gruff voice breaks the silence. "This one carried a weapon." The man behind Étan holds up the fyotor. The guy's busted visor dangles down the side of his head. Good for Étan. He scored at least one solid punch.

Without comment, the big guy in the visor nods, gives Étan a final glance, then moves to me. His head cocks. With a glove of metal fabric, he moves my chin left and right, studying me.

If they're trying to freak us out—it's working.

When the visored one addresses me, the voice surprises me. Instead of the deep bass I expect, the voice is rough, yes, but the pitch is higher than expected. "Where do I know you from?"

I shake my head. "I don't believe we've ever met."

Without so much as the flick of a hand, his visor pops upward.

He is a she! True, her physique resembles that of a body-builder, and the hair is cropped shorter than mine, but this is a woman scrutinizing me. The realization does nothing to lessen my foreboding. She's like a wacky biker chick overdosed on steroids. As I gaze at her sculpted marble cheekbones and fierce eyes, my fearful heart beats double time.

She lets go of my chin. "When I ask a question, I expect a better answer than that one." Without warning, her knee rams my groin with the impact of a sledgehammer. Pain streaks through my body, and my legs buckle. Next thing I know, I'm crumpled on the ground and gasping for breath.

Amazon lady steps backward. "Tell me, impudent little fool, if I give you a choice, is there any particular way you would prefer to die?"

28

KALISTA

Gasps from Theena and Salexa are the only sounds. All eyes rest on me. Despite waves of pain emanating from below the waist, I manage to rise to one knee, expecting a kick to the face any second.

A quick glance shows Prahv standing with wide eyes. Two men grip his arms just below the shoulders. If he knows who Dragon Queen is, he has no way to inform me.

"Forgive me, please, if my first answer wasn't satisfactory. Your men had just woken me from deep sleep. My brain was groggy. I meant to say that I have never seen you before, and as far as I know, you have never seen me. Possibly, my face resembles someone else."

No way I'm going to lift my palm and ask if she happened to catch the latest Unizem show.

"Your excuse is flimsy. However, I accept your apology. You may live. For now. Five participants will make the sport more enjoyable than four." She snaps her fingers. "Shackle them."

Sport? A queasy feeling develops in my gut.

From the samkas, men retrieve manacles that resemble black plastic. But the instant they snap around our wrists, I sense they're made of much tougher material. More shackles lock around our ankles. Sixty seconds later, Prahv, Étan, Theena, Salexa, and I stand in a chain.

I'm dying to ask Prahv who these people are. But when our eyes meet, a half shake of his head warns me not to speak.

"Get them aboard," the female commander orders.

"Right away," one of the men responds. "Standard preparation for the sport?"

"Standard preparation."

Again with "the sport"? No time to ponder the word. The cold knife tip piercing my tunic and nicking the flesh of my back encourages me forward. They herd us to a black bolsamka, which stands outside the ring of illumination.

Unlike regular samkas, which are barely larger than a playground merry-go-round and open on top, this bolsamka is long and enclosed, tube-shaped, with round portholes along the body. Only its bottom is flat. It makes me think of an airplane without wings or tail. Various gizmos extend from the sides, maybe extra tyagil pods for lift. Back in Lotan's quarry, similar vehicles were the workhorses used to lift massive stone blocks and maneuver them into position for his new citadel.

A panel in the fuselage lowers to the ground, providing a ramp to the interior.

"Get in."

Another poke to the kidney speeds my feet up the ramp. Inside the craft's body, we find benches lining both sides. It's similar to old movies I've seen of how paratroopers sat before they jumped.

"Don't just stand there, meat. Sit!" A hand crushes down on my shoulder, leaving no choice.

Meat? What a weird expression.

Nine of Dragon Queen's lackeys enter and take seats beside and across from us. A tenth heads up front and dons the piloting helmet. Our captors don't hide their leers as they ogle Theena and Salexa from head to toe. Watching them causes my blood pressure to rise.

The moment the hatch is shut, our captors break into conversation.

"What a catch."

"Five at once, and hardly a struggle. Can you believe our good fortune?"

"She'll be in high spirits tomorrow. Do you suppose she'll run them all at once? Or maybe spread them out, do one every few days?"

The guy who's fondling Étan's fyotor shrugs. "Hard to say. The main thing is, when Kalista is happy ..."

"... everyone is happy!" the others finish in unison. Riotous laughter erupts.

I seize my chance and risk one word out the side of my mouth to Salexa. "Kalista?"

She tilts her head closer. "Sister of Lotan and Entizar."

A lead weight drops into the pit of my stomach. Just great.

"Say there, little beauty, no communication. Another word, and I'll soon be communicating with you in a way you might not enjoy."

More coarse laughter. Using my eyes, I try to apologize to Salexa for putting her on the spot. So Lotan and Entizar have a sister. Why does this family overshadow everything I do on Zemna?

Our captors break into overlapping conversations.

"Do you remember that scrawny boy we once caught hiding down by the coast?"

"The one surviving off dead fish and waterweed? Ha. I'll never forget that boy."

"No good with his hands, but by Feebia, how that bony boy could run."

"And don't forget how he could jump!"

This elicits another burst of laughter. Must be an inside joke.

"That scrawny kid sure tried Kalista's patience. Kept her away from us for days. We could use more like that one." This time the speaker eyes our group, as if trying to guess whether we'll match the performance of the skinny guy they all remember.

What is the sport they're so excited about? Running must play an important role. If so, maybe my cross-country experience will give me an advantage.

Whatever these people have in store for us, prayer seems the smartest way to spend the ride. I close my eyes.

* * *

A thump blinks my eyes open.

"We're here. Stand up, meat."

As we troop down the ramp, the first sight to greet me is a huge body of water in the distance. Not just a giant lake like Selador, this must be the Palatien Ocean. In the pre-dawn light, its waters appear cold. Ominous. Somewhere out there is Kctaron, the island where Étan once lived. I'd give a lot to be there now. Actually, I'd rather be anywhere instead of surrounded by Kalista's gang with the knives.

A tall man with a crooked nose bars our path. He grips the same kind of inflictor rod Lotan's overseers carried in the quarry. Remembering the agony makes my knees go weak.

"Unbind them."

The same guy who applied our ankle and wrist manacles steps forward and releases them.

With a sneer, Crooked Nose points right, toward a cage in the form of a geodesic dome. "That way, meat. Welcome to your new home."

Rather than metal, the interconnected triangles of the dome are clear, like glass, or maybe acrylic. Beyond the dome, an olive-drab caloid looms above the trees. Unlike the towers in Quel-Tel-Palarim, this one is in pristine condition. It glistens in the sunshine.

"Move out," says Crooked Nose.

As we trudge toward the cage, Kalista's men line the way and offer verbal commentaries.

"I guarantee the bald one is spunky. Look at the storm brewing in those eyes."

"What, spunk out of a son of Ketaron? That would be a first."

"I'll cheer for the fair-haired girl."

"Not me. It's the dark maid with bewitching eyes I'll be watching."

Another guy points toward me as I approach. "What about that one? What do you make of him?"

"Him? Don't pin any hopes on that fellow. Kalista dropped him flat in one second."

The first guy mimics a wince. "Oof. Allergic to knees, is he?"

They laugh as I pass. I'd like to see them handle Kalista any better. At least I'm alive.

Once we enter the geodesic dome, a triangular section of clear bars slides down and locks into place. We're trapped. The entire cage lights up with an electric-blue glow.

"Listen!" Crooked Nose says. "I advise you not to touch the cage. If you do—*Poof.* A pile of stinking ash is all that will remain. Our last guest did not believe me. See for yourselves what happened."

The tip of his inflictor rod points to the ground just inside the dome. On the spot lies a mound of blackened ashes. "The idiot tried to escape."

My cynical side wonders whether he's bluffing. Could the bars be nothing but clear plastic with light passing through them? It would be simple to dump a bucket of campfire ashes and claim they're human remains. But then I imagine Jaylel ascending from a newly recruited Fithian:

"What happened to the Fithian guy before me?"

"Rankin? That nut grabbed a hot power grid even after they warned him."

I grunt. Nope. Even if it's a lie, this is one Fithian who's going to proceed with caution. Better alive in a cage than a crispy critter.

Crooked Nose struts away. Kalista is nowhere to be seen, but her servants peer through the dome's bars. They point and talk back and forth, evidently sizing up our odds for whatever sport they have in mind.

Prahv studies the glowing bars of the cage. "Étan, any idea what kind of plans Kalista might have for us?"

Étan shakes his head. "I've only heard rumors of Kalista. All I know is that she is sister to Entizar and has a high opinion of herself. They say she enjoys belittling others to flaunt her authority."

Salexa shakes her head. "Kalista doesn't merely belittle. She's a fiend. A monster who relishes torture. I witnessed it during a raid on Quel-Tel-Palarim."

She closes her eyes, but that doesn't halt tears from creeping down her cheeks. "My fyotor had malfunctioned. All I could do was watch. Her troop of private guards had overpowered an observation post. They blasted a breach in the wall. Kalista set her solasamka to hover outside the gap while she and several men entered. When she stepped back out, she was dragging a woman. Kalista tied a line to her ankle then proceeded to whip the solasamka back and forth, bashing the woman's body against one caloid then another."

When Salexa bursts into sobs at the memory, Étan surprises me by placing a comforting arm around her shoulders. Good for him.

Theena winces. "How insane."

Salexa wipes her eyes. "Through magnifiers I saw her cackle every time her victim slammed into a wall. Quel-Telan reinforcements drove them off. The last I saw of them, the woman's body still dangled beneath the solasamka as Kalista flew back toward Evron."

The mental image revolts my stomach. I had pictured Kalista as a spoiled biker chick on a flying motorcycle. Now, she sounds

like a cold-blooded Nazi. Or a psychopath who commits atrocities for gruesome entertainment. "Sounds like I should thank
God I'm still alive."

Salexa looks straight at me. "Last night, she was on the verge
of murdering you. Your quick choice of words pacified her."

I glance at Theena. Her pale purple irises are large as her eyes
connect with mine. Some sort of emotion peeks through those
eyes, but I can't decipher it. I step away to stare out the prison
doorway. If I ever gather enough guts to reveal how much I care
about her, I don't want to do it with an audience. Besides, I'd like
some solid clues that the attraction might be mutual. Otherwise,
these romantic feelings could blow up in my face.

Beyond the bars, Kalista's gawkers disperse.

Prahv, who has been listening in silence, picks up a stone and
hurls it toward the glowing bars. On impact, a crackling shower
of sparks explodes from the spot. "So, it is no bluff—the dome
can kill. Kalista might be pacified for now, but she didn't bring
us here for our health. No matter what sport she has in mind,
we're not going to like it."

29

UNNATURAL SELECTION

As Aena inches across the sky, we alternately stand, pace, sit, or lie on the hard-packed ground beneath the prison dome. Me, I'm the one who paces the most. Pent-up anxiety makes me ready to burst. If I had a punching bag, I'd pound that thing until the seams rip open.

I pause when I realize one of Kalista's men is standing outside, gazing at me. "You got something to say?"

He ignores my question, but his thin lips curl upward. Is he gloating in the knowledge of what's in store for us? Another possibility comes to mind. Although it's been months since my image appeared by Unizem and my hair is longer now, somebody still might recognize me as Lotan's enemy.

Please don't let that happen, Lord.

When no one watches, I wander toward the door. Maybe the Intersection could open it, but the access panel is on the outside. My arm can't stretch that far through the glowing bars.

Around midday, we receive a burlap sack of raw vegetables. Two men haul in a kettle of drinking water while a third stands by with an inflictor rod.

"No cups?" Prahv asks.

One of Kalista's men spits. "You've got hands. Cup those."

"Rest," orders the guy holding the rod. "You will need it."

They exit the dome. The leader touches a metallic armband on his bicep, and the triangular gate slides down, clicks into place, then resumes the same blue glow as the rest of the dome.

Theena sighs from where she lies on her side, her head propped on her hand. "Rest, he says. That fellow talks as if he cares about us."

Étan reclines on his back, eyes closed, but listening. "They don't care about us as people, but they do care about their plan for us."

By late evening I've paced away much of my frustration. I recline on the ground and think. Meat, they call us. And we receive about as much attention as a pen full of cows. My tight nerves drive away sleep even though I got little rest during the night. From time to time I pray, but no revelation descends from Heaven.

As I lie here and gaze at the glowing dome above, it's almost mesmerizing. A network of clear, gleaming bars locked into triangular shapes that contrast against the coal-blackness of night. It's similar to the effect of a burning candle—by day you might not even notice a tiny flame, but at night all eyes gravitate toward that light, even from a distance.

That's what I'm supposed to be—the candle that dispels spiritual darkness and summons onlookers to follow Jesus, the true Light.

Where is the spiritual darkness worse, on Earth or on Zemna? The two planets are different in zillions of ways, but both have the same basic need.

Grandma Johnson's face comes to mind. I hope she's getting along by herself. Then again, she has her friends at church, plus her crochet circle and her garden club.

A breeze chills my face, my hands, making the hard ground even less forgiving. I might as well try to sleep on bare concrete. I roll from my back to my side, but that position isn't any better.

Why couldn't Kalista build her cage over a thick patch of matta moss?

And what could Kalista possibly want with us? No way to guess. With an effort, I force my brain to quit rambling. Each time a new thought pops in, I chase it back out. Eventually, sleep takes over.

* * *

"Get up, meat. Everybody, on your feet."

Even without opening my eyes, I recognize the scratchy voice of Crooked Nose.

As I roll over, I accidentally place my hand atop someone right beside me. My sleep-blurred eyes pop open. Now stirring, Salexa has been sleeping next to me.

Theena sits a short distance away, massaging her elbows and gazing at me with the oddest expression.

Salexa blinks and stretches. In a soft voice she says, "Forgive me if I slept too close. I was frightened. Resting beside you gave me courage."

I hustle to my feet, but Theena has already stood and is walking away. Did she hear Salexa's explanation?

Irritated, I splash a handful of water onto my face and wipe it dry with my tunic sleeve as I march over to the gate. There, I cross my arms and stare out. Not for a long time have I come this close to swearing. Maybe Salexa is naïve, but sleeping that close makes it look as if— What must Theena be thinking?

Étan appears at my side, also staring out the gate with crossed arms. When I glance his way, he raises both eyebrows, but says nothing.

"What?"

A mischievous smirk.

"It's not what you think."

"I didn't utter a word," he says, the smirk widening.

"Don't jump to conclusions. I woke up, and she was there. That's all."

He gives my shoulder a squeeze. "No need to get defensive. In a way, it's comforting to know you're more like me than I expected. Might as well make the best of a bad situation, right?"

Étan strolls away before I can object that I'm not like him, that I'm a victim of appearances.

I long to give the glowing gate a hard kick. Only the knowledge that venting my frustration would toast me keeps my running shoes planted on hard-packed ground.

When I do turn around, Prahv is leading the others in a prayer of thanks over the remaining vegetables. Did he call and I not hear? What a crummy way to start the day. I can't even show a little spiritual leadership.

We scarcely finish munching a fibrous breakfast of raw veggies when Kalista approaches our gate. A couple dozen men accompany her.

"Open it," she orders.

Crooked Nose touches his armband. The gate stops glowing and slides upward.

She waltzes over the threshold with an uplifted nose and all the regal pomp of majesty. Two guys with inflictor rods flank her.

Her snooty attitude would make me snicker if this odd creature didn't control my fate.

Examining us from head to toe, she swaggers around our group of five. "Such a pity it's an odd number. Let's prepare this one," she says, pointing at Prahv. "Also, that one." She indicates Étan. "Two males on offense, one male and two females on defense. That might prove interesting."

"You heard the command," says one of the guys bearing inflictor rods. With his weapon, he motions Prahv and Étan toward the exit. "March."

With foreboding glances, our two companions plod out the gate.

"If I may be so bold, my lady," says the other guy armed with a rod. "I suggest you could maximize your entertainment by pitting the captives one against one until only two remain. That way—"

Kalista whirls on him with a snarl. "Did I request an opinion? No, I did not. Your rod, new man." She holds out an expectant hand.

Kalista's troop watches with horrified faces as the offender surrenders his inflictor rod.

"I had assumed my brother would warn new escorts against rudeness before sending them to me. Open your mouth, new man."

"My mouth?"

Kalista's voice erupts in a shriek, "Are you as ignorant as you are ill-mannered? Drop your jaw."

"New man" searches his comrades' eyes for advice, finds none.

"Not tomorrow—now!"

The guy obeys. The moment his jaw drops open, Kalista rams the tip of the inflictor between his teeth and discharges it on full power. Not until his steaming body crumples does Kalista jerk the rod loose.

Topping off the gruesome moment, she throws back her head and cackles to the sky. "I've always wanted to do that. How entertaining!"

Kalista turns and scans her followers. "Korr, congratulations. I promote you to personal escort. Attend me." She hands the rod to him. "The rest of you, drag that fool back to the caloid. If he lives, he can scrub floors with his tongue. If he dies, wash him for grounding."

Grounding? It's the first time I've heard burial described that way. In my experience, dead Zemnans either get vaporized or left to rot as a lesson to others.

Without another word, Kalista whirls and struts back out the gate, the fellow named Korr hustling to keep up. Two men grab the inert "new man" by his wrists and drag him away. Crooked Nose touches the arm band, and the gate slides back into place.

"Wait, please," Theena says with a desperation I've never heard in her. Rushing to the gate, she drops to one knee and bows her head toward Crooked Nose. "Permission to speak. Please?"

The subservient gesture works. Rather than zapping her through the bars with his rod, he says, "Speak, if you will."

"I realize we are less than important in your eyes. The least of the least. But one of those men they took away is my brother. May I inquire what will be done to him?"

"Both will be prepared for the sport."

"If I may be so bold, what is the sport? We hear the expression, but none of us understands."

Atta girl, Theena. With your gorgeous looks and humble attitude, this guy is tolerating you a lot longer than he would me.

Her question elicits a lopsided smile from the guy. "It is a competition of Kalista's own invention. To play it, Entizar permits her to recruit any stray wanderer she can find in this ward. She calls it 'The Chase.'"

"If you will permit a final question, what will they chase?"

"This is a hunt. Those two will chase you three. They will try to kill you—unless you kill them first."

Theena gasps.

Forgetting to bow the knee, Salexa blurts, "But both are friends of ours. One, her own brother. They would never hurt us."

He shakes his head, as if amused by a ridiculous child. "You don't believe me? Wait and see. I guarantee, as soon as they have been prepared, those two will try to murder each of you. Rest. You will need it."

30

DEAD MEAT

"She's not just brutal," Salexa says. "The woman is insane. There's no other way to explain it."

I don't doubt her conclusion. "We need to pray."

Theena, Salexa, and I drop to our knees on the bare ground. I lead with earnest prayer for Prahv and Étan, pleading for God to intervene and save both them and us from whatever madness is taking place in that green tower on the hilltop.

No sooner do I utter "Amen" than Theena opens a floodgate of pent-up emotions in a personal appeal of her own to the Creator. With tears and a quavering voice, she pleads for God to protect Prahv, her one brother. This is no song; yet, once again Theena overwhelms me with her ability to express the deepest heartfelt feelings, to capture the exact nuance of every syllable as she bares her soul before our compassionate Creator. My own prayer had been sincere, but listening to Theena gushing her anguish in a plea, I feel outclassed in the prayer department. All I can do is listen in awe, whispering an occasional "Yes" in agreement. The unyielding ground I had grumbled about during the night becomes holy ground. What a privilege to listen, a companion of a world-champion prayer.

When Theena trails off in sniffs and tears, Salexa pronounces a final prayer. I don't hear all her words. My mind dwells on Theena and the incredible suffering gouging her heart. I place an arm around Theena's shoulders, but she doesn't respond. Unchecked tears trickle down her cheeks. Is she even aware I'm here? Now I wish all the more Salexa hadn't snuggled next to me during the night.

Hours pass. Despite the advice to conserve energy, I resume pacing. First back and forth, then along the inside perimeter. No blackmail, no torture, could force Prahv and Étan to hurt any of us. Just the opposite—with Étan's fiery temper, he's more liable to get himself killed by attacking Kalista or her guardians.

Theena stays pretty much rooted to the spot where we prayed. Occasionally she stands on her knees, lifting more silent pleas to Heaven. Other times, she lies prostrate, but I know she isn't sleeping. Just as Moses and Aaron sometimes did in distress, she's on her face before the Author of the universe and beseeching divine help, not for herself, but for Prahv.

Salexa alternates between us. Some moments she walks beside me, trying to guess what's happening up in the tower and trying to make small talk, which I can't do right now. Other times, she sits beside Theena, even places an arm around her waist, but Theena doesn't respond.

What kind of Fithian am I? The Intersection is still in my hand. Shouldn't I be able to figure out a way to escape?

Around midday, one of Kalista's men shows up and flings more vegetables into our cage. The final potato-like jocassa strays off course and brushes a glowing bar. Just that fast, the jocassa disappears in a brilliant zap and puff of smoke. A thimble's worth of dust filters to the ground.

The jailer cackles. "Anyone like his meals well-cooked?" He strolls away, still chuckling.

About an hour later, Crooked Nose and a dozen or so other guys show up. This time the whole dome stops glowing when he opens the gate.

"Out. It's time."

"Time for what?" Salexa asks.

"You'll see."

As they march us down a winding path to the beach, I weigh the odds of doing the unexpected, maybe whirling and attacking. No, I might be able to get in a few good punches, but I'm outnumbered. Besides, Crooked Nose keeps close with his inflictor rod. As long as that thing is in his hands, he controls the show.

When the path widens onto the ocean shore, Kalista is already there with the rest of her troop, about twenty men all told. The men stand on the pebbly beach while Kalista hovers astride her one-person solasamka. Her smile radiates pure evil. Two other figures stand among her men. Even with burlap sacks over their heads, I recognize Prahv and Étan.

No blood stains their tunics. Not so much as a rip in their garments. Their hands hang at their sides, not even manacled. Perhaps my fears about torture were groundless? But if so, why does it feel like a ghost has dipped his fingers in ice water and tied my intestines into a knot?

"Fanfare," Kalista orders.

In response, three men raise odd-looking trumpets and blare the strains of what might be marching music. They end with a high, triumphal note just as our group halts before Kalista.

"Welcome, welcome," she says, all smiles. "I am so delighted to see you looking healthy and well rested."

Is this the same woman who screeched in delight after abusing the body of her servant? Earlier she was a sadistic lunatic. Now she sounds as sweet as honey. Hovering twenty feet off the ground, she compels us to look up to her.

"My entourage, please be so good as to take your positions."

Wordless, all of Kalista's men spread out to form a human ring, with Prahv, Étan and us in the center. What spooks me most is Prahv and Étan. They don't budge. Not so much as a finger twitch. Not the slightest twist of the head under those sacks. They stand rigid as statues.

Kalista ignores them. Instead, she bestows all of her beaming delight on us three. "By nightfall, I expect that at least one of you shall receive the honor of joining me in my dining hall. You are about to embark on the greatest sport ever imagined. It's a spectacle that I have designed for my personal entertainment. Would you like to learn more?"

She floats in the air, her lips a plastic smile, awaiting a response. Fearful of uttering a wrong word to this bipolar queen, I nod.

"Oh good. Your enthusiasm warms my heart. I so appreciate zeal among my players."

One sideways glance confirms Theena and Salexa reflect dread more than zeal.

"Here is how the sport unfolds. You three will play the role of evil fugitives. Your two companions represent justice. You may run, hide, do anything you wish, including fight back. Your goal is to remain alive as long as possible. In the end, either you fugitives will be dead, or the enforcers of justice will die. I will not interfere, but I will follow the enforcers of justice and observe the entire hunt." She giggles. "Is my sport not ingenious?"

We don't answer. I, for one, don't want an inflictor rod jammed between my teeth.

"Are there any questions?"

Questions galore bubble inside my brain. Still, I hesitate to risk irritating this crazy woman.

"Oh come, come. There are always questions. Glorious though I am, even I cannot have explained everything perfectly. Fear not. Speak up, so we can be assured of the best competition possible."

Yeah, I'm afraid, but my hand rises anyway.

"You have something to ask?"

"Beyond what you've just explained, are there any other rules or guidelines?"

Kalista's mouth twists into a devilish grin. "Do I detect a shrewd player planning his tactics? I like that. But no, there are no additional rules. Of course, you will receive basic weapons to defend yourselves. The enforcers of justice will carry identical weapons. Knives, to be exact."

Kalista's near-childish demeanor raises the hairs on the back of my neck. So creepy. However, as long as she's not shrieking and hurting people, I dare to raise my hand again. "Are there boundaries to the competition? What if someone runs away and never comes back?"

She giggles again. This time, even the men standing around us grin.

"Pretty man, don't you realize? You're no longer on the mainland. I call this place Solace, my private island retreat. Unless you can swim thirty furlahs, you have no way to exit the game. Well, except by death, of course."

An island. That shoots down my idea of ruining her game by sneaking away.

"Anything else?"

Theena steps forward. "If you please, one of those men is my brother. I have no wish to fight him."

Kalista's eyes twinkle. "Better to say, he *was* your brother. All of that is in the past. Tantron, let's give them a brief demonstration."

The guy I call Crooked Nose walks to Prahv and Étan, where he pulls the sacks from their heads. Both men stare ahead, unblinking. On the side of Prahv's head, a patch of scalp has been shaved clean. Embedded in the spot is a device. It's octagonal, like a stop sign, but it's glossy gray, with protective spikes jutting from it. An identical device grips Étan's head. With his bald scalp, nobody needed to shave his head.

Crooked Nose—alias Tantron—glances at Theena. He needs only one second to spot the family resemblance between her and one of the "enforcers of justice." He delivers a series of rapid finger pokes to a handheld tablet. Prahv's eyes become alive, but still aren't normal. "Friend Prahv, do you see that dark-haired girl? She has just insulted your queen. Her lips deserve punishment. Will you please render justice for that offense?"

Prahv marches up to Theena. For a fleeting instant, his gaze sweeps across the three of us, not in recognition, but just making sure he singles out "that dark-haired girl." In a flash, he slaps Theena across the mouth hard enough to knock her down.

Kalista's burst of laughter reminds me of a hyena. "Bravo, the first blow. May many more follow. As I stated, I alone will observe the action live. We wouldn't want the presence of my men to influence the hunt. However, my solasamka is fitted with a holocam to beam the action back to my faithful servants. Mustn't be selfish, you know."

"He doesn't even know who I am," Theena says as I pull her to her feet.

Tantron hands the control tablet up to his airborne queen.

"Final countdown for questions," she says. "Four. Three. Two."

One final time my hand rises. "I'm confused. A minute ago, you said at least one of us would have the honor of joining you in your dining room this evening. But now you make it sound like this is a fight to the death."

A vivacious smile blossoms on Kalista's face. With exaggerated drama, she glides her solasamka lower, closer, staring into my eyes until she hovers only a few feet away. "Pretty man, there is no contradiction. You misinterpret. Perhaps you will be the first to join me? You're so attractive that I do hope so. That would be so tantalizing, so sensual."

I still don't get it, but with her floating right in my face, I'm afraid to utter a peep. This fruitcake might gun the solasamka and ram me before I can leap clear.

She drifts yet closer, still fixated on my eyes. This time her voice becomes conspiratorial. "I will tell you a secret. Of all the delicacies in the world, one rises above every other as the most delectable—human flesh."

The icy knot in my gut yanks tight.

"There's more than one way to join me at mealtime."

Meat. At last, I understand why they call us by that word.

Kalista raises one eyebrow as if we've shared a private joke then guides her little solo craft back up to where it floated before. "Distribute the knives. Open the ring. Fugitives, you have two countas to flee and strategize. After two countas, I release the enforcers of justice, and we shall see what we shall see."

31

A NEED FOR SPEED

Theena, Salexa, and I sprint along the damp sand of Solace Island, just out of the ocean's reach. How big is the island? What's the terrain? I have no plan and downright little time to create one. I calculate two countas equals about ninety minutes of earth time. Right now, the first goal must be to put as much distance between us and our friends as possible. If the waves wash away our footprints, that might buy a little time.

Theena weeps as she runs. "I can't do this. I won't knife Prahv."

I long to draw her close, to place a comforting arm around her. But there's no time. All I can do is hold her free hand as we run.

Puffing, but nowhere near winded, Salexa says, "Theena, you must be ready to defend yourself. He's not Prahv anymore. When he attacks, you won't do Prahv any favors by letting him murder you."

"I don't want to live at the cost of killing my brother. Prahv is all I have left."

Theena's comment pierces my heart. It reminds me of Grandma Johnson.

Despite the need for speed, I grind to a halt, dragging her to a standstill. "Look, we don't have much time. We've got to move, to think of how to survive. But first, I need to say something, and I'm going to say it, especially if this is my last chance to get it off my chest. Theena, Prahv is not all you have left. I love you, and I don't mean like a sister. Maybe Fithians aren't supposed to fall in love. I don't know. But I do love you, and I would lay down my life to save you. I may not be much, but you are definitely not alone."

As usual, Theena's tear-streaked expression is tough to read. Her gorgeous purple eyes gaze deeply into mine.

"For real? You're not just trying to comfort me?"

"Yes, for real. I've felt this way for a long time. But I didn't want to embarrass you if your feelings weren't mutual."

Next thing I know, Theena's arms wrap around me in the tightest hug of my life. Just as quickly, mine circle her. Such bliss has occurred in my dreams, but for the first time I'm embracing this wonderful girl without suddenly waking. The sensation of us pressed together is ideal, practically heavenly. With one hand, I stroke her silky-smooth hair.

Theena pulls back just enough to look me in the eyes. "I love you, too, Rankin, but was afraid to express it. I feared it might be forbidden for Fithians."

Our lips meet at last. Eyes closed, I'm oblivious to the sun, the wind, the ocean's waves, and everything else on this crazy planet. Theena loves me! Right now, this is as big as I want my universe to be—just her, me, and a kiss that communicates our feelings better than words.

If it were possible to freeze time, I could relish this moment forever. The picture would be perfect, if only her brother didn't plan to slice us to ribbons.

The staccato of hands clapping interrupts my brief taste of paradise. Standing nearby, Salexa says, "Excuse me, but this is no time for a Joining Ceremony. We must get away from here."

For the first time, Salexa's voice betrays resentment. She's the last person I would've chosen to witness my declaration of love. On the other hand, maybe it's good that she heard everything.

Still holding Theena, I say, "She's right. We're definitely in danger. If not for your sake, will you promise to stay alive as long as possible for my sake?"

She nods and gives a final quick kiss before letting go.

Reluctant, Theena and I part. When we do, a portion of my heart goes with her. Or maybe part of hers remains in me? Her expression still reflects fear. However, there's a new element that wasn't there minutes ago. Is it hope?

"Let's go." The three of us break into a run.

Up ahead, the strand of beach narrows. In place of the rolling hills on our right, the landscape yields to cliffs that rise straight up from the tossing waves.

An idea leaps to mind. "Those cliffs ahead. Maybe we can find a place to hide."

Salexa studies them. "Do you suppose we could find a cave up high, somewhere we would have to climb to reach? That way, we could defend the entrance easier from inside. Anyone scaling the rock face would be at a disadvantage."

Theena offers an alternate scenario. "On the other hand, in a cave we could end up trapping ourselves inside. If they figure out where we are, all they have to do is take turns guarding the entrance while we die of thirst or hunger."

Tired of carrying the long knife in my hand, I tuck it inside my belt. "I bet Kalista would get bored and interfere. She doesn't want a stalemate."

Another obstacle with hiding among the cliffs is that I can't quite accept the image of myself kicking Prahv or Étan in the face and sending them hurtling to rocks a hundred feet below. But this is all guesswork. There might not even be caves up there.

Theena is panting, but says, "Do you think it's possible Kalista's mind control has any weakness? I mean, what if we surprise them from behind? Could we knock loose the mechanisms? Maybe they would revert to normal."

It's hard to concentrate while running. "We don't know how deep those control boxes are embedded. It might be possible to bash them loose, but if they have tentacles into the brain, that might cause major damage." A horrible image of a chunk of brain tissue ripping loose along with the control device pops into my thoughts. Just as quickly, I push the vision away.

As usual, I can generate more questions than answers. "I can't help wondering if it's possible to talk around the mind control. We don't know how much of their thinking is intact. If there's even a tiny corner of their minds not under control, maybe we can exploit that."

Neither girl comments. They're probably thinking the Zemnan equivalent of "Yeah, right."

We reach the point where the cliffs rise from the water. "Wait here. Let me scout the situation." I wade into the water, then breaststroke farther out for a view of the rocky face. When I halt to tread water, my spirits droop.

"No caves, neither high nor low," I call back.

Theena points and shouts, "What's beyond the cliff? Maybe we could all swim around farther down. That might make finding us harder."

I look left. The cliff face continues to a point that protrudes farther into the ocean. A few hundred yards beyond, a thin strip of shoreline appears where the cliffs diminish in height.

"Let's try it."

The girls plunge into the surf and join me. The wind is raising cold, choppy waves, making it a challenge to swim. Being clothed and wearing running shoes doesn't help. Could a riptide drag us out to sea? But then we round the cliff jutting farthest into the water. We can do this.

"How much time has passed?" Salexa says when we stumble, sodden, back onto shore.

"At least one of our two countas," Theena says. "Maybe more."

Good. They're still on civil terms even if Salexa acts a little stiff. She might be feeling rejected.

"Still no caves. We need to find some kind of high ground. A place where we can see Prahv and Étan long before they reach us. Even better would be a spot that reveals how big this island is."

Salexa tugs loose one of many vines dangling down the cliff face. "Creeping hyatin. When I was little, I climbed them for sheer enjoyment. They're tough as wire, strong enough to hold adults if you two can climb?" She eyes Theena with skepticism.

"No problem," Theena says. Without another word, she selects a hyatin vine, gives it a tug to test it, then begins hoisting herself up.

Her ability impresses me. Between the two girls, I've always considered Salexa the more physically fit, but Theena's hand-over-hand progress would give me a challenge if this were a race.

Salexa chooses another creeper and offers it to me. "Our Fithian goes next."

Hoping I don't make Fithians look like clumsy dorks, I accept the hyatin and start upward. Despite my waterlogged clothing, I make better progress than I expect. Adrenaline, I suppose. Also, the rock here is riddled with cracks and bumps that provide footholds.

My pride does take a hit when Salexa scampers past me on a neighboring vine. "Keep it up, Rankin. You're doing great."

When I reach the summit, rather than seeing a bird's-eye view of the island, I find stout trees, with rope-like hyatins snaking this way and that up their branches. Unlike the woods on the mainland, no one has manicured this corner of Zemna for years, if ever.

After slicing through our hyatins to prevent anyone else from climbing them, I call a halt. "Let's rest a moment and formulate some strategy. We can't just run around in circles."

"We don't have many options," Theena says.

Salexa sits on a dead tree that has toppled to the ground, its roots now exposed. "If we must fight, the three of us might take on the two of them."

"You might be right. But I don't want this to boil down to an all-out battle to the death until we've racked our brains for every option. Besides, even if we did end up putting our friends out of commission—"

"You mean killing them." Theena studies my reaction.

"Even if we did do that—which I have no stomach to do—what would it gain us? A few more days of life? Sooner or later, Kalista will capture someone else to pit against the three of us for her sport. And next time, we might be the ones with mind-control boxes stuck in our brains."

Salexa emits a long sigh. "Or she might match us girls against you."

Her words evoke a hideous image in my mind—Theena and Salexa, eyes glassy, heads partially shaved, with electronic devices mounted on bare scalps. No. I could never plunge a blade into these girls, not even to save my life.

"Maybe we can outwit Kalista," Theena says. "Rankin, you have the Intersection, and they don't recognize you from the Unizem broadcast. Do you suppose we could circle back to Kalista's caloid and sneak off with a samka?"

Salexa's eyes brighten. "Yes. From what you've told me, you can power a samka without an activation disk."

It's the escape plan from Lotan's quarry all over again—but minus Prahv and Étan.

Theena stands and paces while she talks. "Last time we pulled that trick, Prahv used blood to disable the other samkas to slow down pursuit. We don't have any blood. But Rankin, you've learned how to do so much with the Intersection. Could you probe into the controls? Maybe fuse key components to keep them from functioning?"

Months have passed since the one and only day I piloted a samka. However, when I close my eyes, I can still picture many of the inner workings. The power grid, tyagil cell interface, and the velocity control. "You know, I bet I could. The ignition is pretty basic. Plus, there are no locks to stop a thief."

Theena nods. "In the Before Time, nobody needed safeguards. Everybody shared. Nobody stole."

"And nobody tried to cook their neighbors for dinner." The moment I say it, I regret my grim humor, but neither Theena nor Salexa flinches.

While we've been talking, Salexa has spotted a balochia tree and strides to it. With a short hop, she pulls down a branch and snaps off three of the copper-colored fruit. "Catch. Even if we don't feel like eating, we'd better keep our strength up. Plus, the juice will help to keep us hydrated."

"One last thing. Maybe I'm thinking too far down the road, but assuming we really can sneak off the island, I'll want to come back. Maybe under cover of darkness. If Prahv and Étan are alive, I could capture that guy with the crooked nose—what did she call him? Tantron?—and force him to undo whatever he's done to our friends."

Theena brightens. "I'll come, too."

Salexa says nothing. Is she jealous of Theena? Or maybe she considers my idea suicide. If so, she might be right. I wouldn't blame her if she decides to stay far away from crazy Kalista and her death squad.

Back on Earth, life would be so much easier. For the first time, my dream of going home injects a genuine ache into my heart. If I do go back, Theena won't be there. I won't even remember her.

"Something wrong?" Salexa says. "I mean, more wrong than this insane sport?"

"Just thinking. Sometimes I think too much."

Theena stoops, lifts a chunk of rotting log, and hides the core of her balochia beneath it. "Let's not leave any traces of where we've been or what we've done. Try not to leave footprints. Be careful of what we touch. We don't know how much reasoning ability Prahv and Étan have. Maybe none, if she's turned them into biological machines. But we'd better play it safe."

Her statement gladdens my heart. No trace of victim mentality in her words. "You know, you're pretty smart. No wonder I've fallen in love with you."

"I feared you would never say such words."

I tuck a strand of her hair behind her ear and gaze into her eyes. So beautiful.

Salexa clears her throat. "Survival first. Affection later. We need to keep our emotions under control and plan logically. No distractions."

She's right. I release Theena's hand. "Let's go then. I'll lead the way. But first, we have one more important thing to do."

"What's that?" Salexa says.

"Pray."

This elicits a smile from Theena. "I've been waiting for that suggestion. I would be disappointed if you didn't."

"Yeah?"

"Yeah."

That one word sets my spirit soaring. She and I are in tune.

"Allow me." As Theena prays, my thoughts jump back to the statement I had called out to Jaylel in my room at Quel-Tel-Palarim—that even a dinky, yellow Post-It Note with a few jotted lines of encouragement would be nice. But Theena's faith-filled prayer uplifts me better than a note ever could.

"So be it," Theena says in conclusion.

"So be it," Salexa repeats.

Pulling my knife from my belt, I take the lead. "Time to move. Let's try to circle back to Kalista's place and hope all her men are distracted by her holograph of Prahv and Étan searching for us."

As I push through underbrush, for the first time I'm glad to have the dagger issued by Tantron. It's not as long as a machete, and it's narrower, but with its razor-sharp serrated edge, it slices through a gangly hyatin with one swipe. Dumb move. I've just left evidence we were here. Better to lift or push aside these obstacles than to slash them.

Of course, in the hands of our pursuers, a similar blade could slit a person's throat right to the vertebrae.

I swallow and push away the image.

Salexa is right. Better to think logically. Trouble is, I'm from Earth, not the planet Vulcan. Fear is an emotion I can't click off.

IN HIDING

"Well, there's our proof. It's an island all right." The hilltop where we stand isn't the highest elevation, but it's high enough to confirm that much. There's no escaping by foot. Solace Island looks about three miles wide, but longer lengthwise.

Theena points northward. "Look. Kalista's base."

Sure enough, in the distance the green hue of her caloid tower rises above the forest. Sunlight glints from the top of the geodesic dome that had caged us.

"Anybody see her solasamka?"

The three of us strain our eyes in every direction, including straight up through the boughs that shadow our observation point.

Salexa grunts. "No sign of her. I don't like it."

Theena shrugs. "Maybe we gave them a hard challenge when we climbed the cliff."

I consider. "Kalista knows the terrain. If there was an easier route, she'd probably clue them in to save time."

"Not a comforting thought," Salexa says.

Theena settles to her haunches, giving her legs a rest. "There's a lake down there, off to the left. It doesn't lie in a straight path to the tower, but if we don't get water, we'll dehy-drate in this heat."

"You're right, but that presents a fresh danger. They know we need water. They might be watching the lake."

"Or have a sensor grid around it," Salexa says. "Wouldn't be sporting, but I'd be surprised if Kalista believes in fair play."

The mention of water reminds me of how dry my tongue feels. This isn't a balochia tree spreading overhead, but is it fruit-bearing? When I step closer to inspect it, I notice three perfectly round holes bored into the trunk.

"What do you suppose made these holes?" I reach toward one.

"Rankin, no!" Theena tackles me, sending both of us tumbling down the grassy slope.

When we slide to a stop, I spit out sour bits of broad grass. "What was that for?"

"Slishki. Look."

From the three holes protrude black-and-red vipers, each with three wicked-looking eyes and a miniature spike glinting between its nostrils. They ignore Salexa, who stands rigid. However, the creatures latch triple hate-filled eyes onto Theena and me as they sway back and forth. Venom drips from curved fangs.

"Slishki?"

"You don't have them on your planet? Slishki carve dens into trees, then embed their tails in the wood. It's a symbiotic rela-tionship. In the Before Time, they were tame. Children loved to pet them. Now they're evil. They bite and poison anything that approaches their den."

I help her to her feet, and we start back up the slope. "We don't have slishki, but we have similar creatures. Ours don't anchor themselves into trees. They slither through streams, fields, and sometimes hang in trees. Not all bite, but many do."

"Anywhere? That would be horrible."

There's no point in describing the whole range of earth

snakes from garters to pythons. I watch in fascination as the weird creatures withdraw into their dens, still giving us triple evil eyes.

"No matter how much I learn about Zemna, new surprises wait around every corner." Although I don't voice the thought aloud, it occurs to me these slishki came close to stealing Kalista's sport of watching me die. How many more dangers lurk on Zemna?

Salexa glances over her shoulder. "We should get moving. If they're on our trail, they could have heard Theena shout."

"Agreed. Let's go."

Keeping under the cover of overhanging branches whenever practical, we work our way down the steep hillside in the general direction of the lake. Often, the only way to avoid falling is a controlled slide from tree trunk to tree trunk. Weathered roots and hyatin vines often snag our feet.

"Careful. This would be a bad time to break a bone."

Salexa wipes a hand across her perspiring brow. "If the terrain is hard for us, it will be equally challenging for Prahv and Étan, brains or no brains."

Even when we reach the bottom, the interlaced branches and wiry briars continue to bar the way. Our slow progress fuels my frustration.

"The sun is going down," Theena says. "Should we try to push forward under cover of darkness? It would be impossible for them to follow us at night."

Beneath this leafy canopy, I can't see the sun. She's right, though. Fewer than thirty Earth minutes before sunset. "I don't recommend nighttime travel. Darkness is deeper in a forest. We'd soon be stumbling over every root."

Salexa places her hands on her hips, twisting this way and that as if to stretch the kinks from her back. "Kalista might give lanterns to Prahv and Étan. If so, darkness won't hinder them at all."

Flashlights. I hadn't considered that. Another possibility

comes to mind. "Even if Kalista gives them lights, she's only flesh and blood. Sooner or later, she'll need to stop and sleep, same as us. Can you girls push a little farther? I'd like to cover as much territory as possible while we search for a hiding place."

"We're fine," Theena says. "Lead on, Rankin."

With every step, I rack my brain. Isn't there some way to gain an upper hand with the Intersection? Some unexpected strategy? Nothing comes to mind. Here in this island wilderness, there are no portals to open, no devices to power on, no secret codes to crack. Unless I'm missing something obvious, out in nature I'm just a regular guy.

From nowhere, Moses pops into my mind. God gave Moses a staff with power to part the Red Sea and draw water from a dry rock. Yet, the Bible calls him the meekest man. Instead of a miraculous staff, God embedded my tool in my left palm, where I couldn't lose it. A vision of my long-lost New Testament comes to mind. Yeah, God knows what He's doing. If He'd given me a staff like Moses had, I probably would've lost that, too.

"Thinking again?" Theena asks, her voice kept low.

"Trying to conjure up clever tactics. I'm not doing a good job."

"We're still alive," Salexa says. "So far, what we're doing has kept us ahead of Kalista."

When we come across a tall balochia tree, I'm excited to see fruit dangling from upper branches. However, in a forest, trees don't tend to have live branches down low. Neighboring trees block the sunlight down here, often causing lower branches to wither and die, like on this specimen.

I sigh. "We could use that fruit, but climbing so high would be tricky. It would also cost precious time."

"Too bad your Intersection can't communicate with trees," Theena says.

Her statement gives me pause. I've never even considered using the Intersection on a plant, only on devices and people. Is it even possible?

As an experiment, I press my left hand against the tree's trunk and concentrate. Within seconds, my brain merges with a totally new kind of biological song. Mentally unified with the balochia tree, I detect the leisurely movement of sap in veins beneath its bark, the deep roots imbibing water, molecule by molecule, and the mind-blowing process of photosynthesis occurring in countless leaves overhead. The longer I remain merged, the more fascinating the experience becomes. The enormous strength of the stout trunk impresses me as it bears the massive weight of everything towering overhead. Yet, at the same time, I sense the delicate presence of birds perched on twigs—even the exact location of every stem bearing a fruit. Somehow, my tastebuds even perceive the slightly tangy flavor of the sap with its mix of water and nutrients. A flood of joy wells inside me. I'm no longer simply touching rough tree bark —I'm experiencing part of God's glorious creation from the inside out.

"Rankin?" Theena's voice conveys concern.

The urgency of the moment returns to me. Although I could stand and relish this tree's inner symphony for hours, we have no time for luxury. Focusing on three particular balochia stems, I say, "Girls, look up." Then I issue a mental command: *Release*. Those three fruits immediately disappear from my mental awareness of the tree.

Behind me, Theena blurts, "Catch them!"

Reluctantly, I withdraw my mind and open my eyes. As I pull my palm away, soft green and white sparks glitter between the Intersection and the bark. They swirl then fade away. Interesting.

Theena holds two fruit. Salexa cradles the third. Both girls stare at me.

Theena steps closer and hands me one of her balochias. Her eyes never leaving mine, she says, "You are amazing, Rankin Fithian. I never would've believed such a thing is possible."

"God provides."

On the outside, the tree looks like any other to my human eyes. Now, though, I have fresh insight and appreciation for its myriad of inner, invisible workings. And to think there must be billions of trees on the planet, each one playing its own particular biological music. The awesomeness of God's creation impresses me as never before. But now isn't the time to dwell on it.

"Let's have a quick snack then get moving."

* * *

When we continue our trek, Theena stoops to step under a low-hanging vine. "Do you suppose Kalista lied about pursuing us? Could they be waiting for us to trip a motion detector?"

"That maniac is capable of anything."

When we push through a thicket, a dry channel cuts across our path. In wet weather, rain water must run down it. With aching feet and parched throat, I'm tired of struggling for every inch of progress. "Let's follow this channel awhile. Walking will be easier where there aren't any vines or briars. Our feet will scuff the sand, but I'm willing to risk it if we can pick up the pace."

"Whatever you think," Salexa says, fatigue in her voice.

Our senses on the alert, we walk along the stream bed for five or six Earth minutes when Theena whispers, "Yadi."

I freeze, ready for whatever danger the unfamiliar word might mean. In contrast, Theena and Salexa scamper into a patch of thigh-high ferns. Theena plucks an aqua-colored berry the size of a ping-pong ball and pops it into her mouth. "They're ripe. Delicious!"

Salexa plucks one and presses it to her lips. She takes a small bite and sucks the juice. "Dreamy." She picks another. "Rankin, eat some. They'll quench your thirst and restore your energy."

As soon as the juice washes over my tongue, I recall the tangy sweetness with its pleasant sensation tickling my taste buds. "I haven't tasted this flavor since my first day on Zemna. I found a pitcher of this juice in a partially wrecked caloid."

Theena pops another plump berry into her mouth. Her eyes close as she savors it. "Ever since I was a little girl, yadi have been my favorite fruit. So succulent."

As the light fades, we pick enough to fill our stomachs. "I was worried about finding that lake before we dehydrated. Now water isn't so urgent."

Theena smiles in my direction as she licks juice from her lips. "Praise the Creator. We asked Him to guide our steps. He led us to what we need, precisely when we needed it, didn't He?"

Her childlike faith inspires me. Here I am, the Fithian, and I was ready to chalk up the yadi patch to happy coincidence. I take her hand and kiss the back of it, just like they do in old movies. She smiles and surprises me by performing the same gesture on my hand. I nearly laugh.

"There's something else," Salexa says. "Over there. Matta moss. If we spend the night here, the moss will keep us comfortable. Plus, the ferns will provide a visual barrier if anyone passes this way."

I survey the deepening shadows. A comfortable spot to rest, with refreshments nearby for breakfast. Seems ideal. Yet, one thing worries me. The dry watercourse is close. Our feet left tracks in the sand and moldering leaves. "We'll spend the night here, but to be on the safe side, I want to take one precaution. Come on."

Theena wipes her fingers on her tunic. "Where are we going?"

"I'll explain."

Without returning to the waterless path, we parallel its course about twenty feet to the left. After five minutes, we encounter an intersecting trickle of water flowing to the right, probably to the lake we spotted.

"Perfect. I couldn't have planned this better myself."

"Planned what?" Salexa asks.

I motion for them to stick close as I veer right and follow the flow. "Don't step near the muddy bank. Walk only on grass and leaves. Don't break any ferns.

"I still don't understand what we're doing," Theena whispers.

"We're creating a deception. Do what I do." When we reach the spot where the stream encounters the dry watershed, I take one long, sideways step out of the ferns and right into the center of the dry stream bed, ending with my toes at the water's edge. Motioning to the others, I say, "Now you two do the same."

First Theena, then Salexa, imitate my maneuver. We end in the same positions we'd been walking earlier.

"Now what?" Salexa asks. "We're leaving prints."

"Right. From here, we walk backward until we reach our resting place. It might be a futile effort, but this way anyone tracking us would see our three sets of footprints leading straight down to the water. The logical conclusion would be that we've stepped into the stream to cover our trail as we head toward the lake."

Theena's eyes fairly glint in admiration. "How inventive. Only you would think of that, Rankin."

Should I confess I learned this trick from an old cowboy movie I once watched with Dad? Nah. No time to explain Hollywood. Easier to let her believe I'm a genius.

* * *

Late that night, some time after I've stood first watch and settled into exhausted sleep, I awake to an insistent hand patting my shoulder. I blink in darkness. "Wh—?"

A soft hand covers my mouth. Hair tickles my cheek as Salexa whispers, "Shh. Lights."

Her warning startles me into full wakefulness. I roll onto my stomach, glad for the soft and silent bed of matta, and peer between the ferns as Salexa rouses Theena. Sure enough, three lights move along the dry watershed, coming from the same direction we did. The girls join me, one on either side.

Taking shallow breaths, I dare to ease aside one fern leaf but can't see much. Against the blackness, two twinkling gleams bob along, followed by a third steady glow, which must be the head-lamp of a hovering solasamka. From our concealed position, we watch as they draw closer.

My heart thumps faster. Will they discover us? Could we flee through this underbrush without stumbling and breaking our necks? Or will we have to fight for our lives, with Kalista cackling in the background?

Almost against my will, my fingers comb through the matta until they locate the object I'd placed beside me before yielding to sleep—the razor-sharp dagger issued by Tantron. Will I use it if my friends attack me? Even I don't know. Still, it's my only weapon. Not smart to leave it behind.

Keep walking, you guys. Don't stop. Don't even pause. The longer we avoid contact, the better for all of us.

Despite my mental plea, the first two lights do pause, causing the one floating behind to halt as well.

"What is it?" Kalista's voice snaps. "Have you found something?" Her tone brims with irritation. No more sweetie pie schoolgirl. The irritated biker chick is back.

A male voice mumbles something indistinguishable.

"Well, check it out, fool. If all three stepped off the trail, there must be a reason."

Twin beams of light crisscross in our direction. The girls and I hunker lower, our faces pressed into the sweet-scented moss. Dry leaves crunch. A twig snaps as Prahv and Étan approach our hiding place.

"Hold up. I see now. Yadi berries. They must have stopped to fill their bellies. Bring me some of those, and you two eat some as well. You're no good to me if your bodies collapse."

Thank you, Lord.

I keep my face averted. Luckily, the olive drab tunics Theena and I wear provide perfect camouflage. Salexa's brown one is a fortunate color, too. However, as the sound of boots swishing through grass grows louder, I remember Salexa's strawberry-blond hair. My arm slides over her head just as a pair of boots stops not three feet away.

Too bad we didn't think to leave berries near the trail so they wouldn't penetrate this far. I make a mental survival note for next time—if we get a next time.

In the following minutes, all we can do is listen to the soft snap of yadi stems and feet shuffling back and forth as their owners pick berries. Étan and Prahv don't speak. Just as well. I don't want to hear them making comments like, "These delicious berries will surely strengthen us to disembowel our friends."

"Enough," Kalista calls out. "Back to the hunt."

Soft plopping sounds reach my ears. Have they dropped their remaining berries? Next comes the sound of retreating footsteps through the ferns. The bobbing lights continue down the watershed toward the stream.

Once our pursuers disappear, we three heave a collective sigh.

"Praise the Creator for your deception, Rankin," Salexa says.

"But do we dare to stay here?" Theena wonders aloud. "If they run out of footprints, they might come back."

"It's possible. Or they might follow the stream with or without evidence we waded down it. We don't know how deep Kalista's mind control penetrates their brains. To be on the safe side, I suggest we creep back the way we came. Thanks to the berries, we don't need the lake anymore. Let's cut across country toward Kalista's base. I want to get ahold of a samka."

33

"DIE!"

At dawn's first light, I clamber halfway up a tree to catch my bearings. Mostly obscured by leaves, but unmistakable, the top of Kalista's abode reflects Aena's morning rays. In other circumstances, the scene would be beautiful, worthy of a painting. However, the sight makes me wish I could kick myself. I climb back down.

"We're off course. We've already passed Kalista's place. No wonder the terrain is getting rough again."

Theena caresses my back. "Don't blame yourself. In the dark, and in a forest, who can plot a straight direction?"

The orienteering course I passed in ninth-grade summer camp comes to mind. Yes, I'd found my way through the woods and located every soda bottle dangling on their twine cords. But in camp, each of us had carried a compass.

Salexa shrugs. "We can angle back to it."

"I don't suppose we have a choice. Still, we've wasted a lot of energy. And we haven't run across other berry patches. Not even a fruit tree. We'll be needing water again."

Theena gives my back a final pat. "Lead on. Do what you must."

Once more, we hike up a steep incline, this time toward our objective. But my new concern is the lack of cover. Trees grow sparsely on this end of the island. I can't win. Either trees conceal us and make our direction hard to guess, or we plainly see our goal in open places that leave us visible.

The climb deepens my breathing, but this is a good chance to say what I've been thinking. "Girls, make me a promise."

Theena's face shows concern when she turns her head. "What kind of promise?"

"If anything happens to me, don't stop. Keep going. Try to get off this island with one of Kalista's samkas."

Theena steps in front of me. "I hope you're not thinking of sacrificing yourself to save us?"

I shake my head. "All I'm saying is that Kalista is totally insane. There's no telling what she might do, even if it violates her own rules. If something stops me or slows me down, don't hesitate. Make a straight line to those samkas and get out of here, if at all possible."

Salexa eases to a squatting position. Even her athletic physique must be weary of the constant walking. "We don't have the Intersection of All Things without you."

"You might not need the Intersection. All you would need is a samka activation disk. If necessary, you two could club that Tantron guy from behind. He's bound to carry one."

Theena clasps my hand between her own. "We've prayed to the Creator. Let's allow Him to guide us."

Part of me wants to force the conversation, make them promise to escape, if possible. Instead, I kiss her on the knuckles. "All right. Let's press on."

When we crest the hill, there's no protective trees or shade. Just a wind-swept summit of sparse broadleaf grass and loose stone. From here, Kalista's home stands out against the skyline. Unfortunately, we can't plot a straight path to it. The direct approach is impossibly sheer. We would need ropes, harnesses, real climbing gear to scale that cliff, and we would hang in plain view if we tried.

"Sorry again. Looks like we'll have to circle our way down and around."

Salexa puffs a wayward strand of hair from her face. "Maybe if we veer left, back toward the ocean? We know for sure the terrain is not so steep on that—"

The shrill blast of a whistle cuts her off. On another hilltop, Prahv stands, clutching view magnifiers in one hand and some sort of whistle in the other. He's looking straight at us. But where are Étan and Kalista?

The shriek of the whistle was already enough to freeze the marrow in bones. When cackling laughter wafts down the wind, panic kicks in. "Girls, quick, down the hill. That way."

We run, slide, tumble, and crawl down the steep pitch of the hill. Within seconds, we're out of Prahv's line of sight, but the repeated shrieks of the whistle echo behind, growing fainter as we increase the distance between us.

"Why doesn't he stop?" Salexa blurts, jumping from boulder to boulder. "She already knows which way we've gone."

"He's not in his normal mind," Theena says. "She must have ordered him to take that position and blow a signal if he saw us. New order blots out old. He didn't even try to chase us."

If that's true, then it's just Étan and Kalista on our tail. Will Prahv stand there blowing his lungs out until she goes back for him?

The moment my running shoes hit the shale, the surface on this whole side of the hill breaks away. Theena, Salexa, and I go tumbling headlong toward the bottom in an avalanche of crumbling stone.

"Rankin!"

Tossing, tumbling, I'm powerless to aid Theena. The most I can do is clench my teeth and try to stay above the avalanche, but I'm failing even in that. Everything is happening too fast.

When at last the tons of debris slides to a halt, I'm buried to the waist and blinking grit from my eyes.

"Rankin!" Only Theena's neck and head protrude from the rubble.

Farther down the slope, Salexa picks herself up. On all fours, she crawls toward Theena.

Ignoring the pain to my hands, I push away sharp bits of shale and dig myself out. Crawling to Theena, I paw away the rubble like a dog, using all the speed I can muster.

Salexa digs on the opposite side. "Hold on, Theena. We'll have you free in a moment."

Theena grimaces. "My knee. It's twisted. Hurts ..."

The next sound is the one I dread—the hyena laughter of an insane woman. When I glance, sure enough, Kalista is about six hundred yards down the ravine and cruising behind Étan, who plods toward us, his glinting blade drawn and ready.

"Faster, get her out!" My breath comes in rapid pants as I scrape at the rubble. But the rocky bits are a like a 3-D jigsaw puzzle, all compacted around her. If only I had a shovel. Or a crowbar.

Salexa switches tactics and uses her feet to push the shale from Theena.

Theena moans. "It's crushing my lungs, my stomach. Hard to breathe."

Grabbing Theena by the armpits, I pull upward so hard my leg muscles quiver. She moans and rises, but only a fraction. She's embedded worse than I imagined.

In front of Theena, Salexa's light boots are kicking up a storm of rocky bits. That should relieve pressure from Theena's ribs. But this is taking too long.

Another quick glance shows Étan and Kalista drawing closer. His expression is blank, but Kalista's face radiates sheer delight. She already expects the finale of her perverse sport.

Pausing just long enough to wipe my sweaty palms on my

jeans, I grab Theena again and heave, rocking left and right. I'm grunting and puffing, but inch by inch, Theena's body works loose, rising higher, higher, until she at last slides free.

Only fifty feet away, Kalista breaks into giddy cackling. "Oh, how heroic. Handsome man, you just might provide the most romantic meal I've ever tasted." She punctuates the statement by double-clicking her brilliant white teeth together.

Never before have I longed to punch a woman in the face, but now the urge is overwhelming. If only Étan weren't between that witch and me. "Salexa, get her out of here."

Salexa helps Theena to her feet. "We have to run."

Theena winces. "I'll try. But my knee ..."

For a split instant, I plan to stand in the gap between Étan and my friends. But Theena's faltering footsteps are too pitiful. Five minutes ago, Theena could sprint as fast as I can, maybe faster. Now a toddler could outrace her. No time for healing.

I run to Theena's other side and drape her right arm over my shoulders. "Hurry!" Bearing Theena between us, Salexa and I make better time. But to what point? Thirty feet behind, Étan keeps pace with steady, leisurely steps. My plan to steal a samka is impossible if he and Kalista follow us all the way. My mind snaps to a decision. All three of us can't escape. Instead of assisting Theena, I slide out from under her arm and turn to face Étan.

"Salexa, get her out of here. I'll stall them."

Theena halts when I do. "Rankin, don't commit suicide. You and Salexa save yourselves. Maybe this is where I'm meant to—"

"No way. You made me a promise. Survive as long as you can, Theena."

"But—"

"Salexa, drag her!"

Salexa grips Theena's wrist and pulls.

"Wait." Theena breaks free and hobbles to me. Before I realize her intention, she places her hands on either side of my face and looks me in the eye. "No matter what happens, Rankin Fithian, you're the best thing that's ever happened to me. I love you."

Theena's lips meet mine, warm and desperate. Her kiss brims with love, caring, passion—a dream come true. But with Étan and his blade bearing down on us, this isn't the moment for romance.

I break away. "Go. There's not enough time to heal you now. I'll catch up."

Once more, Kalista's high-pitched cackle pollutes the air. "Bravo, you who are about to die. Étan, terminate the male first. Then recalculate and eliminate both females."

Salexa wraps an arm around Theena's waist and pulls her. Despite backward glances from Theena, they hobble away as best they can.

When I turn to face Kalista and Étan, my inadequacy sparks a cold sweat. The only barrier standing between death and the girl I love is—me. But I've never studied karate or judo. Never practiced boxing. Never even watched the school wrestling team. How can I possibly defeat an experienced warrior?

In a bid to buy the girls time, I sidestep. Then again. Then backward. Étan follows.

God, help me.

Kalista's expression has grown crazier than ever. With victory apparently only seconds away, she actually closes her eyes, runs her tongue along her lips as if already relishing my death. Too weird. But no time to watch the maniac.

Étan's own face registers no emotion whatsoever—just single-minded determination as he marches closer, closer, his hand now raising the blade.

"Come on, Étan, think. You're no robot."

Backing up is the only defense that comes to mind. The girls need me to stall. My mind races as I try to recall a movie, a book, anything that might provide last-moment inspiration.

"Cease moving," Étan says.

A thought springs to mind. "Étan, your father died because

he refused to be the puppet of a petty tyrant. Resist her mind control. Fight back."

Without a flicker of sentiment, he plods forward, adjusting his direction every time I do.

"You look so romantic, pretty warrior. So brave." Kalista actually bats her eyebrows at me.

"Be quiet!"

"I can hardly wait for tonight's feast. You should thank me for liberating you from that disease-ridden harlot."

Étan is ten feet away and closing, but Kalista's slur ignites my pent anger. In blind rage, I cock my knife hand to my ear then hurl it at her face just as she begins another licking motion.

Étan tries to intercept my blade with his own but misses.

Caught off guard, Kalista shrieks and zips the samka upward.

Too late. My knife misses her leering face but plummets instead into her abdomen. Her scream is deafening, and I'm as astonished as she is. But now there's time only for Étan. He lunges, knife poised, still operating on her last command.

Like an amateur bullfighter, I sidestep and suck in my gut. The knuckles of Étan's knife hand graze my tunic as he races past and trips over a chunk of rock. Evidently, the device over-riding the morality and personality centers of Étan's brain affect his agility and reaction time. Back in Quel-Tel-Palarim, this guy could have skewered me.

When he rises and turns, there's no animosity in his features, but no robotic stare, either. He's Mr. Spock—unemotional, but intelligent. Blood drips from his lacerated hands, but he ignores the wounds.

"Recalculating."

"What do you mean, 'recalculating'? Étan, you're no machine. You're a man. We're friends."

Can I get through to him? Maybe he's too far gone, but every second I delay buys more time for the girls. A fast peek up the ravine places them about a football field away.

This time when Étan thrusts the knife forward, it's a fake attack. Some flicker of reasoning inside that skull gauges my reaction. He advances a step, crouches, then slashes at chest level. Another test, but by the time I realize it, I've jumped backward.

"Étan, you don't have to do this. We're friends. I saved your life, and you saved—"

He rushes straight at me, eyes fixed on my chest.

I manage to grab his knife wrist with both hands, but with his stocky build and thirty-pound advantage, he's still pushing, driving me backward. I'm amazed he doesn't yank the blade free and then plunge forward with it. Yet, as long as he's advancing and the deadly tip points toward my chest, he seems satisfied.

But how many backward steps can I take before I stumble over one of the countless boulders littering the area? My desperate grip on his wrist tightens, my nails digging in. Even if Étan can't acknowledge pain, if I squeeze his wrist hard enough maybe his muscles will drop the weapon.

And what about Kalista? Could that wounded lunatic be leveling a fyotor at me this precise instant?

With all my might, I squeeze my fingers around Étan's wrist. Harder. Harder. I clench my teeth. My fingers are strong, thanks to hours of toil with Lotan's hammer and chisel. Surely his wrist bones will crunch if I increase the pressure.

Not until the knife clatters to the ground does Étan's gaze falter. His focus slides from my chest, to my eyes, then to his empty hand. But he's already stepped over the knife, and it's nowhere to be seen.

"Recalculat—"

"No, you don't!"

Without the blade to worry about, my instincts revert to fourth-grade playground tussles. I purposely fall down backward, dragging Étan off-balance toward me. Whether he feels pain or no, when my Nike running shoes catch him in the midsection, an audible "Oof" escapes from his lips. Another half second, and my legs heave him over me, onto his back.

I scramble to my feet, but Étan is already doing the same.

"Étan, concentrate. The real enemies are Kalista, Entizar, Lotan."

He crouches, curling both hands into fists.

"Use your brain, buddy. Kalista programmed you to fight me. Do your own thinking."

He no longer telegraphs new strategy with the word "recalculating." Étan snaps a fist toward my gut. I jerk backward. When he throws a punch to my jaw, I dodge, but feel the wind on my cheek. Once again, he's forcing me backward, always backward.

"Étan, resist Kalista's orders. You're not her—."

Out of nowhere, his battering-ram knuckles bash my eye. I stumble backward, blinking, struggling not to fall as agony radiates from the spot. My vision on that side is gone. Is it possible to punch an eyeball so hard it bursts? I've got to change tactics—do something different, anything unexpected.

Overexaggerating, I flash my good eye to a point over Étan's shoulder and shout, "Now! Knife him in the back!"

Incredible—Étan falls for the oldest trick in the book. He whirls to meet the non-existent attacker. When he does, I deliver a clumsy kick to his kidney.

No murmur of pain escapes Étan's lips, but my kick knocks him off balance. He crumples face forward into loose shale.

Seizing my chance, I sprint away. When I'm a safe distance, I dab my fingers to my throbbing eye. As I pull them away, my fingers glisten with blood. Only one working eye left. Can't let him whack that one.

When Étan turns and starts toward me, for the first time a flicker of genuine emotion registers in his eyes—the granite-hard glint of rage.

Beyond him, Kalista's solasamka rests on the uneven ground,

cocked on an angle. She lies on her side, knees drawn into a near fetal position. Good, she's not aiming a weapon at me.

As Étan plods toward me, I walk backward, glancing about as I go. To my relief, Theena and Salexa are out of sight. Now, if only I can keep Étan distracted, without getting myself killed. The girls need more time.

Étan charges. I turn and bolt the opposite direction, leading him away from the girls. My running shoes are old and battered, but in a foot race they'll give me an advantage over Étan's heavier boots. I glance back and—no! My left toe has caught on something hard. I pitch forward, sprawling into the shale.

Streaks of pain shoot from my ankle. Not now. God, not now! The second I try to stand, stabbing pain radiates from the ankle. It's broken or sprained, or both.

Étan bears down in a dead run. His eyes blaze at me with dead-set determination. He lunges. The impact feels like a refrigerator ramming into me. Next thing I know, he's sitting on my stomach, hands closing around my throat.

"Étan, sto—"

His vice-like grip cuts off all air flow. Étan squeezes, then throttles my throat up and down, banging my head over and over into broken shale. My vision fogs. Whining screeches in my ears.

I can do something—but what? With my air cut off and my skull slamming the ground, I can't think.

By the time my hand closes around a rock, my one good eye sees Étan's face as through a darkening tunnel. I slam the rock into his nose once, twice. Blood spurts from his nostrils, but the force crushing my throat continues.

Strike higher, to the head.

I latch onto that thought and bash the rock into the top of Étan's bald scalp. Then my clouding vision sees it—the device embedded in his head. With failing strength, I target the implant and swing.

Nothing.

I bash it again.

Nothing.

With my last ounce of fading strength, I rear back and slam the rock into the implant one last time.

I hear the sickening gurgle before my brain comprehends the source. It's me. From air rushing through damaged windpipes. I burst into coughing spasms and try to sit up but can't.

When my vision clears, I realize Étan isn't holding me. He's collapsed atop me. Mere inches from my eyes, Kalista's mind-control thing just dangles there. It's dented, but still hanging from his head, tethered by dozens of thin filaments leading into a bleeding hole in his skull.

Horrified, I shove Étan's body off. Like a wounded crab, I scuttle backward, dragging my injured foot as I go. Will he lift his head? Pounce on me?

What was once Étan just lies there. Face down. Unmoving. I stare through my one seeing eye.

That fast, the fight is over.

Swallowed by a tidal wave of emotion I've never experienced before, I burst into bitter tears.

"God, why? Why do people have to die every place I go? Étan wasn't ready. He didn't know You. I hate this. Let people live! Give them a chance to know You!"

The lavender heavens don't answer. So, I lie there, one functional eye weeping for my dead companion and for all the violence on this messed-up planet.

When the tears finally slow, I wipe my nose with the sleeve of my tunic. "There are still good people on Zemna. Wonderful people like Theena and Salexa."

Where are the girls now? Sticking to the plan, just like I instructed. Praise the Lord for Salexa dragging Theena away. They'll be heading for Kalista's place, searching for a samka. I promised to follow. But how can I? With one blind eye and a useless ankle screaming with pain, how can I catch up?

The solasamka. With an effort, I rise on my one good leg and hop toward the vehicle.

"Ow, ow, ow." Each hop jolts my bad ankle and tortures me with renewed shots of pain. When at last I reach the solasamka, I crawl onto it. Behind the seat, a coil of stained rope hangs from a clasp. Salexa's grotesque tale about bashing bodies against caloids comes to mind. I don't want to touch it.

I slide onto the seat and examine the controls. Awesome, they're almost identical to a regular samka's, just smaller and more compact. The power disk sticks tight. The console lights still glow.

"Hallelujah. Finally, something in my favor."

But wait—the guidance helmet. I need a helmet to command this thing.

There's the helmet. Not ten feet away, still on Kalista's head. I sink to all fours and crawl to where she lies, still in a fetal position. Her hands are locked around the blade protruding from her stomach.

Although Kalista looks helpless, I crawl with caution. She's moaning. Although mortally wounded, Dragon Queen might have one last bite in her.

From a prudent distance I stretch my arm and—yes. Her guidance helmet slips right off. Kalista doesn't resist. She simply whimpers.

I scuttle backward with my prize. From a safe distance, I examine it. Instantly, my heart sinks. A spider web of cracks radiates from an impact point. Can it still function?

Dear God, please let the internal components be intact.

Only one way to know. With a grunt, I heave myself to my feet once again then turn toward the solasamka. But there—standing directly in front of me is Étan, the bloodied mind-control gizmo dangling against his ear, but still attached. The marrow freezes in my bones.

"Die!"

Étan's knife hand flashes.

Searing pain explodes in my chest. In shock, I collapse to my knees.

When Étan extracts the blade from my body, every tooth of the serrated edge slides with a nick-nick-nick against a rib bone. Limper than a rag doll, I collapse backward onto unyielding rock. Blood spurts from my chest.

"First objective, male—terminated. Second objective—two females." Étan strides away.

34

THE MIND OF ÉTAN

I've failed.

In shock, with excruciating pain emanating from my chest, my eye, and leg, I simply lie in loose rubble. My killer trudges away, trailing the girl I love and Salexa.

Can't think. Every aching part of my body screams for relief. Every tortured attempt to catch a wheezing breath creates a grotesque gurgle of fluid and air from my punctured lung. What was it the Scouts taught in First Aid class? Direct pressure to slow blood loss. As more duty than hope, I flop one hand over the spot.

The solasamka. How ironic. It's pointed straight at Kalista and me. If her men are watching by holocam, they'll see me kick the bucket. Can't a guy die with privacy?

"Pssst."

Did I imagine the sound?

"Pssst. Pretty warrior."

I manage to turn my head. Kalista faces me with—surprise—a smile back on her pallid face.

"So romantic, isn't it? You. Me. Together in our final moments. Fate binds us, even in death."

Her final fang isn't the one I expected.

"You're sick, Kalista." I cough, spluttering blood. "Sick in the head."

A whimper. "You wait. You're mine. We'll depart this world together."

Hideous thought. I twist my head to observe Étan's shrinking figure.

Hurry, girls. *God, please help them escape.*

With fading strength, I close my eyes and wait for the end. Strange. Death isn't as bitter as I feared. But Heaven is my real home. Not Earth. Not Zemna.

Heaven. I'll finally see Mom and Dad again. I can tell them that, even though I rebelled for a while, I still followed Jesus. After all this time, my wounded heart will be healed.

Okay, Jaylel. Bring the next Fithian. I give up.

Unbidden, a voice whispers into my mind. *Which planet would you choose if you weren't dying?*

Huh? Did that come from God, or Jaylel, or from my own hallucinating brain?

Crazy question. Since the moment I arrived here, I've wanted to return to Earth. But if I wasn't dying and could choose either planet? To my surprise, memories of Earth and dreams of attending college fade. Despite all the death and misery on Zemna, God used me here. I made a difference. Yeah. If I could pick either planet, I'd stay here and be a Fithian.

That realization comforts my heart. Yes, I'll die, but on the planet I *want* to be on, not one I'm stuck on against my will. Poor Grandma will miss me. But who knows, maybe she's already in Heaven by now?

Thank You, God, for allowing me to be a Fithian, even if only for a short time.

To the accompaniment of Kalista's moans and the air wheezing between my slick fingers, I let my final thoughts wander. Of all possible memories, my mind floats back to Quel-Tel-Palarim. Like déjà vu, I feel as if I'm there again. No, not in the city. Beneath it, in the Medical Section. Something is similar.

Once more, some fragment of my brain hears the cacophony of ruptured cells, of discordant biological music that needs repair, recomposing the notes to rejoin the symphony. Yet, the clanking and scraping in my thoughts is a new breed of noise. Despite the months that have passed, I'm vaguely aware that I've never encountered a biological noise so screechy and distressed as this one.

"Pretty man. What are you doing?"

Both my eyes flutter open, even though only one sees. Won't this witch let me die in peace?

"What is that light?"

With an effort, I lift my head. From beneath my left hand peeks a puny glow. Of course—the Intersection. If all this agony hadn't scrambled my brains, I would've thought of it. The Intersection is attempting to heal me, but it needs my brain to interface. Do I have enough consciousness to do it?

All thoughts of Kalista blocked, I shut my eyes and try to concentrate. Healing comes harder this time. My mental energy is a feeble minnow struggling upstream as I descend into the disharmony of my own biological song. The chore seems impossibly tiring, the damage too severe. Still, note by note, I calm the dissonance, beginning with the ugliest sounds then moving on to others that need less intense mending. At last, the music inside me hums pleasantly. I sense no more tissue to repair.

When I open my eyes, they can both see! The glow is gone, and so is the wheezing. There's no chest wound, just blood stains. When I stand, praise God, both legs work. I literally jump for joy.

"Thank you, God!"

"How did you do that?"

I stoop in front of Kalista and flash her the Intersection. "Lady, never underestimate a Fithian. Now to stop Étan."

The guidance helmet still rests where I dropped it. However, falling onto rock a second time has widened the cracks. Instead of being clear, the helmet is lackluster gray. Defunct.

I smash the useless thing to the ground. "I was so close to making it work. So close."

The busted helmet sits there, directly in front of my running shoes, taunting me.

My running shoes. I recall an old advertisement. *Just do it.*

The solasamka practically beckons.

Wait, that won't work, will it? Not without the guidance helmet to link my brain. I step aboard anyway, seat myself, and place my left hand atop the power disk. Just as I do when healing an injury, I allow an inner portion of my brain to connect, to unify my consciousness with the craft. The sensation is different from using a helmet. No digital readouts appear in my vision. No yellow tint colors the landscape. Yet, when I think *Up*—the solasamka eases into the air.

Higher. We rise more.

"Wait. Help me." Kalista reaches a begging hand toward me.

Her pitiful request stabs my conscience. After everything Kalista has done, I shouldn't feel one twinge of pity. But I do. Especially since my own hand threw that knife into her gut. Maybe the Intersection could save her. Maybe it can even cure insanity. Problem is, healing extensive wounds requires lots of time. If I delay to heal her, the girls die.

Enough thinking. Priority One is to save the girls. If I can do that, then I'll come back and see about helping Kalista.

To the solasamka I command, *Forward*. It responds!

In no time, I reach the bend in the ravine and follow its course. The solasamka is a hot little vehicle. No wonder Kalista loves it. With the wind rustling my hair and clothes, it's like an airborne Harley.

But this is no time for thrills. The girls are somewhere ahead, and Étan is dead set on wiping them out. But where are they? Theena was limping. Could she have gotten this far? Or maybe I lay bleeding longer than I realized?

My tongue scrapes inside my dry mouth. The Intersection

has healed me, but it did nothing to replace body fluids. That canister. Could it be water?

When I unsnap the canister from the front of my seat stand, I find that it does contain liquid. Not water, but something sweet, fragrant. Yadi juice. With the Intersection clamped over the power disk, I chug down gulp after gulp with my other hand.

Better save some for the girls.

When at last I spot them, my heart lurches. The ravine is a dead end, with steep walls on three sides. The girls are trapped as Étan approaches, closing the distance with steady strides despite my damage to the device controlling him.

The sight of my craft causes the girls to recoil. Of course, with the sun behind me, they can't see. They think I'm crazy Kalista, come to gloat over their corpses.

Descend. Lower, lower. Cruise on this level.

I'm six feet off the ground. What to do? Jump from the craft and surprise Étan from above? No way. He still grips a knife, and I'm down to bare knuckles.

Instead, I zoom past Étan and lay the solasamka on its side as I twist into a tight spin to confront him.

"Étan, halt."

He glances at me, tries to circle around me. So much for my hope that he'll respect any pilot of the solasamka. "Must destroy secondary targets."

"What are you talking about, dimwit? You haven't even destroyed target number one. Look. It's me, Rankin, alive and well."

This comment does give him pause. He scrutinizes me as I hover before him. Loosening the filaments in his brain seems to have returned a portion of humanity to him. "That target was terminated. You merely resemble that target."

He sidesteps to get around me, but I maneuver my craft to block. At the same time, I keep an eye on his knife hand. He saw me throw mine. I don't want to fall victim to the same tactic.

He stops and stares. "You block my path."

"You bet I do, buddy."

"You are not a target, but you block my path to the targets." He steps sideways in the other direction.

Just as fast, I reposition. "We're done killing. The sport is over. Kalista is dead."

He doesn't pronounce the word, but I read "recalculating" in his eyes. Aloud he says, "The mission ends when all targets are terminated. If non-objectives block the mission, they become targets of opportunity."

When his gaze clicks to a stop on my face, it's not hard to guess what he just labeled me. I gun the solasamka upward as Étan leaps. From twenty feet up, I pause and watch him pick himself off the ground. How much abuse can a human body absorb? Even if he can't sense pain, there must be a limit.

With me out of his path, Étan reverts to his original direction, straight toward the girls.

"Rankin," Salexa calls. "Do something!"

This is madness. How can I stop Étan without crashing my craft down on top of him?

Crashing? Bashing. Kalista used a rope to bash bodies against caloids!

Ignoring the repugnant blood stains on its fibers, I reach behind me and seize the coil. Working fast, I tie the end into a wide loop with a slip knot. Not large enough to lasso a cow, but wide enough to fit around a man.

"Rankin, he's getting closer!"

When the line of hemp falls around Étan, he halts. Recalculating, no doubt.

"Sorry, dude. Can't give you time to think." I gun the craft backward, cinching the loop tight, then, keeping the line taut, I flash the solasamka in circles around him, revolving over and over in a game of human tetherball. By the time I stop, my own head is spinning, but there's Étan, trussed up with both arms pinned to his sides.

"You hinder my mission."

All I can do is shake my head. "You're breaking my heart. Forgive me, but I have to do this."

Gunning the solasamka backward pulls Étan crashing to the ground. Fortunately, the knife lies out of his reach. If he'd recalculated a little faster, that rope might be in shreds.

When I step to the ground, Theena hobbles to my side. "What should we do with him? We can't take him along if he keeps trying to kill us."

"First things first." Without another word, I kneel and place my left hand over Theena's knee.

Even without looking, I know she winces. The Intersection detects the damage and allows me to pour healing virtue into it. Compared to repairing my chest wound and busted eyeball, fixing a twisted and swollen knee is child's play.

"Incredible," she says when the deed is done. She hugs me.

I turn and survey Étan. "I'm not sure if I can do this, but I want to try something. You two, hold him still."

Trussed as he is, Étan poses little threat when I kneel over him and close my eyes. Still, after all I've endured, it's comforting to have Salexa sitting on his legs and Theena pinning his shoulders.

I place the Intersection over the hole where the bundle of corn-silk filaments still binds his brain to Kalista's device. There, my mind encounters exploding impressions, warring noises more jarring than every kid in a school clanging on pots, pans, broken glass, and metal pipes as they attempt to drown out an orchestra. My brain—it's sizzling!

Inexplicably, both girls' faces appear in my thoughts. Their names evaporate from memory. Instead, to me, they suddenly represent secondary targets. Knife them! With a cry, I jerk my hand free and topple backward.

Theena lets go of Étan to help me up. "What happened?"

"It's not a simple healing job. With that device attached, it's active warfare inside his brain. Scary stuff." What I don't tell Theena is that, for an instant, I pictured my hand gripping a blade and stabbing straight toward her. Trembling, I stand and blink away tears. My brain needs a bath.

"You hinder my mission," Étan repeats.

"Forget the stupid mission."

"Not possible. Targets must be eliminated."

Fascinating. Kalista's last order remains stuck in his gray matter, yet Étan is closer to conversation than he's been since they operated on him. What would happen if I grabbed that bundle of contacts and gave them a solid yank? Most likely, I'd kill the guy.

"Can't you help him?" Salexa asks.

"I'm not sure. I'll try again, but first I need to do something. I stoop and pick up Étan's knife. Dry blood from my chest coats its entire length. I hurl the knife high onto a rocky crag.

"Why did you do that?" Theena asks as she once again places her hands over Étan's shoulders to hold him steady.

"Tell you later. This time I'll place the Intersection under his neck and work up from that direction. And Theena, let's try another experiment. While I work with the Intersection, I want you to sing to Étan."

"Sing to him?"

"Might not help, but he's responding to our words more than he was. I want you to pick the most beautiful song you can think of then sing straight to him. Keep him calm."

This time I lie on the ground to slide my left hand under Étan's neck. My mind is already melding with his neurons when Theena's angelic voice breaks into song. I've never heard this one before and would love to stop and listen. Instead, I take a breath and let my mind merge, drifting upward and through the lower regions of Étan's spinal cord and brain.

Approaching the damage from this direction, the earlier din and clash seems muffled, more tolerable than when I entered through the same hole as the mind-control gadget. Something else is different, too. Easier. His brain still resists my efforts, but the raging chaotic river I faced the first time now flows slower.

Maybe it's distracted as Theena's voice inputs glorious thoughts about the Creator, grace, mercy, and love.

Whenever I encounter a filament, I will it out bit by bit, much as the epidermis of a finger gradually forces out a wooden splinter. Encountering them this way, I understand these threads are far more numerous than I realized. All thoughts of time vanish as I locate and ease out filament after filament. The things are everywhere. Some are broken and dead. Others aren't. But with the elimination of each one, the chaos inside Étan relaxes another degree. Along the way, I repair nerve damage, revive centers I find disrupted.

A new experience—passing through his brain cells, I glimpse images, overhear bits of conversation, relive flashes of Étan's past as if I myself am there. The experience embarrasses me; yet, these snippets help me to appreciate him on a deeper level. For his privacy, I back my presence away from that sector.

At last, my thoughts push out yet another strand—and I find no more. Étan's mind hums calmly now, a normal biological song ebbing and flowing in peaceful rhythms. Except for one spot. From inside the gray tissue of Étan's brain I "look" up and out the circular hole in his skull. It's the last of the damage and relatively simple to heal. I relax while the Intersection regenerates the necessary tissues.

When I disentangle from Étan, I'm exhausted. Never has a healing session demanded so much concentration.

Theena kneels and places a hand on my shoulder. "Are you all right?"

"Let me lie here a moment. How's our patient?"

"Sleeping. Can we take off the rope?"

"Let's wait about the rope. I want to make sure all thoughts of his 'mission' are gone." Feeling like an arthritic old man, I stand, then trudge to the solasamka. Kalista's beverage is calling. After a couple swallows, I offer the canister to the girls. "Drink?"

Theena takes a sparing drink, then passes the canister to Salexa. While Salexa quenches her own thirst, Theena slips one arm around my waist and rests her head against my shoulder. I kiss the top of her head and slide my hand around her waist, grateful for this reprieve from the emotional roller coaster.

If Salexa harbors any jealousy about my coziness with Theena, she doesn't show it. In fact, she hands the canister back to Theena for another sip. Thank goodness, she seems to accept the situation. I have zero energy for dealing with a love triangle. I'm pretty sure the Intersection doesn't know how to handle one either.

"Save some of that juice for Étan. He's going to need it."

Theena gazes toward distant hilltops. No need to explain. I'm worried about him, too.

Salexa sinks to the ground and sits cross-legged. Her clothes are torn and coated with dust. Her hair is scragglier than I've ever seen it. On her chin is a scrape. She looks exhausted. "Rankin, what happened back there? Whose blood is on your tunic?"

"The blood is mine. Étan stabbed me. In fact, he left me for dead. Kalista took a knife to the stomach. She was still moaning when I left her."

My comment catches Theena off guard. "Still moaning? I assumed you had trapped her, maybe tied her up like you did Étan."

I shake my head, but Theena detects something in my demeanor.

"You're thinking about healing her." When Theena gazes into my eyes, it's as if she reads my soul, and not with the aid of a symbol on her palm. "You intend to go back and heal that detestable creature, don't you? Even before looking for Prahv?"

"I'm not even sure she's still—"

"But you intend to find out." Theena slaps down her statement like a challenge. "And if she's alive, you actually plan to heal her."

With a sigh, I cross my arms and hang my head. I can't look at her when I say this. "Theena, I love Prahv like a brother. At the moment, though, his life isn't in danger. As a Fithian, my job isn't to destroy life. I'm here to point people to new life in the Creator. Kalista makes me sick to my stomach, but if I can repair her wound and her mental illness ... Well, I need to try."

She lifts my chin. "Rankin, this planet is better off without Kalista's breed. Let her die. We need to find Prahv and get as far from this blood-soaked island as we can."

Never before have I seen a flash like steel in Theena's eyes. However, I've seen similar hardness in other eyes—in a mirror. After terrorists murdered Mom and Dad.

I take her hand. "Theena, I never told you how my parents died. They were visiting old friends in a distant land. While they were there, fanatics just as despicable as Kalista chopped off their heads. I was far away, living with my grandmother."

I hang my head, ashamed of what I'm about to say.

"On the day they flew away on a type of Earth bolsamka, I was angry at them."

"Angry with your own parents? Why?"

"For a stupid reason. Back then, I believed in God but had no interest in loving or serving Him. My mother and father wanted me to attend a private school for believers, one that taught about God. I hated the idea and rebelled. When my grandmother took them to the—well, the place where the air vehicle waited for them—I didn't even go along. Never even said goodbye."

"What did you do?"

Tears well in my eyes. "I went to play ball games with my friends. My plan was to stay angry long enough that my parents would change their minds. A few days later, they were dead. Killed by men who were even angrier at their faith in God than I was. Since then, not a day has passed that I haven't wished I hadn't been so stubborn, that my parents and I had been at peace when they died."

Her hand tightens in mine. "But you still yielded to the Creator."

"Eventually, yes. The point is, when I heard about their

murders, I swore revenge. I wanted to find those fanatics and hack them to pieces. But my hatred was destroying me from the inside. It kept me from becoming the person God wanted me to be. If Kalista is dead, she's dead. But if not—and if I can heal her insanity—she might embrace the light of the Savior. Jesus teaches to love our enemies and do good to those who abuse us."

Now Theena is drooping her own head. Surprising me, she bursts into tears. She presses her face into my chest.

Is this good? Is she crying because she agrees, or because she disagrees? Or neither? My arms circle her, but I'm so dog-tired. All I can do is offer comfort and let her tears flow.

Jaylel, wherever you are, couldn't you give my right hand a second symbol to decipher the female mind?

No reply.

I guess some requests are too tough, even for angels.

The next moment, Étan's unexpected voice catches us by surprise. "All right, who's the hilarious person who tied me up in my sleep? Get this rope off me!"

Salexa, Theena, and I burst into laughter.

35

GRUESOME MEMORIES

Now free of his bonds, Étan lowers the canister and licks his lips. "Somebody tell me everything that's happened. Last I recall, they were leading Prahv and me into her caloid."

Before we can even begin explaining, Salexa looks skyward. "Uh-oh. Trouble."

Five samkas loaded with fyotor-bearing men descend in a circular pattern around us. We're surrounded.

Crooked Nose—Tantron—marches straight to me, his weapon leveled at my chest. "You're the one."

"I'm which one?"

"You threw the knife that mortally wounded the sister of Entizar, ruler of this entire ward. Now you're going to save her life."

Étan cocks his head. "You did what? I must've been unconscious quite a while."

As if noticing him for the first time, Tantron studies Étan up and down with wide eyes. "You restored him."

Then, stepping closer to me, Tantron presses the fyotor against my chest. "You should be dead meat. We watched by holocam as you conjured some sort of magic to heal yourself. Who are you?"

"They call me Rankin Fithian."

When I raise my left palm, some of Tantron's warriors gasp. Others curse.

"Lotan's Unizem broadcast. That's why you look familiar. I don't know how you energize that hand, 'Fithian,' but we're wasting time. Bring her."

From one of the craft, four men bear a litter with the body of Kalista. They set her before me.

"Do it," Tantron orders. "If she dies, Entizar will slay us all. But if I have to die, you and your band will burn first."

I drop to my knees beside Kalista. "Believe it or not, I was preparing to go back and try to help her." Fortunately, they've left the knife in the wound, which minimizes blood loss. "I will try. But know this—if I succeed, it won't be by magic, but by the power of the Creator. Plus, she might not be the same person she was."

"Enough talk. Do it."

When my consciousness descends into Kalista's mind, I'm immediately overwhelmed by indescribable sordid sensations that raise goosebumps on my skin. "Oh, my word."

"What is it?" Salexa asks.

"She's ..."

The nearest comparison that comes to my mind is stepping into a forest clearing and finding myself in the middle of a satanic ritual. Her mind is unclean. Contaminated. Revolting. Until now, I'd assumed Kalista was the victim of horrible insanity. And yes, there's insanity here. But I also experience snippets of unholy memories—Kalista praying to demons. Kalista raising her arms and urging murky spirits to fill her body, to lend her their power. Scarier than the most gut-wrenching horror movie, this is real—and I want out of here.

Hands trembling, I say, "Can't explain. Somebody, hold her arms and legs in case she begins to thrash."

The life force inside Kalista is ebbing. I switch my attention from her brain to the biotic cacophony emanating from her stomach. Releasing her limp fingers from the handle of the knife, I withdraw the hideous blade. Once it's out, I press the Intersection to the wound and concentrate.

Each healing is unique. In this case, Kalista has lost so much blood the procedure is more complicated than usual. The Intersection doesn't create new plasma. It works with what's there, and in her case the missing body fluid proves a grim hindrance. A good, old-fashioned IV drip would go a long way right now.

Theena's hands rest on my shoulders. "Redeem her, Rankin. Fix Kalista, both body and mind."

The knife wound is only half repaired when I ease my thoughts out of those tissues.

"Done already?" Salexa says.

"No. Before continuing in that spot, I need to ..." Better not to voice my plan to purge the demonic influence. If I cure the belly wound but leave her mind insane and open to demonism, we'll still be cooked before sundown.

I return to Kalista's head and lay the Intersection across her brow, my own forehead resting on the back of my hand. Immediately, my mind is wading through demonic mental muck that defies description. No previous encounter has prepared me for this. I detest the need to submerge deeper, but it's the only way to purify her mind.

God, help me. I can't do this alone.

My mind plunges in. The cerebral mire hits me, swallows me—a tidal wave that feels like sinking in a sea of spiritual dung. I'm immersed in her insanity plus a veritable cesspool of dark memories and experiences. There's no stench, but my mouth automatically clamps shut. With Étan, I backed away from his memory centers, protected his privacy. In Kalista's case, there's no choice. I must navigate those dark corridors to pinpoint the nucleus of her madness. Tears well in my eyes as I witness glimpse after glimpse of atrocious memories. Previous "hunts." Murders. Gruesome dishes. Ungodly perversion. No human should see such atrocities, yet the emotion that

Kalista's mind drapes around each one is sensual pleasure. I'm weeping as my consciousness flits between the grossest graphic images.

Theena's hands tighten on my shoulders. "Rankin, are you all right?"

All right? At this moment, nothing is all right. As my brain darts past each window into Kalista's vile memories, each vision threatens to make me vomit. If only there were some other way to localize the origin of this perversion.

When my awareness enters the compartment I'm searching for, I sense the truth more than see an injury. Goosebumps prickle my skin when I detect other beings' "fingerprints." Demonic traces, and more than one. I don't know how I recognize them, but devilish residue clings like slimy cobwebs. I'm careful to avoid brushing them with my consciousness. What if the demons that possessed her had still been here when I entered? I shiver. Maybe they vacated to find a new host body. Whatever the reason, I'm glad they're gone.

Just as a sanitary worker might hose away a leak of foul sewage, I engage the virtue of the Intersection to wash away her cerebral pollution. When at last all traces of demons are gone, the Intersection reacts in a unique way, illuminating this corner of Kalista's intellect with healing brightness. The slimy cobwebs dry, disintegrate. I bow my own psyche before this medicinal glow. It's warm, tingly, cleansing my mind as well.

I've lost track of time, but eventually I realize the mental and spiritual healing is finished. I replace the Intersection over her stomach wound to complete the job.

My eyes are closed, but within a few moments a male voice breaks the silence: "His hand. It's not shining anymore."

I blink. He's right. "Whatever I can do is done."

Kalista's eyes flutter open, mere inches from mine. They reflect puzzlement. "You were in my dreams. Or am I dreaming still? I feel so weak. Can't even recall how I came to be here."

I stand and look at Tantron. "She needs water. Lots of it. Then food, followed by bed rest. Her own body must complete the healing process."

As if snapped from a trance, Tantron clicks his fingers. "You men—don't just stand there gaping. Fetch water. Now!"

Three subordinates scramble to obey.

Tantron still grips his fyotor, but now it points to the ground, not at me. That change is comforting.

Kalista studies my face, then everyone else's, while taking long sips from the canister they give her. She pauses. "Tantron, I don't understand. I feel as if my mind has been wandering in barren places. You're the only person I recognize. Why are we here?"

For the first time in my experience, Kalista speaks like a normal, rational woman. Not as a tyrant. Not like a sadistic cannibal. Just as a confused human being. Praise God.

"Most of them are your personal escorts, appointed by your brother Entizar."

She turns her eyes to me. "And this man? We've never met. Yet, his face—even his posture—he seems hauntingly familiar. Did Entizar send him as well?"

Tantron drops to one knee. "This man has been your physician. His name is Rankin. When we lost all hope of saving your life, he pulled you from the jaws of death. They call him a Fithian."

"A Fithian? But there's no such thing." Her gaze drops to my left hand.

I extend my palm. "Fithians do exist. More important, the Creator is real. He has instructed me to bring a vital message for you and everyone willing to hear it. Will you listen?"

Her eyes stray to Tantron. "How do you advise me?"

Indecision passes over his face. "I've seen enough evidence to consider whatever this unique visitor has to say. But not here. Let us bear you to your home."

To me, she says, "If you will, please follow us. Tantron will guide the way to my home."

Another "please." Judging by Tantron's raised eyebrow, he's going to pay close attention when I tell the story of the Savior. Amazing. Only by surviving the madness of Kalista's sport could I turn persecutors into a willing audience.

When I glance heavenward, Aena emerges from behind a cloud. Coincidence, or a positive sign?

Theena appears beside me. She takes my hand as Tantron's men carry Kalista to a samka. "What about Prahv? My brother is still out there somewhere."

Tantron cuts her off. "We know the hilltop where Kalista stationed him. We can nullify the search-and-destroy program. What I can't do is remove the control mechanism without damaging his mind. Can you heal one more person, Lord Fithian?"

I laugh. "I'm no lord. Call me Rankin Fithian. Or just Rankin."

Another man leans and whispers into Tantron's ear. Despite the lowered voice, I catch every word. "We still have a problem. Don't forget Loruk and Dorn. When Entizar hears their report, he will react."

"What's this about Entizar?"

Tantron frowns. "Two spies placed here by Kalista's brother to ensure I treat his sister with respect and loyalty. They have ever criticized me for allowing Kalista to pursue her sport without bodyguards—as if I could overrule her. The moment we saw the vision of you hurling the knife at her and then the eye of the holocam skewing around, they tried to open a comm-link to Entizar. When I caught them, they fled. Grabbed a samka and raced for the mainland. By being first to reach Entizar's ear and implicate me in Kalista's death, they will seek to curry his favor. At the cost of our lives, if Entizar isn't satisfied when he comes. And he will definitely come."

Listening to this exchange, Étan looks totally perplexed. "But Kalista did not die. All is well that ends properly, right? Won't

Entizar be irritated at his own spies for barging in with a false report?"

Tantron stares at Étan, zeroing in on the side of his head. Not so much as a scar remains on the shaved scalp. Maybe it's tough for him to swallow the fact that I've freed someone from his mind control. "You must understand, Entizar is Entizar. His actions are unpredictable. However, given a choice between raging anger and rational thinking, his typical reaction is anger. He will be glad to find Kalista alive, but when he learns that his sister's personality has been altered, he might yet lash out. Her body lives, but by Feebia, that woman is no longer the Kalista that Entizar knows."

"Thank goodness," Salexa mutters.

Tantron snaps his fingers. "Team Two. Locate the other Defender of Justice—the one they call Prahv. Neutralize the conditioning and bring him to base." He hands an electronic tablet to the leader of Team Two.

"Thank you," Theena says.

Tantron strides toward a samka. "You four will have to squeeze in with us. I'm not sure how much time we have before Entizar arrives. Whatever it is you have to say, Rankin Fithian, I want to hear it before he gets here."

36

A STARTLING MESSAGE

"So be it."

When I conclude my prayer, Tantron and the dozen men alongside him rise from their knees. Joy swells my heart at the sight of Étan, too, standing and brushing off his knees. He notices me watching, clasps his hands together and raises them high. The victory gesture of a Quel-Telan warrior. I grin and mimic the gesture back. He's made a decision for the Creator. Now *that* is a giant-sized victory.

Fewer than half of Kalista's men responded to the Gospel invitation. Her other followers hang back. One obviously wrestles inwardly. Fear distorts other faces. A couple guys sneer at those who just now prayed to the Creator requesting forgiveness and salvation. I'd been hoping for one hundred percent. I should know better. The Good News always results in mixed reactions.

Tantron wipes moist eyes with his fingers. "I can't recall the last time anything moved me to tears. Rankin, what else must we do to join the Creator's family?"

"To join God's family, nothing else. Jesus did it all by paying your debt of sin when He died in your place, Tantron. All you needed to do was repent and accept that sacrifice. But to grow in

God's ways, pray to Him daily. Love the Lord. Listen for His quiet leading in your heart."

A feminine sob. Not yet strong enough to stand, Kalista sits on a divan, her face buried in her hands. "Oh God. Oh God. Oh God."

She isn't "taking the Lord's name in vain" as people say on Earth. I suspect the Gospel message illuminated more than enough hideous memories to cause anguish. Tantron starts toward her, but I catch his sleeve. Theena kneels beside her and —after the slightest pause—wraps a tender arm around Kalista. I can't hear what she whispers, but now I'm brushing away tears of my own.

I force myself to look away. There's Prahv, standing in the rear of Kalista's audience chamber. Thanks to the Intersection, he's healed of the mind implant, but the confused way he twists his head left and right makes me chuckle. We'll explain everything to him later.

Tantron claps his hands for attention. "Men, as you know, we have good reason to expect Lord Entizar to arrive for inspection. I cannot predict the outcome. However, I advise each man to prepare his quarters. Check all equipment. Make sure not one grain of sand is out of place, or you'll invite unnecessary wrath. At the first sign of his approach, we will gather in the courtyard. Dismissed."

The men disburse.

Tantron grips me by the shoulder. "Rankin Fithian, I have much I would like to discuss with you. So many questions. However, there's no time. You and your friends must get away from Solace Island immediately."

"Are you sure the situation is that dangerous? I mean, Entizar needs the Good News, too. If you and Kalista vouch for us—"

"Tantron is right, Rankin. You must leave." It's Kalista, her eyes red and swollen, tears glistening on her cheeks. "I don't recall all of the evil I've done in my life, but I remember enough.

Entizar is more malicious than I ever was. And now I recall the Unizem broadcast from Lotan. Please, for all your sakes, leave us."

When I hesitate, Prahv steps forward. "I'm still collecting pieces of my own memory, but if you have a spare samka, I can pilot it."

Tantron motions toward the exit. "Follow me."

* * *

When we reach the samka corral, Tantron removes a power disk from the pocket of his armband and hands it to Prahv. "Take my personal craft, the azure one over there. It's in perfect condition and should serve you well. You'll find the helmet on the pilot's seat."

Two men are already stowing canisters of food and drink aboard.

Another man hurries up to us. He's one of those who stood in the rear during my explanation of the Gospel. "Tantron, two messages for you."

"Messages?"

"The first message is that a large armada of samkas has been detected—approaching from the direction of Evron."

Tantron's expression remains firm, but the color drains from his face. "Entizar and his forces. Is the second message good news or bad?"

A hint of a sneer appears on the man's face. "That depends on your point of view. The message is this." He steps to Theena and aims what looks like a pistol-sized fyotor at her head. "The Fithian and his friends are not leaving. They are going to wait right here for Entizar. Keep your magical hand down, Fithian-trickster, or the pretty lady goes up in flames."

I'm speechless, but Tantron isn't. "Malkud, what do you think you're doing?"

"The same thing you would be doing, if you were smart,

Tantron. Lotan has offered a life of luxury to anyone who delivers that rebellious thief. Lotan's brother will arrive any moment. So, guess who has called you 'sir' for the last time."

Prahv had taken a step toward the samka, but now stands frozen, watching the scene unfold. His eyes reflect the same fear I feel. "Friend, you do not have to do this. If you want to escape your old life, come with us. We will take you anywhere you want to go."

Malkud laughs. "Anywhere? I want to go to Lotan. And surprise—you all get to ride along."

Tantron tries again. "Malkud, I'm senior supervisor on Solace. I command you—"

"Too late!" Theena blurts. Her gaze is on the sky. "Entizar is here."

The instant Malkud looks up, Theena's fist smashes his Adam's apple with astonishing force. He staggers backward and collapses onto the stony ground. Wheezing, he struggles to breathe but also fumbles to pick up the fyotor pistol.

In that instant—*Foosh!*—Malkud erupts into flames. I'm so close that the flash of heat feels like someone has hurled open the gates of hell. It's my turn to jump back.

Grim faced, Tantron holds up one sleeve of his tunic, revealing yet another version of a mini-fyotor strapped above his wrist. "One does not become a senior supervisor for Entizar by being naïve."

"Expect the unexpected," I comment. Then to Theena, "You were awesome."

"I wanted to stop him but didn't mean for him to be killed."

"Malkud sealed his own fate," Étan says. "Those who live by the fyotor, die by the fyotor. Now come. You must flee before Entizar descends on us for real."

One after another, Étan, Salexa, Theena, and Prahv press raised right palms to Tantron's in farewell.

"May the Creator bless you," Prahv says as he gives the gesture. "I hope we meet again."

Tantron nods. "We will. If not in this life, then in the next. For now, fly fast and far. Keep your altitude low until you clear the horizon."

I'm last. Tantron claps both hands on my shoulders then sighs. "Countless questions churn inside me. But so little time. Maybe some day."

All my friends have already said goodbye. What can I add that will sound fresh and worthy of a Fithian? An answer pops to mind. When I raise my right hand, instead of pressing it against Tantron's, I split my fingers in the middle. "Live long and prosper, Tantron."

With difficulty, he duplicates the gesture. "Live long and prosper? Is that the standard blessing on your home planet?"

I can't control my smile. "Not among all of us. Only some of us."

"Same to you, Rankin Fithian. Live long and prosper. Now hurry."

The grin on my face grows wider as I take my seat aboard the samka. The safety harness deploys over me. I love these aircraft.

Prahv inserts the disk. We're in business. Yet, the samka scarcely clears the ground when a voice shouts, "Wait!"

Ignoring the gate, one of Kalista's men vaults over the low wall and runs up, arms flailing for attention. He's one of the men who hung back during my message. Even now, conflicting emotions register on his face. This could be a trick, but my gut tells me to release my safety harness.

"Fithian, please—may I ask a question?"

Tantron scans the sky. "So far, no sign of Entizar, but there's not a second to spare, Rankin."

"What's your question?"

"Today you gave an invitation to place faith in the Son of the Creator. I did not do it. I wanted to, but I couldn't. What I mean is, the first time I heard this message, I rejected it. Worse, I mocked it. Because of that, I considered myself unworthy to accept it when you shared it, too."

"What do you mean, the first time you heard this message? Did you hear me speak in Lotan's ward?"

He shakes his head. "It happened far away. Another man spoke of a Lord Christ. I never saw him perform miracles the way you do, but his followers declared him a Fithian."

His words blow me away. "Prahv, lower the samka!"

The craft settles to the ground, but Tantron once again studies the lavender heavens. Drops of sweat bead his forehead. "Rankin Fithian, I insist, you must leave."

I ignore Tantron. "What can you tell me about this other Fithian?"

The man shakes his head. "Not much. I didn't talk to him personally. His build was heavier than yours, but he was shorter than you. Dark brown hair."

"What about his name? What did people call him?"

His eyes light up. "He had the most extraordinary name I've ever heard. So bizarre. Like a name from a fantasy tale dreamed up for children. I'll try to pronounce it right. 'Fithian Al-ex-an-der.'"

"Alexander is an Earth name! Tell me more."

Tantron pulls the man from the samka. "Mikkos, Rankin must go."

"One more moment," I plead. "Mikkos, what else can you tell me about this Alexander?"

"He carried an object. A collection of writings, but not in a normal tablet. Al-ex-an-der called it 'Word of God.' I got only a glimpse, but it contained bizarre symbols I had never seen before. Line after line of them covering flat, rectangular sheets all bound on one side. I laughed at him and his writings. Is it too late for me to trust in Christ?"

Now I feel exactly like Tantron—brimming with questions, but no time to talk.

Tantron changes tactics. Ignoring me, he appeals to Prahv. "You must get Rankin out of here. For your sakes and ours."

The samka lifts from the ground.

"Prahv, stop." Then to Mikkos, "It's not too late. You heard the invitation. The door to God is open. Tantron repented. He can help you to pray. But first—where was this Alexander?"

"Far away. In Taralah. But you can't talk to him. He was killed."

The hairs on my arms stand up. *He was killed.* Jaylel's exact words.

Obeying Tantron's urging, Prahv eases the samka a few feet off the ground.

"Mikkos, what about the writings? What happened to those?"

"The followers of Al-ex-an-der stole his body so no one could vaporize it. The rumor was they buried him in a secret spot, with the writings in a separate box above his heart."

Another warrior runs to Tantron. "Sir, Lady Kalista sends word of approaching craft. Entizar, plus countless others."

"Prahv, let's go," Étan urges.

"Go, go!" echo Theena and Salexa.

All I can manage is half a wave before Prahv guns the samka past the dome of bars then straight out to sea, mere feet above the rolling whitecaps. I reactivate my safety harness, which locks me into place.

Étan cranes his neck backward. "I see them. The first ones are landing already."

Salexa watches, too. "Do you think they spotted us?"

Étan continues gazing toward the island. "I don't believe so. Otherwise, they would give chase. Hopefully, all their attention will be on the island."

Solace Island. *God, bless and protect those people, especially Your new children. They need Your intervention.*

Part of me wishes I could've stayed and explained his sister's newfound faith in the Creator. Yet, my smarter side realizes that would've been an enormously dumb move. Entizar might kill strangers first and ask questions later.

The time was ripe for leaving. Better to boldly go places I've never gone before.

Theena slips her hand onto mine. "You're quiet. Was that other Fithian—Al-ex-an-der—a friend of yours?"

When I gaze into her purple eyes, all the sweat and grime and pain behind us fade away. I shake my head. "I once heard about another Fithian who was killed. I can't help wondering—can we find Alexander's grave? I need his copy of the Word of God."

I don't try to explain the concept of a side quest. But now that I'm resolved to remain on Zemna no matter what, the goal of locating a functioning Unizem portal no longer seems as urgent as before. My heart has already said goodbye to Earth. I'm in this ministry for the long haul.

Theena tightens her grip on my hand. "We could try to find the writings. But Mikkos was right. Taralah is a long distance from here, even by samka." She leans forward and taps her brother on the back. "Prahv, how many days do you think it would take to reach ... Wait. What's that?"

I stiffen. "What, another samka?"

Prahv, too, glances left and right.

She points. "Not in the sky. On the control panel. What is that yellow thing?"

Stuck to the spot is a small, yellow rectangle of what looks like paper. Markings cover the surface, but it's too far away for me to make out details.

When Prahv peels the thing loose, goose bumps rise on my skin. It looks just like—

"What is it?" Salexa asks.

Prahv studies it, then shrugs. "Symbols. Perhaps Tantron developed a private code."

I stretch out my hand. "May I see?"

When he passes it over his shoulder, my fingers tremble at the mere touch. How in the world did a Post-It Note get stuck to a samka on Zemna?

One glance tells me this is no code. These are words. *English* words, printed in blue ballpoint pen. My heart lurches as my American brain reads what Prahv couldn't:

Dear Rankin,

I have a message for you: "Well done, good and faithful servant. Carry on!"

—Jaylel

P.S. Your Grandma Johnson arrived in Heaven two of your days ago. She and your parents ask me to say, "Go get 'em, Rankin!"

Instantly, my tears flow. My vision blurs. Mom, Dad, and Grandma—they know where I am. They're proud of me!

Theena leans over as far as her harness allows. "Rankin, can you decipher it? What's wrong?"

Words evaporate. I don't want to blubber in front of my friends. After shaking my head and wiping my eyes, I say, "Everything is perfect. I'll explain later. Right now, I need to spend some time in private prayer."

No clock has dinged. No whistle blew. Somehow, though, I know—phase one of my mission on Zemna is complete. My internship is over. I've crossed an invisible line separating the Rankin who wanted to flee back to Earth from the Rankin who wants to stay. Best of all, I've received the one thing I've wanted more than anything—closure for the rift between my parents and me.

I doubt I'll be the best Fithian in history. Still, it's encouraging to know I don't totally stink at the job. Better yet, I now have a definite goal—go to Taralah and locate Alexander's grave. I must find his Bible.

I close my eyes.

Thank You, Lord, for these friends. Thanks for guiding me, even when I don't see Your hand. And thank You for choosing unimportant, imperfect me—out of all the believers on Earth—to become the next Fithian.

THE END

A NOTE FROM THE AUTHOR

Dear reader, thank you for joining me in *The Next Fithian: An Ordinary Teen on a Strange, New World*. It's a book I hadn't intended to write, but once the idea took root, I couldn't shake it. As the story progressed, I grew to love working on it.

If you, too, enjoyed your trip to the planet Zemna with Rankin, may I ask a favor? Actually, several favors …

First, please tell friends and family how much you liked the book. Enthusiastic word of mouth is the #1 form of advertising.

Second, jot a review of *The Next Fithian* at online book vendors and Goodreads. Don't tell what happens in the story. Spoilers ruin it for others. Just rate it with however many stars and tell what you liked about it or how it made you feel. The more reviews, the more likely others will give the book a try.

Last, visit me at **rickcbarry.com** and sign up to receive my emails. After all, if you liked Rankin's adventure, you're my kind of reader. Stay in touch so you'll know when future titles release. While you're on my site, check out my other books. Maybe you'll discover your next adventure?

Blessings to you!
~Rick Barry

GROUP DISCUSSION GUIDE

1. Although Rankin is eager to leave the U.S. to join an archeological dig, he's careful not to trample his grandmother's feelings. Do you think such thoughtfulness is normal among today's teens? Why or why not?

2. The instant Rankin's airplane explodes, he blurts what he believes is a final prayer before death. Everyone expects to die someday; yet few people seem to prepare their soul in advance, even if they believe in God. Why do you suppose that might be?

3. Rankin feels inadequate for the Fithian role and tries to wriggle out of it even though he knows God hand-picked him for it. Have you ever felt inadequate to do something God wanted you to do? What are some ways we can cope with feelings of inadequacy?

4. On Zemna, Rankin notices that people think differently. Their sense of humor is sometimes different. The way they consider things such as the sun and people's ages surprise him. Have you ever interacted with someone and experienced misunderstandings due to cultural differences? If so, share an example.

5. Working in Lotan's quarry, Rankin struggles with doubts. He's living an exhausting, dangerous life and wonders whether he's messed up and God is punishing him. Yet, in the middle of misery, he meets Prahv and Theena, who become his best friends. Have you ever gone through a tough situation, only to look back later and see blessings that resulted from it? Can you think of one to share?

6. In Quel-Tel-Palarim, no matter what Rankin does, Étan doesn't like him and is hostile. In that situation, it would be easy to automatically dislike a person back. What are some positive ways to respond to a person who is negative toward us no matter what we do?

7. When Étan gets wounded, Rankin begins to realize the Intersection has healing powers. At the same time, he realizes he's hindering the healing process. In order for the Intersection to heal, Rankin can't just go through motions. He must consciously set aside dislike for Étan and truly care about the man. What things in us can hinder God's ability to use us for good in others' lives?

8. After Rankin saves Étan's life, his popularity rises. Suddenly many Quel-Telans admire Rankin. Such treatment might tempt anyone to get a big ego. If you won a million dollars or received massive praise for an accomplishment, you might be tempted to gain a high opinion of yourself. How can we stay humble despite praise?

9. When Rankin and his friends flee Quel-Tel-Palarim during a raid, Étan informs them he's coming, too. Rankin doesn't want Étan in the group but has little choice. Have you ever had to tolerate someone who irritated you? If so, did you ever learn to appreciate that person?

10. At various times, Rankin decides not to show certain individuals the Intersection of All Things, the symbol that pegs him as a messenger of God. In those situations, was he being wise or cowardly? Why do you think so?

11. In the story, we learn that, although Rankin is the son of missionaries, he didn't enter a personal relationship with Jesus Christ until his teen years. Do you think it's common for the kids of believers in ministry to delay coming to the Lord? Can you think of influences that might delay such kids from developing a personal relationship with God?

12. More than once, Rankin recognizes his own struggles with living a consistent Christian life. Because of his shortcomings, he considers himself unworthy to tell people about God. Can you relate to his feelings? If all Christians stayed silent about God until they become perfect, flawless examples, would any of us ever share our faith in Him?

13. With Theena, Rankin finds himself in a frustrating situation. He's growing to love her, but she treats him the same way she treats her brother. When Rankin finally confesses his love, Theena reveals she loves him, too. But in real life, romantic attraction isn't always mutual. What advice might you give a friend who has become romantically interested in someone who simply doesn't love back?

14. When Rankin tells Theena he wants to try to heal Kalista, she objects. After all, Kalista hurt her brother and nearly got them all killed. Can you recall a circumstance where you (or someone else) wanted to do right, but that decision angered friends or family?

15. As Rankin lies dying of a knife wound, he realizes he no longer wants the goal he's worked so hard to achieve—returning

to Earth. He has made more of a difference for good on Zemna than he could on Earth. In light of all the danger and misery he's experienced on Zemna, does his wish to stay make sense?

16. In the final chapter, Rankin receives a brief but encouraging message. Has anyone ever given encouragement that truly touched you? Is there anyone in your life you could encourage, either in person or through a written note? (Think about it. No need to discuss this question aloud unless you wish to.)

ABOUT THE AUTHOR

Rick C. Barry has climbed mountains, jumped from perfectly good airplanes, toured WW II battlefields, and visited Eastern Europe over 50 times in Christian ministry. He holds a degree in Foreign Language Education and speaks Russian. His fiction and non-fiction have been published by Kregel Books, Focus on the Family, JourneyForth Books, Answers in Genesis, and others. His previous novels are *Kiriath's Quest, Gunner's Run, The Methuselah Project,* and *Methuselah Project S.O.S.* Visit him via his website at rickcbarry.com.

ALSO BY RICK BARRY

The Methuselah Project: A Novel

In WW II, Captain Roger Green becomes an unwilling guinea pig in a bizarre German experiment. The war ends, but the Methuselah Project doesn't.

Methuselah Project S.O.S.

In this sequel, Roger Greene is determined to rescue the captive woman who once risked her life for him. But a conspiracy wants him dead. Can he succeed without getting both of them killed?

Gunner's Run

Over Nazi Germany, machine gunner Jim Yoder tumbles out the open bomb bay of his B-24 Liberator. His parachute saves his life, but now he's alone, on foot, and on the run across Hitler's Europe.

Kiriath's Quest

When the barbarous Grishnaki capture Kiriath's father, the kingdom cannot pay the ransom. To rescue his father, Kiriath devises a bold plan to sneak into the Grishnaki's valley—alone if necessary.

Learn more or buy at **rickcbarry.com/book-table**